Someone was watching her...

She felt the strangest tingle along her spine, almost as if she'd been touched. Nonchalantly she turned, into the mocking gaze of James Tenet. "Damn! You scared me."

James had been wickedly amused by her volley of fire when she'd argued with him a few weeks back. Now her face flushed at the memory of how he'd made her pulse jump. It had only been the heat of combat, she told herself.

She could tell by the delight in his eyes that he had more grist for the horrible newspaper mill. "I hope you realize those allegations against my friend are contemptuous lies," she said.

"Possibly...but very entertaining lies." His gaze swept Jennifer from head to toe.

Why was she suddenly so fluttery? She knew all he wanted was information.

"There's an old saying. You can lead a horse to water but you can't make him drink. I think that's been updated." Jennifer's smile was challenging. "You can lead a reporter to the truth, but you can't make him think."

ABOUT THE AUTHOR

Caroline Burnes is the author of six Familiar books and lives with Familiar's alter ego, E. A. Poe, a black cat who was once a stray. As an animal lover, Caroline urges all pet owners to spay and neuter their cats and dogs. "A lucky few stray animals find homes, but most of them suffer and starve," she said. "If you have a pet, please have it neutered. If you don't have one, think about adopting a stray from a local humane society or animal shelter. You might luck up and find your own Familiar."

Books by Caroline Burnes

HARLEQUIN INTRIGUE

86—A DEADLY BREED
100—MEASURE OF DECEIT
115—PHANTOM FILLY
134—FEAR FAMILIAR*
154—THE JAGUAR'S EYE
186—DEADLY CURRENTS
204—FATAL INGREDIENTS
215—TOO FAMILIAR*
229—HOODWINKED
241—FLESH AND BLOOD
256—THRICE FAMILIAR*
277—SHADES OF FAMILIAR*
293—FAMILIAR REMEDY*

* FEAR FAMILIAR Mysteries

Familiar Tale

Caroline Burnes

Harlequin Books

TORONTO • NEW YORK • LONDON
AMSTERDAM • PARIS • SYDNEY • HAMBURG
STOCKHOLM • ATHENS • TOKYO • MILAN
MADRID • WARSAW • BUDAPEST • AUCKLAND

This book is dedicated to Susan Haines,
an animal lover and rescuer of many cats and dogs

ISBN 0-373-22322-6

FAMILIAR TALE

This edition published by arrangement with Harlequin Enterprises B.V.

Printed in U.S.A.

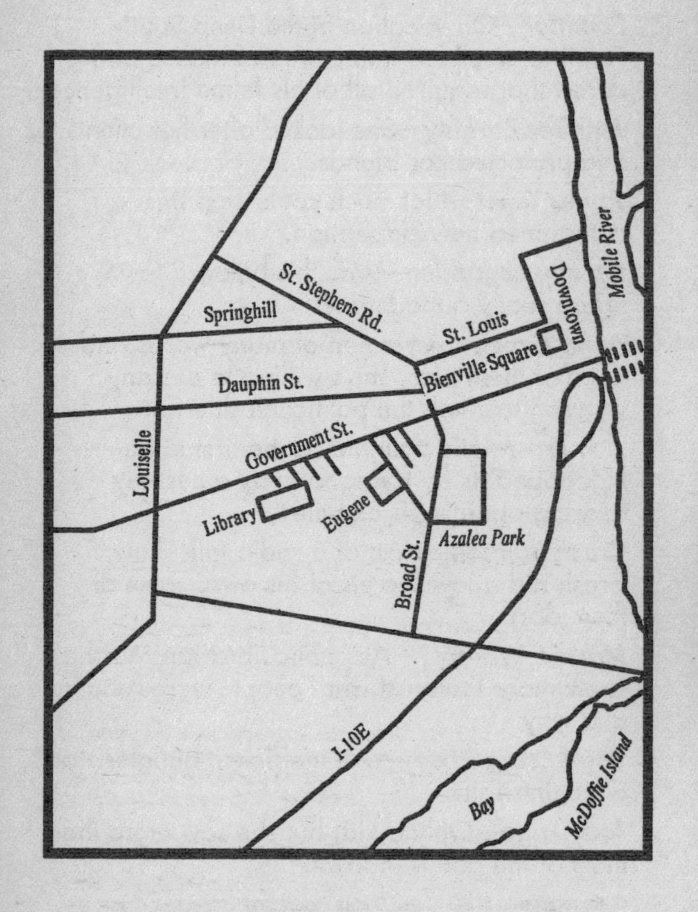
St. Stephens Rd.
Springhill
Downtown
Mobile River
St. Louis
Bienville Square
Dauphin St.
Government St.
Louiselle
Library
Eugene
Broad St.
Azalea Park
I-10E
Bay
McDoffie Island

CAST OF CHARACTERS

Familiar—On vacation in the Deep South, Familiar stumbled into a web of malice and deceit that required all of his feline intelligence.

Jennifer Barkley—She looked after her clients... and protected her friends.

James Tenet—Not much could stop this determined newspaperman.

Eugene Legander—Was this beloved town figure really a madman?

Anna Green—A woman of many words and none of them nice, she's willing to use any weapon to climb the political ladder.

J. P. Frost—His daughter is the first to be kidnapped. Is he trying to sway a custody hearing against his ex-wife?

Crush Bonbon—Host of a radio talk show, Crush hid a few secrets of his own, some of them dark.

Martha Whipple—As public librarian Martha knew more than just what people were reading and why.

Chief Craig Bixley—An inefficient bungler...or a villain's foil?

Judy Luno—Only a kid, but she saw more than most of the adults in town.

Chapter One

Never one to be smitten by floral scents, I must admit that the magnolias and honeysuckles that surround the palatial Adams estate have intoxicated me. What a beautiful day in a tropical paradise. From the upstairs balcony I can see the front yard aflutter with those frilly azalea things, and the wisteria is clinging to the old bricks of this place, such a sweet-sad perfume. The Old South, alive with romance, beauty—and beneath all the color and trim, the odor of fine vittles.

The lovely Eleanor thinks she has me securely incarcerated in this room. Don't bet on it. My keen olfactory system detects an abundance of culinary delights on the buffet tables downstairs. The pitch of laughter also tells me that the party is in full swing. A sleek and sly black cat will never be noticed.

Eleanor is so busy with her bundle of joy, little Jordan Lindsey, that she forgot to lock the hall door to the bath. Ah, a small oversight in a woman as intelligent as she is good-looking. Perhaps it was a psychological blunder. It could be that she subconsciously wants me at the party. After all, Eugene Legander, the guest of honor, is not only a legendary author but a cat lover. I believe he is owned by eight felines, descendants of some highly elite Roman cats. His latest children's book is a literary success—and this is one party I don't intend to miss. No matter that Eleanor has still not completely forgiven me for my escapades at the White House last year.

Ah, a bump with my muscled kitty rump and the door opens. The hall is clear and the smell of something delicious will lead me unerringly to the food. Is it ham, baked with those cloves and pineapple? And there's a teasing odor of spicy boiled shrimp. Maybe I've died and gone to heaven.

A little peek between the banister railings and a perfect view of graciousness, Mobile, Alabama style. The lower floor is buzzing with laughing folks, and look at that platter of chicken livers wrapped in bacon. One of my favorite hors d'oeuvres. I'd say Mrs. Adamses' party for Eugene Legander is a smashing success. Champagne flutes floating in the air, beautiful women in such lovely, vivid dresses. There's the white-haired author. He's playing an air guitar! And reciting poetry! I simply must meet this man.

But who is that lovely young woman approaching him with an urgent look on her face? She's devastating with that cascade of mahogany hair! And those eyes, shattered blue crystal! She isn't as tall as my lovely Eleanor, but that peacock silk dress clings to every slinky curve. I wonder why she's so very disturbed. Oh, to wipe that look of consternation from her lovely face.

But first things first. I must hear what she's whispering to Eugene. She looks likes she's going to burst.

"HE'S PULLING UP in front of the house," Jennifer Barkley whispered, unable to hide her fury. "He's going to crash the party and try to start a fight." She gave a worried glance to the fifty-odd guests who were chatting and laughing all around the lower floor of the Adamses' beautiful home. This was definitely not the place for a scene. "Now, Eugene, whatever you do, don't let him provoke you. Everyone knows he's a fat bully!"

"Crush Bonbon is no match for me!" Eugene Legander straightened his cravat and put his glass of burgundy on the table where he'd been signing copies of his highly acclaimed children's book, *Tribe of the Monkey Children.* At the look on the author's face, several guests stopped talking and moved closer.

Jennifer Barkley looked at the author with serious doubt in her spangled blue eyes. Her grip on his shoulder tightened as the front door opened with too much force and a mountain of a man blocked out the beautiful spring day. His roving glare caught Eugene's and held.

A whisper spread through the elegant old house—Crush Bonbon had arrived—uninvited.

Jennifer put her other hand on Eugene's shoulder, hoping to hold him in place. As if sensing the building tension, the front parlor where Eugene had been sitting began to fill with curious partyers. Jennifer took a deep breath. "As your publicist, I order you to sit still and keep your lip zipped. You know how he gets your goat."

"He may get my goat, but today I'm going to rattle his gizzard." Eugene stood. Though he was in his seventies, he was spry and fit. "I'll go more than one round with that cockatoo." He assumed the stance of a fencer, daring Crush to advance with a wave of his hand.

Jennifer rolled her eyes. Eugene, or Uncle Eugene as he was known to his millions of young fans, was the most lovable, dearest—most stubborn—man she'd ever met. And he enjoyed a good verbal sparring match with Mobile's most conservative and obnoxious radio talk show host, Crush Bonbon. The two had been at each other's throats since Crush had moved to Mobile a decade before.

"Well, well, Crush," Eugene said as he stepped forward, the gleam of battle in his eyes. "I didn't realize you were so lonely you had to crash parties uninvited. Crush the Crash. How fitting."

"I've come to uncloak you for the sick man you are," Crush replied, his double chin quivering with indignation. "Your books are a source of wickedness in a world already filled with evil. You encourage mischief in children, foolishness in women, and—" he looked around the room, making sure he had everyone's full attention "—moral decay."

A tall, slender woman with chestnut hair touched only lightly with gray stepped to the door. "Mr. Bonbon, this is a private party. Please leave now."

"Mrs. Adams." Crush gave her a courtly bow. "I have no wish to show discourtesy to you, but you've been conned by this man." He pointed at Uncle Eugene. "He pretends to love children, to write for their entertainment. But look at the children in his books. Terrible things happen to them. They swing through trees like monkeys. They mock their teachers and their parents. His books teach insurrection and anarchy. He must be stopped—" he pointed at Eugene dramatically "—before another child disappears."

Victory glinted in his small eyes as he watched the shocked adults in the room. The meaning of his words didn't take long to sink in. A low rumble of murmurs spread among the partygoers.

"Why, I never!" Martha Whipple, the local librarian shook her finger at Crush.

"What child has disappeared?" Eleanor Curry asked as she stepped forward, baby Jordan in her arms.

"Mimi Frost is missing. She disappeared in the park this morning. *After* she was seen with Eugene Legander, feeding the pigeons."

Eleanor shifted Jordan to a more comfortable position. "Get out of this house as Mrs. Adams has requested." Her normally pale face was stained with anger. "I've known Eugene Legander since I was a small child. He loves children, and I won't allow you to stand here and make unwarrented innuendos." She stepped forward. "Get out now."

A hush had fallen over the rest of the room. Mrs. Adams put a hand to her mouth. "I can't believe it. Little Mimi. I must call her mother immediately. There's been that terrible custody battle. Maybe her father took her..." She didn't complete the thought as she realized how damning it could be.

"Maybe Eugene can tell us where she is." Crush held his ground. "Especially since a page from his ridiculous book was found with her hair ribbon. The exact page where the first child is kidnapped by the monkeys. 'Kidnapped' is, of course, the operative word."

Another murmur ran through the room. Eugene stood frozen.

"I've asked you politely..." Eleanor was breathing rapidly and she turned to find Jennifer Barkley at her side. "Now I'm telling you, get out or I'll have you removed."

"Mr. Bonbon," Jennifer said, completely in control. "Your accusations are grounds for slander. I suggest you leave before your mouth gets you into more serious trouble. Most of the time intelligent people can overlook your ugly drivel, but this time you've gone too far."

"Ah, Ms. Barkley. Eugene is your meal ticket. No wonder you protect him so fiercely. I'd—" He stopped at the sound of a low, deadly growl. His eyes widened at the sight of a big black cat, crouched between Eleanor and Jennifer, staring directly at him.

"Grrrr—grrrr—grrrrr!" Familiar swatted at his pant leg with one sharpened set of claws.

"Mark my words." Crush backed up, his gaze on the angry cat. "If Eugene Legander is allowed to roam free, more children will disappear. He's a sick man. A child hater. A very sick man!" He threw up both arms and turned to run as Familiar leapt into the air at him.

Eleanor closed the door on his hasty departure and looked down at the cat. Familiar stuck out a back leg and nonchalantly began to clean it, as if he were sitting at home in front the television. "Haven't I taught you not to growl at strangers?" Holding the infant in her arms, she bent to stroke the now purring cat. "Good work, Familiar, you little escape artist. How did you get out of the bedroom?"

"Meow." Familiar basked in her praise, then wound around Jennifer's extremely attractive ankles.

"What a cat." Jennifer bent to lift him so that she could look into his golden green eyes. "He was defending you."

"Yes." Eleanor nodded. "He was. Familiar is a very special cat." She gave him a knowing look. "And like all special creatures, he can sometimes cause more trouble than you could ever imagine. That's why I didn't leave him in Washington."

"What an extraordinary creature!" Eugene rushed forward and took the cat from Jennifer's arms. "I do believe it must be the soul of Lancelot returned to us in feline form."

"Meow." Familiar puckered his whiskers and yawned to show his disdain of human evaluation, but he made no effort to move away from the stroking hands.

Backing slightly out of the group that had now resumed chattering with full force, Jennifer hid her frown. The party had resumed as the guests drifted back to the buffet table, the bar, or the gardens. But Crush Bonbon had greatly disturbed her—and Eugene. He was doing a good job of hiding it, but she could see the distress in the set of his shoulders. Had one of the local children really disappeared, or was that some gambit on the part of Crush Bonbon to start a controversy? His daily talk show fed off rumor and fear. If he could start a stampede of mothers worried about the safety of their children, he would do so. Simply for the fun of it—and the audience it would draw.

The uncanny sensation of someone watching her made Jennifer pause. She felt her pulse quicken at the strangest tingle along her spine, almost as if she'd been touched. Nonchalantly she turned into the mocking gaze of James

Tenet. "Damn," she whispered under her breath. Tenet was a journalist with a sharp eye and an even sharper wit. They'd gone a round not more than two weeks ago when Tenet had opined in a column that fiction, in general, had become too dollar-driven. It was true the column had not addressed Eugene's books, but the general tone of it had set Jennifer off and she'd lowered both barrels at James when she'd met him in the mall.

The trouble was, he'd been wickedly amused by her volley of fire. In fact, had goaded her. And something more. Her face flushed at the memory of how he'd made her pulse jump. It had been the heat of combat, *and* something else. Something she refused to acknowledge.

Now she could tell by the delight in his eyes that he had more grist for the horrible newspaper mill. The scene between Crush and Eugene—and the ugly accusations—would be sensationalized in the morning newspaper unless she could somehow defuse the story.

Jennifer took a steadying breath and walked over to the reporter's side. "I hope you realize Crush Bonbon's accusations are contemptuous lies."

"Possibly. But very entertaining lies." James kept his expression coolly neutral, but he couldn't keep his gaze from sweeping Jennifer Barkley from head to toe. She was one of the most attractive women he'd ever seen. She hummed with energy, especially when she was angry. When she'd accosted him in the mall, he'd been unable to resist teasing her. She was so beautiful when aroused, and her flashing eyes had done a little arousing of their own. In fact, he'd come to this writer's shindig for the express purpose of seeing her again. He grinned at the expression on her face. And it was going to be well worth his time and effort. She was one publicist who took her job a bit too seriously.

Watching his expressions, Jennifer felt a sudden drop in the bottom of her stomach. The man was difficult to deal with and required complete cool. Why was she suddenly so fluttery? To hide her discomfort, she flagged a passing waiter and picked up two glasses of champagne. She handed one to him with a carefully constructed smile. "Surely you're too intelligent to allow the likes of Crush Bonbon to manipulate you. He's a great shepherd to the sheep, but you aren't a sheep." She raised her eyebrows in question.

"Neither sheep nor goat." He smiled and sipped the champagne he'd accepted with one arched eyebrow. "Is it true that a child has disappeared?"

"I don't know," Jennifer replied. "I was hoping you could tell me." Whether she liked to admit it or not, there was something about the tall, dark-eyed reporter that tempted her to linger beside him. His slightly tilted eyes and golden skin reflected his Filipino heritage, but his mocking smile was all his own.

"The police reporter will know. I'll check before I write the story." He grinned. "I'm accurate, and I'm not led around by the nose."

"There's an old saying. You can lead a horse to water but you can't make him drink. I think that's been updated." Jennifer's smile was challenging. "You can lead a reporter to the truth, but you can't make him think. I hope you enjoy the party." Her perfect exit was ruined by the loud, distressed wail of a young child.

"Mama!"

All eyes turned to the garden entrance where an eight-year-old girl stood in the tatters of a once beautiful yellow organza sundress. "Mama!" She held out her arms but did not move. Dirt covered her legs and hands, and tears had tracked through dirt on both cheeks.

"Daisy!" Amanda Adams rushed to her daughter and quickly inspected her for serious injuries. When she was certain she wasn't hurt, Amanda pulled the child against her, heedless of the expensive silk of her own dress. "What is it, darling?"

"He pinched me!" Daisy wailed the words, her face pressed into her mother's side.

"What?" Amanda ignored her guests as they clustered around. "What did you say?"

Daisy pulled away from her mother long enough to throw Eugene Legander a look that managed to hold both horror and betrayal. "He pinched me. Hard." She held out her arm. In the tender flesh under the muscle there was a bright, angry red blotch where the abused tissue was collecting blood.

"Who pinched you?" Amanda's voice was controlled, but concern was giving way to fury.

"He did!" Daisy pointed at Eugene and then pressed her face against her mother and sobbed. "Please, make him go away."

Jennifer started to step forward, but the look of hurt on Eugene's face stopped her. Would it be better to confront the child and make her admit her lie, or to get Eugene out of the party? Her first official duty was to guard his reputation, but in the time she'd worked as his publicist for Grand Street Press, she'd come to regard Eugene's feelings as most important. He was a generous man who gave without expecting anything in return. She could see that Daisy Adams's accusation had cut him to the bone.

"Daisy, you must be mistaken." Eugene took matters into his own hands as he knelt beside the child and spoke softly to her. "I would never pinch you."

"You did," Daisy said on a cry as she pressed tighter to her mother's side. "You pinched me, and then you pushed me into the garden shed and locked me there. I've been trying to get out for hours!"

Eugene started to reach out to the child but thought better of it. He stood, shaking his head, all color drained from his face. "I should be leaving, Amanda," he said to her mother. "I didn't do a thing to Daisy. Perhaps when she calms down she'll—"

"I'm sorry, Eugene." Amanda Adams spoke stiffly. "I think it would be best if you go. Daisy doesn't tell fibs."

"And neither does Eugene." Jennifer stepped forward. She bent to Daisy. "Did you see Eugene when he pushed you into the shed?"

The little girl paused in her crying to remember. "I was picking flowers. For Uncle Eugene's jacket." She hiccuped and her breath caught several times before she could continue. "We'd been talking about the impatiens, the red ones." She hiccuped again. "I went to pick a carnation for him, and then he came up behind me where I couldn't see and he pinched my arm and pushed me into the shed." She peeked a glance at Eugene from behind her mother's leg.

Eugene didn't move, but he spoke directly to the little girl. "I didn't do that, Daisy. I was sitting on the bench. When you wandered off, I came into the house for a glass of wine."

Daisy ducked back against her mother's leg. "He hurt me."

"Someone hurt you," Jennifer corrected. "But it wasn't Eugene."

"We should go," Eugene said, touching Jennifer's arm. He glanced at Eleanor, his blue eyes sad. "What a terrible ending to a fine day," he whispered to her as he kissed her cheek. "I'm so sorry your visit to Mobile was ruined by this."

Eleanor, holding Jordan in one arm, hugged the author. "Hardly ruined. You know excitement is my middle name. I'm sure this will all be straightened out by dinnertime. I'll speak with Amanda after Daisy has had a bath and rested."

"Thank you, darling," Eugene whispered. "And take care of the lovely black cat. A handsome rascal."

"Handsome and very fond of trouble." Eleanor finally caught sight of Familiar as he sat on the top step eating something he'd stolen from the buffet tables. "And he's going to die of cholesterol if he doesn't quit stealing party food."

"Posh. Cholesterol makes his coat shiny," Eugene said, something of his spirit returning at Eleanor's promises. "Call me later," he said as he took Jennifer's arm.

He kissed Amanda's cool cheek and left as discreetly as possible.

At the door, Jennifer found James Tenet waiting to walk out with them.

"Headed for the newsroom to crank out a story?" She could have bitten her tongue, but it was too late to take back the words.

"Exactly my game plan." He smiled down at her.

"It was a lovely party," Eugene said, a sigh escaping. "What a terrible way for it to end."

"Indeed," James said, ignoring the blue fork of lightning Jennifer shot at him with her gaze. "I don't believe the little girl was hurt. I think she was more upset at being locked in that shed. I went out and took a look. She finally managed to knock the door off its rusty hinges. There's no doubt she was locked in there."

"I wonder which of the children did that to her," Jennifer mused as they made their way to her car. "Tommy Franklin and Chris Estis were both there. Either one of them is capable of playing such a trick, but I can't think they'd pinch her so hard." Jennifer knew all of the children who attended Eugene's very popular story hour readings at the local library. Many of the children also made Eugene's house a regular visiting place. He enjoyed their company and they helped him in his gardens—and with his adventures.

Eugene shook his head emphatically. "Those children are mischievous, but they aren't mean. They wouldn't do that to Daisy. I mean, they might lock her in the shed, but they would *not* have left her in there crying. And they wouldn't have pinched her like that."

James looked past Eugene to catch Jennifer's eye. "I'm sure it will sort itself out," he said calmly. He stopped at Jennifer's car and opened the driver's door for her. As she slid behind the wheel, he leaned down. "Don't coerce any confessions out of those children just yet."

"I would not force—" She stopped as she saw that he was deliberately provoking her. "If I decide to do any arm-twisting, it will be directed at the press," she said as Eugene settled himself in the passenger seat beside her.

James laughed as he shut her door and waved as she pulled away from the curb.

"That man is awful," Jennifer said, watching him in the rearview mirror.

"Awful. Now that's an interesting way to describe him." Eugene nodded. "Awful can be very intriguing."

"Eugene." Jennifer had a warning note in her voice.

"I once knew an *awful* woman in Rome. She could provoke me into a terrible temper with just the arch of her eyebrow. Strangely enough, whenever I got the chance, I spent every moment I could in her company."

"Eugene..."

"Don't sound so awfully threatening," he said, completely ignoring her as they pulled into his driveway. "I think I need a nap, Jennifer. Just drop me off at the front door."

Knowing there was no point in arguing with Eugene, Jennifer sighed. She had a little running around to do—regarding the disappearance of Mimi Frost.

As soon as Eugene was out of the car, Jennifer turned on the radio and tuned into Crush Bonbon's afternoon talk show.

"Mrs. Sharon Frost is still in tears with no sign of her daughter on the horizon. Police have been notified, but as usual, our local blackjack carriers are slow to respond. Maybe if little Mimi had been snatched from a doughnut shop they'd be all over the scene."

Jennifer gritted her teeth at the sound of Crush's know-it-all voice. If she had a car telephone, she'd disguise her voice, call in and point out that Crush looked like he ate three meals a day, plus at least eight snacks, in a doughnut shop. He sure as hell wasn't missing any Twinkies. Lucky for Crush she hadn't given in to the craze of trying to drive and carry on a sensible conversation.

She put a lid on her ire and listened to Crush again.

"I'm not casting any aspersions on poor Mrs. Frost. I know she's beside herself with worry about nine-year-old Mimi. But I must point out that Mrs. Frost *allowed* her beloved child to play in the park with a very disturbed individual."

Jennifer turned the dial up as she made the corner in front of the local police station. She was going to see if there was any "official" word on Mimi Frost. And then she was going to—

"Part of the problem facing this great country is the fact that women are shirking their duties as mothers. It seems harmless enough, sending little Mimi out to the park to play with...this person. But why didn't she accompany her daughter? Was she too busy painting her nails or watching some feminist talk show? Why trust our most precious possessions to a solitary figure—a man who makes his livelihood imagining the destruction of our children? What were you thinking, Mrs. Frost? Or were you thinking of anyone except yourself?"

As mad as Jennifer was at Crush's innuendos regarding Eugene, she was furious at his remarks about Mrs. Frost. The woman was probably tearing her hair out trying to think where Mimi had gone—and Crush was double-loading the guilt right on top of her. What an ass! What a total chauvinist!

The ringing of the on-air telephone made Jennifer take notice.

"Crush, this is Jasmine Finley. Stop this foolishness right now. I know Mrs. Frost, and I'm sure she felt certain Mimi was in good hands. It's a sad day when we can't let our children play in the park for an hour. What are we supposed to do, chain them in their rooms and let them rot their brains with television and radio? Why don't you get off your big duff and go and patrol the parks on Saturday morning? Lend some support to mothers who want their children to get a little sunshine rather than mold in the house."

"Thank you, Mrs. Finley." Crush cut her off. "But it isn't my place to guard someone else's child. It's the mother's responsibility. Fathers bring home the bacon, and mothers cook it and rear the children. That's the way it's always been, and the way it should be. This show is meant simply to alert parents to the dangers of allowing their children to go unprotected, even with someone they think is harmless. I predict that other children will disappear. Mobile is in for a time of great sadness. And it's going to fall at the feet of women too busy to attend to their duties."

The telephone was ringing in the background, but Crush ignored it. "Now, on to another topic. Cats in the house. I wouldn't have believed it could be true, but I saw it with my own eyes today—a very exclusive party where a nasty, hairy cat was allowed to roam the premises. Yes, that's right. Cat hair in the food. Cat hair on the sofas. It was disgusting. And what's even more troubling, no one in the room seemed to notice but me.

"As we all know, cats are filthy, disagreeable animals that eat rodents. And that may be their only redeeming quality. They do eat rodents. But the cat isn't my topic of interest. It's the women who find it necessary to have cats. Do you see the link? Cats are feline power, feminine power. And women who view themselves as powerless like to pretend to have more power by owning cats. Now let's take this one step further and talk about men who own cats. Wow! Did you know that the author, Uncle Eugene, owns eight cats!

Eight! And they live in the house with him. I've heard they eat at the table with him. He *actually* sets places for them."

Jennifer found her heart pounding with fury. She was tempted to turn the car around and drive straight to the radio station. Crush would be far more appealing with part of the antenna tower stuck through his black and evil heart. And she was just the woman to do it!

Just as she reached to turn off the car, she heard Crush pick up the telephone.

"Hello, Crush. This is Marvella Mayhem. I want to tell you that cats are superior creatures. I believe you dislike them because you realize they're much, much smarter than you are. You fear their feline abilities, their discriminating natures. As a fat little boy I imagine cats clawed you. See, cats don't care for sweaty, fat little hands."

Jennifer closed her eyes and leaned back against the seat. She recognized Eugene Legander's voice—as, undoubtedly, did Crush. Eugene was only making matters worse, but it was just like him to call in and defend cats instead of himself.

"What kind of kook are you?" Crush asked. "You sound like a woman with a hormone imbalance. Maybe you should get a shot, or a patch, or maybe just go shave." He laughed and picked up the next telephone call.

Jennifer opened her eyes and had a feeling of trouble to come as she saw Mrs. Sharon Frost coming out of the police station in tears. She was being supported by two other women while her ex-husband trailed behind.

Obviously, Charles "J.P." Frost had not taken Mimi for the afternoon. She was actually missing.

Chapter Two

Jennifer sat at the wheel of the car as Mrs. Frost and her entourage, still trailed by Mr. Frost, passed by her car. The women were distraught, concern for Mimi evident in every utterance. Mr. Frost was grimly concerned and visibly angry.

"How could you allow her to ramble around the park alone?" he demanded of his wife's back.

"She wasn't alone. She was with Uncle Eugene," one of the women responded. "He loves Mimi. He'd never allow anything to happen to her."

"Then why isn't she at home? Or better yet, with me?"

"He said she told him she was going home," the woman responded, her own anger showing.

"The police should pick Eugene Legander up and bring him in for questioning," Mr. Frost continued.

"He's a kind man and he loves children." Sharon Frost turned to confront her ex-husband. "There's no evidence that he knows anything more about this."

"You were perfectly willing to tell the police that I'd kidnapped Mimi—without any evidence." J.P.'s anger was at the boiling point. "They came to my business and none-too gently brought me down here for questioning. Why is this writer person so different from me?"

"Because he's never been cruel to me, or anyone else," Sharon Frost pointed out before she turned and marched toward her car, her friends hustling to keep up. She turned back to fire another volley. "You threatened repeatedly to take her from me. You even said it in the courtroom. That's why you were picked up for questioning, Charles." She got in the car.

Jennifer sat, a silent witness to the painful domestic scene. Divorces were often difficult, especially where children were involved. The Frosts were no exception, apparently. Was it possible that Mimi had grown tired of having her parents fight over her and had hidden out somewhere? The little girl was a regular at Uncle Eugene's story hour, and Jennifer remembered her as a shy, retiring child with big blue eyes that were always too wide, always a little upset.

The idea that the little girl might be tucked away somewhere, frightened and alone, made Jennifer desperate to figure out a course of action, but there was really nothing she could do. The police had been notified. Wheels had been set in motion. Surely the child would turn up unharmed in the next few hours.

She got out of her car and went into the police station. A helpful sergeant explained that since Mimi had been missing only a few hours, the police had taken no official action, but unofficially the park and surrounding area had been thoroughly searched, and now officers were going door-to-door to question Mimi's friends. The hope was that she'd decided to visit a friend and had forgotten to tell her mother.

Although Jennifer was normally good at reading people's faces, the young sergeant kept his opinions carefully hidden. He was smooth, professional, and very reassuring.

"Could I see the page from Eugene Legander's book that was left with her ribbon?" Jennifer smiled, knowing that many times in the past her simple smile had worked wonders. It wasn't that she was flirtatious. Men simply liked her smile.

He hesitated, then shrugged. He got a plastic bag that contained a page torn from what Jennifer quickly identified as Uncle Eugene's latest book. She scanned the paragraphs of type. It was the part of the story where the unhappy young children had begun to sneak out of their windows at night to meet in the park. They'd realized that the adults in their lives were no longer fulfilling their parental duties and were deciding, for the first time, to band together in the trees. But first they had to rescue a little girl who'd been terribly unhappy. The "monkey" children had lured the little girl away from her mother and were swinging with her through the trees to a hiding place.

As she read the passage, Jennifer felt distinct uneasiness. The parallels were obvious to anyone who knew Mimi Frost's family situation. She was an unhappy little girl. Perhaps she'd gone to hunt the monkey children for herself.

She handed the page back.

"Did you think of something?" The sergeant watched her, his face eager now and his gaze lingering on the low-cut bodice of her party dress.

"It's a sad part of the book," Jennifer said carefully.

"I heard the chief is going to question that writer," he offered. "He does write some very unusual stuff. Might be he has an odd relationship with children."

"I doubt that very much." Jennifer kept her face as controlled as he had earlier. "Thanks." She hurried out of the police station and got back into her car. Grand Street Press wouldn't be happy with the recent turn of events, but she had to report in.

FAMILIAR SAT OUTSIDE Daisy Adams's bedroom door and listened to the little girl tell her mother what had happened that afternoon. A hot bath, fresh pajamas and a dinner upstairs had put Daisy in a calmer frame of mind.

"No, I didn't *see* Uncle Eugene," Daisy admitted. "But it had to be him. We were in the garden all alone. There was no one else there."

"We'll look into it," Amanda assured her daughter. "There has to be some logical explanation. I can't believe Eugene would do such a thing." She spoke softly.

"I'm not lying," Daisy said, her voice breaking with the strain of her emotions.

"I know you're not," Amanda soothed. "We believe you, sweetheart. Certainly someone pinched you and locked you in the shed, and your father and I intend to find out who did this to you."

"I can't believe he did it," Daisy whispered. "He's always been so nice."

The ringing of the telephone ended the conversation and Familiar dodged back into the shadows as Amanda Adams left her daughter's room and picked up the phone.

"Peter." She was surprised. "Just a moment, she's right here."

She put the phone down and went to get a concerned Eleanor.

For several minutes Eleanor listened. "I'll pack up Jordan and we'll be right there, Peter. How much is the bond?" There was another pause. "I'll get it. Just hang in there until I arrive. We love you."

She replaced the receiver and looked at Amanda. "This hasn't been a very good day. Peter's in jail in Texas. He was arrested when he tried to take pictures of one of those fake safari hunts where men pay outrageous amounts of money to shoot tigers from zoos."

"How terrible." Amanda touched Eleanor's arm. "He isn't injured, is he?"

"They roughed him up some, but he's okay. He needs me to bail him out." Eleanor looked back to the room where Jordan was sleeping.

"I'll book a flight for you. Is there anything else?" Amanda put her arm around Eleanor. "You can count on me. We were like cousins when we were growing up."

"It's Familiar." Eleanor looked around for the cat. She sensed he was listening. "I can't take him to Texas."

"Then he'll stay here, as our special guest. Daisy will love having a cat, even if it's only for a few days."

"Are you sure?" Eleanor looked under the table. "Familiar has a mind of his own. He can be quite a handful."

"If he gets too rowdy, I'll take him to Eugene." Amanda smiled.

"Then you don't believe that about Eugene pinching Daisy?" Eleanor had intended to talk with Amanda and her husband as soon as Daisy had fallen asleep.

"I honestly don't know what to believe. Daisy doesn't lie, but neither does Eugene." She ran a hand lightly over her right eyebrow. "It's a mystery, but one we can look into. At least Daisy is here, safe. I called Sharon Frost. There's been no sign of Mimi, and it'll be dark in another twenty minutes."

"I'm so sorry, and I'm worried." Eleanor pushed her straight black hair back from her shoulders. "I feel like I'm abandoning Eugene in his time of crisis. I'll get Peter out of this mess, and then we'll both come back."

"And don't worry about the cat. He'll be perfectly fine."

Eleanor kissed Amanda's cheek. "It isn't Familiar I'm worried about. It's you." She put her hand on Amanda's shoulder. "Listen, Familiar is...special. He has some peculiarities that go beyond a taste for gourmet foods."

"What are you trying to tell me?"

Eleanor hesitated. No one ever believed her when she tried to tell them about Familiar's adventures. They thought she was exaggerating. "Nothing." She smiled. Sometimes it was simply better not to know.

THE PLOT DOESN'T THICKEN, it simply twists. I can't believe Eleanor is going to take off for Texas, but Dr. Doolittle is in something of a bind, it seems. I'm telling you, Peter is a one-man-make-trouble machine. I'll bet when he was taking pictures he was trying to get those people's faces so he could press charges. Good for him. It's horrible the way they take broken-down lions and tigers—many of them are declawed and have never been out of a cage—and shoot them ten feet from the cage door. That's a great safari. That's really something to brag about. And those so-called hunters pay thousands of dollars for the privilege.

I feel my blood pressure jacking up, and it doesn't have anything to do with cholesterol, caffeine, or lack of exercise. What I have to do is focus on the fact that now I'm the only one left to find out what's at the bottom of the accusations made against Uncle Eugene. I know that kindly old gentleman could never do such a terrible thing to a little girl, but if there was no one else in the garden... I checked for footprints, but it was useless. Hundreds of feet had trod all over the place. Little feet, big feet, wide feet, narrow feet. And the shed offered no clues. The door was latched with a rusty nail on a string. Not very technical, but effective enough to keep a small girl prisoner. The only clear fact is that Daisy was deliberately imprisoned. The door didn't accidentally stick.

I'm wondering why. Who would want to frighten Daisy Adams like that? She's a nice little girl. Not loud or mean. Who would want to pinch her and lock her in the dark? Some of the other children, those little savages, playing one of the vile pranks they find so amusing? Or someone trying to set up Eugene Legander? Or Eugene? Those are the possibilities.

I'd like to blame it on that big fat boor who crashed the party. He has a bone to pick with Eugene, and this afternoon I heard his little spiel on the radio about cat owners. That man is a menace to society. He doesn't like cats because even the dumbest cat I know is smarter than he. That Uncle Eugene told him, though. Yes, sir! Eugene to the battle. He's one feisty guy.

Eleanor is packing her bags, and I'm at sixes and sevens. The evening outside is balmy. Perfect for a stroll. I think a visit to Uncle Eugene's home is in order. Luckily it's only a few short blocks away.

Mobile is a beautiful city. The oak trees are magnificent the way they canopy the streets. And some of the old homes here are mansions. Too bad they're crowded on those little bitty yards, but I guess development takes a toll in one way or another.

I love the way the people here talk, so slow and easy. It adds just another degree of charm to a city already brimming with wonderful things.

If I'm not mistaken, that's Eugene's house. Listen! It's the sound of...my word—a manual typewriter going ninety to nothing. And it's coming from the backyard.

Was that a growl? Surely not. Uncle Eugene is a cat man. But it sounded distinctly like a bark. I'd better have a peek. Why, it's Eugene writing away. And he's excited. And he's growling with excitement. Jeez! This man loves his work.

But look at his porch. I can't believe my sharp kitty eyes. Who is that lovely creature silhouetted against the back door? What an elegant neck! What a supple back! Look at the way she arches and stretches! My God, I'm smitten! I must know her name.

This Eugene, he attracts lovely creatures. Feline and human. Speak of the devil, here's that blue-eyed spitfire now, Jennifer Barkley. Ah, the perfect name. Miss Spitfire. And while she's here to keep Eugene company, I'd better check back at the Adamses'. I want to be there to tell Eleanor goodbye and at least pretend I'm going to behave. My little stay in Mobile holds a lot of promise. I'm going to have to figure out a way to get introduced to that sexy kitten I saw at Eugene's. My heart belongs to Clotilde, that's true, but there's no harm in admiring the feline form. Especially when it is grace in motion. Ah, the swish of that tail. Perfection.

"JENNIFER." Eugene stood up at his writing table and went forward to greet her with a hug and kiss.

Jennifer hugged the writer, but she saw the deep concern he tried so hard not to show. Eugene's solution to worry was to work like a maniac. "There's been no sign of Mimi," she said. "And I spoke with Amanda a few minutes ago. Daisy believes it was you. She doesn't want to believe it, but she can't remember anyone else in the garden. And more bad news, Eleanor has had to rush to Texas to help Peter with a project he's become involved in." Jennifer left out the detail that Peter Curry, internationally respected veterinarian and animal protector, was in jail. She crossed her fingers behind her back, hoping for forgiveness for the omission. The news would only upset Eugene and there was nothing either of them could do about it. They had their hands full. In the span of the afternoon, suspicions about Eugene had begun to grow. Ugly suspicions and dark rumors—fed by Crush Bonbon and his outrageous, dangerous radio commentary.

"Mimi will turn up." Eugene's chin lifted. "She's a very intelligent child. She has my complete confidence. And as for Peter Curry, Eleanor will get him out of boiling water. She's been doing it for years now."

Jennifer knew that much of Eugene's calm was bravado. He was a man who kept his worries private and, out of respect for that, she changed the subject. "How is the book coming?"

"I've almost finished the final draft of the last chapter," Eugene said, signaling to his worktable. "*The Lizard King* is almost complete. I'll be ready for the reading next Saturday."

Jennifer glanced at the neat stack of manuscript. She was always amazed that Eugene could work on a manual typewriter and produce pages without error. He said it was a talent he'd developed as a secret agent after World War II. She didn't actually believe him—but then again, with Eugene Legander, anything was possible. Anything at all.

"I can't wait, Eugene." She gave him a hug. In the time she'd worked with him, he'd become more a father to her than a client. It wasn't that she failed to take her work seriously. She did that, and she knew she was good at it. But she couldn't deny she was personally involved with Eugene. He was family to her—and invaluable to the publisher.

"Why don't we invite that interesting young man from the newspaper over for a glass of brandy?"

Eugene's question caught her off guard. "James Tenet?" She couldn't believe it.

"That's his name. He seemed rather charming." Eugene's look was innocent.

"If we asked him over, he'd think we were trying to bribe him not to run that story." The idea of James Tenet's company made her panicky. She felt a prick of excitement at the mention of his name, and also a little dread. He liked tormenting her. He enjoyed getting her riled. And he was so damnably good at it.

"The man isn't a fool, Jennifer. He can't possibly believe we're trying to control the press with one glass of brandy." Eugene stacked his already neat pages. "I'll give him a call."

Jennifer knew there was nothing she could do to dissuade Eugene once his mind was set. Now she had to think up an excuse to leave. But she couldn't leave Uncle Eugene alone with Tenet. The reporter might worm all sorts of information out of the writer—and then twist it into a story. Eugene never suspected that anyone was up to anything, but Jennifer's experience was very different. It was her job to make sure no one—especially no newspaper reporter—took advantage of Eugene Legander. And Eugene had no inkling of how ugly the rumors had already become all over town.

With a sigh, she followed him into the house. She had to stay and she might as well accept it. Her only hope was that James Tenet was tied up with a story.

Night had fallen over the city while she and Eugene had talked in the garden. She went around the small house, turning on lights and making sure the brandy decanter was filled. Her job had become part hostess, part publicist, part friend. She was smiling when Eugene replaced the phone and announced that Tenet would be over in less than fifteen minutes.

"He was almost speechless when I told him you were here. Waiting."

"Eugene!" Jennifer whirled around, her blue eyes wide with disbelief. "You didn't tell him I was waiting for him to come here?"

"It flattered his ego tremendously." Eugene poured a small measure of brandy and handed her the glass. "You young people are so terribly complex."

Jennifer rolled her eyes. "The man will think I have some kind of interest in him."

Eugene poured his own glass of brandy, declining to comment. He moved to the sofa, adjusted the stereo to a classical station, and pulled a delicate black-and-white cat onto his lap. "Come along, AnnaLoulou," he said, scratching the cat beneath her chin. "You enjoy a nice scratch and aren't afraid to show it." He looked up innocently at Jennifer. "Cats don't mind letting you know what they want. It's one reason they're hardly ever dissatisfied."

Jennifer bit her lower lip. Eugene was a perceptive man—too damn perceptive for his own good sometimes. She lifted her glass of brandy. "To satisfying our needs, Eugene." She grinned at him over the lip of the glass as she drank. He could play games, and so could she.

It was only moments later that James knocked at the front door. Jennifer poured another brandy while Eugene let him in. He greeted them both with a handshake and a smile, but his gaze lingered on Jennifer, almost a touch against the blue silk blouse she wore tucked into jeans.

"The police chief has issued a formal missing person's report on Mimi Frost," Tenet said as he took a seat on the sofa beside Jennifer. "We're going to run a front-page story on the little girl, with her picture." His brow furrowed. "I certainly hope she's okay."

"Surely she's visiting with another child," Eugene said. "Mimi was always quiet, but there was a hint of the adventurer about her. I wouldn't be surprised if she turns up at the beach."

"I hope you're right," Tenet said. He glanced at Jennifer. "Chief Bixley said you were down at the station house."

Jennifer nodded. "I saw Mr. Frost. Obviously he doesn't have his daughter."

"Mr. Legander, I don't want to upset you, but is there anyone who might benefit if your...reputation...suffered?" James asked the question as he stared into the amber depths of his brandy.

"Everyone has enemies," Eugene answered. "But who would possibly benefit? No one."

James looked at Jennifer. "Do you agree?"

She thought a moment. It was one of the questions she'd been asking herself, and the answer wasn't as simple as it had first seemed. "There's no one apparent who would benefit." She framed her answer carefully.

James looked down into his drink, then back up at her. His brown eyes watched every flicker of emotion on her face. "You see, I was wondering if it might be some publicity stunt you'd cooked up to promote Mr. Legander's new book."

Chapter Three

"Get out!" Jennifer stood. She pointed to the door. "Get out before I tie you in a knot and throw you off the porch."

Eugene stood, also. "Mr. Tenet, that's an unfair accusation. I think you owe Jennifer an apology. She's one of the most professional publicists I've ever known, and whether you know it or not, what you're accusing her of is an ethical violation."

James stood. He'd caught one full blast of the scalding anger in Jennifer's eyes and almost—almost—regretted his statement. He'd meant to bait her, but it had gone much further than that. She wasn't merely angry, she was injured, too. Perhaps he should apologize.

"I didn't mean . . ."

"I know exactly what you meant." Jennifer pointed to the door again. "Get out now while you can still walk."

"Jennifer." Eugene's reprimand was gentle. "I think we can discuss this in a civilized way. Mr. Tenet obviously isn't aware of the accusation he's made. Surely he—"

"He knows. And he did it deliberately." She took the drink from his hand. "I knew it was a mistake when Eugene invited you over. At least now I'll be prepared for the lies that will be printed in tomorrow's paper. Just let me warn you—there's a little girl missing tonight and if your newspaper does anything to jeopardize her safety, you'll be sorry. Very sorry."

Blue sparks leapt from her eyes. James regretted that he was being thrown out, but he knew that retreat was his best policy now. "It wouldn't be the first time a publicist used a stunt to great advantage. I wasn't accusing you of actually doing it."

"It just crossed your mind that I might be capable of such a thing. To use a child, to frighten the child's parents, to get the entire town stirred up and concerned simply to promote a book. It just crossed your mind that I might be capable of such behavior."

James saw the anger deepen in the flush of her cheeks. He'd better leave before she picked up something and brained him. Jennifer Barkley struck him as a woman of action, not of words. "There are plenty of publicists who wouldn't hesitate."

"Well, I'm one who would." Jennifer could feel her body beginning to tremble. "I would very definitely balk at such a thing. And Grand Street Press would not allow it, Mr. Tenet. So keep that in mind if you have any more brainstorms about my involvement in the disappearance of a child."

"I will." He nodded at Eugene and left.

Jennifer shut the door with more force than necessary. "The nerve of that man." She found she could draw a deep breath at last.

"Indeed, the nerve." Eugene was completely unperturbed.

"He accused me of using a child to further your book."

"He did," Eugene agreed. "That's rather original, don't you think?"

"I do not think it is original. I think it is reprehensible. He's a slime to even have thought of it. *He* probably wouldn't hesitate to use such a ploy. That's why he thought of it. But to accuse me..."

"It isn't as if he knows you well." Eugene went to the decanter and brought it over to refill her glass. "Sip a little, dear. You're all aflutter."

"I don't want to sip. I want to punch him in the nose." She sipped the brandy. Now that the first rush of anger was over, she realized her feelings were badly bruised by his accusation. Did he really think she was the type of person who would callously use a small child to gain publicity for a book? He must have a very low opinion of her indeed. "He must think I'm scum." Jennifer spoke the words aloud without really meaning to.

Eugene's look was sharp. "I doubt that." He didn't bother to hide his growing amusement.

"It isn't funny."

"I disagree." He chuckled, knowing he was only making her more angry.

"What's so blasted funny?" She put her hands on her hips.

"You are, my dear. And Mr. Tenet. I believe he stepped off the end of the pier before he tested the depth of the water." He chuckled again. "He didn't intend to accuse you, but it just happened."

"He said it in plain English." Jennifer couldn't believe her ears. "He didn't stutter. And I'm not dreaming. How can you defend him?"

"It's a guy thing," Eugene said, laughing again at her furrowed brow and dark blue, sparkling eyes. "You see, you're one of those unfortunate people who are truly beautiful when you're angry. I believe he intended to tickle your anger. Instead he fanned a real flame. Then he had to retreat." He laughed harder. "His expression was priceless. Very much like the young boy who breaks the window with a baseball."

At Eugene's explanation, Jennifer felt her anger dissipate. Her favorite aunt, Beth, had delighted in teasing her into a fury, as had her grandmother, grandfather, and all of her classmates. They'd claimed she was amusing when she was angry.

"You threatened to tie him in a knot and throw him off the porch." Eugene finished his brandy and laughed softly. "He was impressed. And more than a little smitten. I think he relishes the idea of you laying hands on him in any fashion."

"Eugene!" Anger had given way to complete shock. Eugene Legander was playing matchmaker—and he was actually championing James Tenet's cause. "He's a muckraking reporter. A scandalmonger. A troublemaker. A..."

Eugene covered his ears. "Enough. To quote a very famous literary figure, 'the lady doth protest too much.'" His blue eyes twinkled. "Now go home before you pop a blood vessel. You're far too excited by this to be able to deny the fact that you find Mr. Tenet attractive. You forget, my dear, that I've spent the last five decades observing behavior—human and feline. The little rituals between the male and female are obvious to me."

Jennifer couldn't stop the blush that crawled up her neck and into her cheeks. She wasn't angry, she was caught. She did find James Tenet attractive—God help her. But she'd never lower her personal standards to actually go out with the man. Even if he did ask her.

"Go home." Eugene waved her toward the door. "Why don't we go to Billie's for breakfast? I want to ask around the neighborhood about Mimi. If she hasn't returned home, I think we should look for her. I have some ideas, some secret places she's told me about."

Jennifer hesitated. It was an awful thing, but she had to calculate the reaction if Uncle Eugene found the little girl. There would be those—particularly Crush Bonbon—who would say that he'd found her because he'd put her there. But finding the girl was the priority. She'd handle the fallout from there, if there was any.

"Are you okay?" Eugene asked as he gave her a hug at the door.

"Yes. I was just thinking about my job." She didn't tell him the details. She was almost as bad as James had accused her of being.

"You work too hard." Eugene kissed her cheek and gently pushed her out the door.

As she walked down the walk lined by tallow trees and willows that had just budded into electric green leaf, she heard Eugene singing to the cats. He liked Italian opera, and he insisted that the cats did, too.

Jennifer smiled as she drove toward home.

WITH A CUP OF COFFEE in her hand, she walked out onto the sidewalk of her small cottage and picked up the morning newspaper. She dreaded looking through the stories to see what James had written about Eugene's party. It was just plain rotten bad luck that he'd witnessed Crush's attack. Just rotten luck. How often had she invited reporters to attend social events honoring Eugene and none had shown up? And of all the reporters the newspaper could have sent, why had it been James? He normally covered hard news, courts and trials and murders—the big stories. What was he doing at a book-signing party, drat it?

She took her coffee and the newspaper to the small sunroom at the back of her house and sat down to read. Mockingbirds, grackles, bluejays and cardinals clustered around the bird feeder she'd installed, filling the air with their gossip and arguments.

She skimmed the national news, cringing at the reports of war-ravaged countries, then turned to the Metro section. The headline stopped her: Author Feted And Accused. There it was, in black and white. She read James Tenet's story, saw that it was mostly focused on the success of Eugene's book-signing party, with a mention of the accusations made by Crush Bonbon.

She had to bite her lip to keep from laughing at Tenet's description of the big Bonbon careering into the room and dramatically pointing his finger. And Tenet had accurately captured Eugene's posture of defense—the fencing master with the pretend rapier. It was very funny stuff.

And Crush Bonbon came off looking like a fool, while Eugene had style. There was no mention of the accusation made by Daisy Adams, and Jennifer took a long, deep breath of relief. James had done a very fair job of it. She felt a tingle of remorse at her hasty words to him.

When the phone rang, she picked it up, still scanning the paper. "Hello?"

"I heard an eruption of Mount Vesuvius was due at the Barkley residence this morning—after the newspapers were delivered. My editor wants me to take some photos."

Despite herself, Jennifer couldn't help laughing. "I'm sorry, Mr. Tenet, you were misinformed. No eruptions are planned for today."

"This is a pity. I do enjoy a good display of fire and molten lava. Not to mention, heated blasts of air."

"Is there a purpose to this call?" Jennifer could not control the sudden beating of her heart.

"Only a humble apology. And to beg your forgiveness. Eugene cautioned me to wait until this morning, when you'd had time to cool down."

"I see." Jennifer sipped her coffee. Instead of being angry, she was shamelessly pleased. It mattered to James that he had falsely accused her. And, drat it all, it mattered to her that it mattered to him!

"I am sorry, Jennifer. I know you're ethical. I'm on my bended knee. In my bedroom." There was a wicked pause. "Wearing nothing but my—"

"I get the picture." She felt the heat travel up her body. She did get the picture. All of it. In perfect detail. And it made her decidedly unsettled. "Your apology is accepted, and I want to thank you for calling. Now *I* have to get back to work. Goodbye."

She replaced the receiver, her heart pounding. He was a demon. And she could almost hear him laughing at her once again.

To gather her wits, she spread the paper out on the white table and forced herself to focus. The story about Mimi Frost stopped her cold. The little girl had still been missing at press time, and none of her friends knew anything about her whereabouts.

Jennifer finished her coffee, folded the paper and hurried into the shower. She would help Eugene hunt for the girl. Mimi had to be somewhere. And Jennifer prayed that she was safe.

Twenty minutes later she pulled up in front of Eugene's house and blew the horn. He came out, dressed in boots and trousers, ready to poke among shrubs and abandoned buildings. To Jennifer's surprise, a big, handsome, black cat was also sitting on the porch. As soon as Eugene came toward the car, the cat followed. With complete aplomb, the cat hopped into the back seat when Eugene opened the door.

"I didn't think you let your cats out," she said, glancing into the back seat. Did they really need to baby-sit a cat? It might get sick in the hot car.

"It isn't mine. That's the cat that Eleanor brought with her. Familiar. He's extraordinary."

"Meow." The cat rubbed against Eugene's neck and cast a long, green look at Jennifer.

She saw the intelligence, and the wit, in the animal's glance. "Is he going with us?"

"Meow."

"I assume he is. He seems to want to go." Eugene shrugged. "Cats are very independent creatures. I think we should let him come."

"I don't know." Jennifer gripped the steering wheel. Before she could do anything, the cat leapt over the seat and swatted the key, seemingly demanding that she turn the ignition switch.

"I think he wants to get the show on the road," Eugene said, looking straight ahead as if it were perfectly normal for a cat to hijack a car.

Jennifer raised her hands, palms up. "I give up. He can come."

SHE HAS AN INFLAMMATORY temper, but Madame Spitfire is a piece of cake for a cat like me. She likes a challenge. Definitely. And I like her. She even smells delicious, like one of those fragile white blossoms that grow in all the yards here. I think I'll just stay here on the front seat, beside her. Ah, breakfast. Good. This looks like a place for sausage and eggs. Maybe some grits. I haven't had any really good grits since I left Cassandra's house in Tennessee. Eleanor, that darling thing, isn't much on breakfast foods.

Now that breakfast is going to be taken care of, I'll turn my brain power toward the missing kid. I have a few ideas about this little girl, and I think I can train Eugene faster than any other human around here. Too bad Eleanor had to cut and run. We've gotten to where we work very effectively as a team. She's sort of my Watson, if you will. A few bites to give me the energy necessary to put my feline brain into high gear, and then we'll have this little girl home where she belongs. I want to have this concluded before Eleanor and Peter return to take me home.

"I STILL CAN'T BELIEVE they allowed that cat in the restaurant." Jennifer gave Familiar a skeptical look. The cat acted for all the world as if he had every right to go wherever he chose. He'd even pointed out his breakfast selections from the menu with one quick black paw. Eugene had interpreted, and darned if the cat hadn't eaten every single thing put in front of him. He was like a garbage disposal. "And I thought cats were supposed to be finicky eaters. I've never seen a cat eat grits!"

Eugene picked up the cat as they crossed the street. "He is finicky, dear. He's just very Southern and finicky. He did enjoy those grits." Eugene kissed the top of Familiar's head as he put him down. "If only he knew where little Mimi has gone."

They'd driven to the park and gotten out. Azalea Park was in a residential area with ducks and lakes and plenty of space for children to run and play. Eugene enjoyed it for the botanical gardens located up on the hill and the many nature trails that extended back through the woods.

They were out early, and it was a weekday, so attendance at the park was light. Eugene stood and watched as Familiar went directly to the bench where he'd sat and talked with Mimi. The big black cat sniffed the bench as if he were a dog, and then began circling the ground.

"Cats have a very acute sense of smell. Some scientists believe their olfactory systems are more highly developed than those of the dog." Eugene watched Familiar work the area.

"Then why aren't cats used for tracking?" Jennifer thought it was a good question.

"Have you ever seen a cat that would take orders?" Eugene sniffed the question back at her, then turned and went to the cat. "Tracking cats, indeed. What an absurd idea."

Whether cats could be trained to track or not, Familiar seemed intent upon doing exactly that. He took off down a trail that led away from the playground and lakes and toward the botanical gardens and the wooded trails.

"Mimi liked to play back here," Eugene said. He motioned to the south. "Her home is just over there, a nice little subdivision. When she left me on the bench to finish my chapter, I'd assumed she'd gone home. She was always coming up unexpectedly in the park, and then going home." He tried not to show the worry, but it was evident in his voice and in the way he pushed his long white hair back. It was a gesture he used only when greatly worried.

"If she's hiding out in the woods, we'll find her." Jennifer tried to bolster Eugene. She didn't believe they could find anything the police had missed, and the newspaper story had stated that officers had searched the park, the woods and the surrounding neighborhood.

"Meow!" Familiar marched back to her and swatted her shin with a big black paw. He turned and hurried down the trail.

"I think he wants you to speed up a bit," Eugene said.

Jennifer was so surprised, she didn't bother to reply. She picked up her pace and followed the black cat as he wove through the trails as if he knew them by heart. Her only concern was that the cat wouldn't be able to find their way out when he decided it was time to leave. That very thought made her sigh. She'd turned over her destiny to a black cat that had hijacked her car and wormed a free breakfast out of her. What was happening to her life?

At a fork in the trail, Familiar hesitated. He took the left turn and hurried even faster. Jennifer and Eugene were breathing hard when he veered completely off the trail and disappeared into a thick wall of honeysuckle and scuppernong vines.

"Familiar." Jennifer got down and pushed the thick leaves aside. To her surprise she discovered a narrow passageway tucked among the vines. Familiar, only his golden eyes showing, was waiting for her to follow. "That cat's found a hidden trail." She crawled through the vines, not caring now that she snagged her pants or that leaves fell down the neck of her blouse. Eugene was right behind her.

The path ran only twenty yards and culminated in a small, vine-shrouded clearing that contained a flashlight, a book, a glass jar filled with water, a box of cookies that the ants had not yet discovered and an old quilt.

"So this is Mimi's hideout." Eugene looked around, impressed by the leafy green walls. "She did a good job. This is very private."

"She told you about it?"

"Several times. She used to make up stories about who lived here with her and tell them to me. She has a charming imagination, and she's a very lonely little girl."

There was something so solitary about the secret place that Jennifer felt her heart constrict. How sad that the little girl had to bring her fantasies into the woods, alone. "Did any of her friends know about this place?"

"I think I was the only one, because she knew I would never hunt it or try to use it. She needed something of her own, Jennifer. I think you can understand that."

"I do, but I don't like it." She picked up the cookies. The box was half full. She broke one in two with a snap. The humidity hadn't ruined them yet, either. "She was here yesterday, I'm sure." She had a thought that perhaps she shouldn't have touched anything.

"Meow!" Familiar's sharp cry drew their attention, and Jennifer decided that since she'd touched the cookies she might as well use the flashlight. She picked it up, flicked it on and surveyed the enclosure. She stopped when she found Familiar pawing at a small book. As she picked it up, she knew she'd found Mimi Frost's dairy.

"That's personal, my dear," Eugene said.

"It may lead us to where she is." Jennifer hesitated. She understood the violation of reading someone's personal writing, even that of a child. But the nine-year-old's safety was in question. She opened the book and read by flashlight, scanning the neatly printed passages as she looked for some mention of a plan to run away.

"She seems happy enough." Jennifer frowned. "There's no plans about running away." She closed the small book. Mostly, it was a journal about the stories the child was making up. She wrote about her characters and ideas. Mimi

Frost would undoubtedly grow up to be a writer. If she grew up at all.

"Meow!" Familiar snagged the leg of Jennifer's trousers and pulled at them.

"What now?" Jennifer followed the cat, using the flashlight to search as she went. She stopped at the place Familiar indicated. A small transistor radio had been smashed to pieces, and beside it were signs of what looked to have been a struggle. The ground, damp and rich, was furrowed where fingers had clutched. And there was a small piece of cotton covered with violets. Jennifer found that her fingers didn't want to pick it up, but she did.

"That's a piece of the dress Mimi was wearing." Eugene's voice was troubled. "I remember clearly she was wearing a little sundress because she was telling me how she was going to plant violets at her grandmother's next week."

Jennifer tucked the material into her pocket. Like it or not, she was going to have to take this information to the police. And she'd never make Chief Bixley believe that she and Eugene had been led to the hideout by a black cat from Washington, D.C. She turned the problem over in her mind. Eugene was going to look twice as guilty—why hadn't he told the police yesterday about the hideout? That was going to be Bixley's primary focus. She had to think of a counterploy before they got downtown.

"She could have torn her dress on that thorned vine." Eugene pointed to the two-inch barbs on a bamboo vine hidden among the honeysuckle.

"Yes." Jennifer didn't believe that and neither did Eugene.

"What now?"

"I think there's no doubt Mimi has been taken away, and I'm afraid it was by force." She swung the light back to the finger marks in the dirt. "She fought hard."

"Oh, dear." Eugene put his arm around Jennifer. "She's okay. I can't help but believe that. We can't give up hope of finding her, Jennifer. We're all she has, the people of this town who won't give up on her."

"You're right, of course." Jennifer replaced the flashlight. "Let's go to the cops. Maybe they can take some fingerprints and all of that. You know, modern forensic science." She swallowed back the feeling of defeat. Eugene was correct. They had to keep the faith—and keep searching.

Even Familiar was silent as they hurried back to the car and to the police station. When Familiar followed them inside, Jennifer discovered that she took great comfort in the cat's presence. As if he understood, he curled around her ankles and gave her a gentle bite on the shin.

"No pets allowed." The young desk sergeant Jennifer had talked to before was glaring at the cat.

"Tell him," Jennifer said flippantly. "We have to see Chief Bixley. We have new information in Mimi Frost's disappearance."

"No pets—"

He didn't get to finish the statement as Familiar hopped onto his desk and casually knocked over a foam cup full of coffee, spilling the contents down his uniform front.

"Hey! Cat!"

The resulting noise brought police officers from all over the building, including Chief Bixley.

"What the hell is going on in here?" Bixley, a slender man with a perfectly groomed mustache, said as he stepped into the room. All noise ceased. Even the desk sergeant muffled his cries of dismay as he mopped at his shirt with paper towels.

"Well?" Bixley pinned the young man with a glare like burning torches.

"The cat knocked coffee all over me. It was hot." With each word, the desk sergeant's voice faded.

"Cat?" Bixley's gaze swept the room, ignoring Jennifer and Eugene. "What cat?"

"Meow." Familiar walked up to the man and sat down, his golden green gaze mesmerizing.

"Get that animal out of here." Bixley's blood pressure rose with his voice. "Eugene Legander, this is some of your foolishness. Everyone knows you're cat crazy." He waved his hands at Familiar. "Scat. Get out of here." He looked up at Eugene. "I hate cats. Get him out of here."

Familiar walked past the fuming Bixley and went straight into the chief's private office.

"Watch your coffee," the desk sergeant advised.

Before Bixley could say another word, Eugene swept past him, dragging Jennifer by the arm. "We need a word with you," Eugene called over his shoulder.

When they were inside the private office, Eugene closed the door. Jennifer pulled the cloth from her pocket and gave Bixley a succinct rundown on what they had discovered in the woods. "I touched the cookies and the flashlight," she admitted before she yielded the floor. She could see the anger in Bixley's eyes. Mobile's finest had searched the woods and found nothing. Now an old man, a publicity flack, and a black cat had discovered vital evidence. He was furious.

"Don't you find this situation a little...convenient?" His voice registered his sarcasm.

"I find it reprehensible that your men didn't discover the hideout. It was easy to find." Jennifer crossed her fingers behind her back. She'd never have seen it without Familiar's guidance. "I'd say this reflects more on the lack of ability of your men than it does on my tracking abilities." She could see that she'd scored a direct hit.

"I'll have the crime scene guys over there within half an hour." He picked up the material that Jennifer had deposited on the desk. All thoughts of the cat in his office had completely left his mind, and Familiar had taken a seat beside Eugene's legs.

"Mimi was a favorite of Eugene's," Jennifer said as she leaned over the desk. "He loves children, especially those from Mobile. Let's keep that one thing clear between us, Chief. You know how easily a town can be torn up by ugly rumors."

Bixley's gaze stared directly into Jennifer's. He understood her totally. "I'll keep that in mind."

"I'm going to speak with Mimi's friends," Eugene said as he prepared to leave. "If I discover anything, I'll call you."

"It would be better if you allowed the law to handle this." Bixley squared his shoulders. "We have the training...."

"Save your breath," Eugene said, completely unruffled. "You might consider the fact that these children trust me. *I've* spent hours and hours with them, listening to their ideas and dreams. They'll talk with me faster than they'll even confide in their parents. If they know anything, I believe I can get them to tell me."

"As usual, Eugene is right." Jennifer dared the chief to deny it. "If you refuse his help and the girl is injured in some way, the public is not going to be forgiving." Rumors could work in both directions, and she wanted to remind him of that.

Bixley nodded. "Go ahead. But don't get in our way." He waited until Eugene, the woman and the cat were out the door before he spoke again. "And remember, Mr. Legander, I have serious doubts about you in this matter. Serious doubts."

Chapter Four

Jennifer sat in her sun-room and held the portable telephone at least six inches from her ear. Nonetheless she could still clearly hear Maji Call's twangy voice going on and on about how critical it was for Jennifer to keep the story of Mimi's disappearance—linked to Eugene's name—away from the national media.

Jennifer's mind was on the local media, and a conversation Eugene had had with the very interesting James Tenet. James had called Eugene and proposed a guest column regarding the influence of literature on young minds. Jennifer had supported the idea, but Maji had given a firm veto. It was a dead issue, but still, Jennifer couldn't stop thinking about James's motivation. Was he trying to stir the pot? Or was it a legitimate ploy to give Eugene the same advantage that Crush Bonbon had—accesss to public opinion? James was a man to watch!

"Jennifer! Jennifer?"

Maji's sharp voice brought her back to the present. "Yes, Maji?"

"Eugene's reviews are excellent. The best ever. *The Children's Guild* review has acclaimed him as the finest living writer of children's stories. They find his work has 'depth and compassion for children, with sage advice and the wisdom of an adult who has retained the innocence of a child.'" Maji liked to quote directly from the reviews. "Jennifer, it's your job to see that some dreadful child in Mobile, Alabama, doesn't ruin this for us. If the big papers even get a whiff of what that moron on the radio is saying, it could be dreadful. Dreadful." She took a deep breath. "Worse than dreadful. Especially for you."

"Right, Maji." Jennifer was used to the publisher's dire threats. Grand Street Press was a small operation by most standards. They produced quality books, and Uncle Eugene was their symbol of excellence. His loyalty to Grand Street showed that mutual respect between writers and publishers still existed—and could be profitable for both. Eugene was the most important element of the publishing house. That was why she'd been assigned full-time to promote, and protect, the author's career. It was a fact that Eugene was the best living writer of children's fiction. It was a fact that he was wise and kind and generous. So up until Mimi Frost's disappearance, Jennifer's job had been a piece of cake.

"The local paper has played all of this down," Jennifer reassured Maji. "Most people in town realize Crush Bonbon is a bigot, an idiot and a fool." Most people, but that didn't mean Bonbon couldn't stampede the masses into a mob mentality. She just wasn't going to mention that to Maji. She'd learned not to fan the flames of Maji's pending-disaster complex.

"Well, make sure that no one pays any attention to that wretched radio person."

It was time for a change of subject. "We have a reading at the library. Eugene is going to try out the manuscript for his new story, *The Lizard King*." Jennifer found it fascinating that Eugene tried his work on live audiences of children as he honed and polished the final draft. The author liked to watch the children's reactions. Few living writers were willing to risk so much, but Eugene was a perfectionist.

"Promote that angle heavily. And for God's sake, don't let any more of those little snot-nosed brats disappear."

"Yes, Maji." Jennifer couldn't help smiling. If anyone in the media heard Maji Call talk about children, they'd think *she* might have kidnapped Mimi Frost.

"Keep me posted."

"Sure thing." Jennifer replaced the telephone. It had been a long and stressful day. None of the children she and Eugene had interviewed had known anything about Mimi. And she got the feeling they weren't lying to Eugene. There had been a frantic call to Eugene about the cat, Familiar, from Amanda Adams. Familiar had disappeared from the Adamses' luxurious accommodations and Amanda was worried sick. Jennifer smiled. The big black rascal had taken up residence at Eugene's and had refused to leave. He seemed to have been completely charmed by Eugene's youngest female, AnnaLoulou. Jennifer had been amused at the goofy expression on Familiar's face as he'd watched the young female strut and flick her tail. Eugene was right—there were definite signs of interest between the genders, no matter the species.

As if her thoughts were telepathic, the telephone rang and she answered to discover James Tenet on the other end.

"I know I'm risking decapitation or something worse at your hands, but I was wondering if I might get a press pass to Eugene's reading at the library tomorrow?"

Jennifer heard the amusement in his voice and knew instantly that Eugene had been right. James Tenet intended to needle her. He liked to get her riled—to see what outrageous things she might say next.

"I'd be delighted to arrange a press pass." Butter wouldn't melt in her mouth. She'd die before she'd give him the pleasure of losing her temper.

"Why, Ms. Barkley, you sound as if someone spanked some manners into you."

Jennifer's high-minded resolve flew out the window. "You arrogant pencil pusher. I wouldn't give you a press pass to hell. I—" She caught herself when she heard him laughing. Damn! He'd done it to her again. "But I would be glad to invite you to the reading as my special guest." She recovered herself as best she could, even though her ears were burning with her chagrin at being so easily tricked by him.

"If I didn't know better, I'd think you had a split personality. One second you're delightful and the next you're calling me names and threatening me with dire destinations."

"You bring out the best in me," Jennifer said sweetly. It crossed her mind that James Tenet didn't have to call and ask for a press pass to the reading. It was a *public* reading. Anyone could attend. He knew that, so he had to have some other reason for calling. The idea gave her a tiny chill of pleasure.

"I've been at the paper all day, and now that that deadline's over, I wanted to get a bite to eat. How about joining me?"

Even though she'd anticipated it, the question startled Jennifer. Less than twenty-four hours before she'd declared she'd have nothing to do with the man, even if he asked her. And now...

"I have something I want to discuss with you, Jennifer. Something about Eugene, and you aren't going to like it."

"What?"

"Meet me on the causeway. The Calypso. Say, in about thirty minutes?"

Jennifer automatically checked her watch. Where James Tenet was concerned she had no idea whether she should meet him or not. Every time she heard his voice it was as if her brain went on the fritz. Was he asking her on a date and using Eugene as a ploy, or did he really have something to tell her? Or, worse yet, some plan to trick her into acting like a fool?

James sensed her hesitation and realized that, once again, he'd bungled the situation. In more than one instance he'd been considered better than smooth with the ladies. But Jennifer Barkley had the most infuriating effect on him. He took everything just a little too far—his teasing, his seriousness, his thoughts. Lately he'd discovered that he was sitting at his computer staring at a blank screen and visualizing Jennifer's eyes or lips. It was a terribly distracting habit to form at the ripe age of thirty-five.

"Jennifer, I'm asking you to dinner, and I also have something to tell you about Eugene." There. He'd straightened it out with simple directness.

Jennifer responded in kind. "I'll meet you at the Calypso in half an hour."

"See you there." James was grinning as he replaced the telephone. But the grin faded as he scanned his computer screen. He'd pulled up the state wire to see what stories were breaking across the nation, and much to his surprise, he'd come upon a very brief reference to the developing feud between radio host Crush Bonbon and children's writer Eugene Legander.

The story quoted Crush as saying he was launching a campaign to get the author's books "banned and/or burned in all God-fearing cities and towns." Crush did not go so far as to claim that Eugene was a man who would like to injure children, but he implied it. James's lips quirked as he read the story again. Crush had a personal vendetta against Eugene, that was plain to see. At least for the moment he wasn't accusing Eugene of kidnapping that missing girl. For the moment. That was what he had to alert Jennifer to.

He picked up his coat, tightened his tie and started toward the parking lot. He had bad news for Jennifer, but he could certainly appreciate the pleasure of her company for dinner—before he had to break it to her.

JENNIFER had ten minutes to decide on what she would wear. The stubborn part of her urged her to go in her faded blue jeans and red silk blouse. She looked perfectly fine for the island atmosphere of the Calypso restaurant. Still... She snatched her favorite blue sundress out of the closet and slipped into it. The full skirt and fitted bodice showed off every firm curve. Let James Tenet eat his heart out. As her aunt Beth had often told her, "Look, look. But lookin' and gettin' are two different things." It would do her ego a lot of good to see James Tenet want something he couldn't have. The man had too much charm by far, and she'd seen him around town, squiring the most eligible of Mobile's bachelorettes. Even as she recalled the instances, she was aware that she'd never seen him with the same woman more than once or twice. He seemed determined not to show a public preference for any one lady.

The night was slightly cool and Jennifer picked up a soft white sweater and got in her car. The strip of highway that connected Mobile and Baldwin counties and crossed the Mobile River delta and Mobile Bay was called the causeway. A newer, safer, superhighway had been constructed above the water, but some of the tough old-timers who'd weathered hurricanes and floods still owned restaurants and lounges along the old highway where the water lapped the edge of the road. There were bait houses and a few hotels, but mostly there was tall saw grass whispering in the gentle April breeze and the sound of water beating a soft cadence against rowboats and black wooden piers.

Jennifer loved the smell of the water and the gentle sounds of the night as she drove with her window down. A full moon was slipping over the trees on the Mobile side of the bay, a silvery globe of pale spring magic. It was definitely a night for romance.

The thought surprised her, and embarrassed her. And it was Eugene's fault. He'd put foolish notions in her head where James Tenet was involved. And the tropical spring night was having an effect on her. She was normally a sensible young woman with her future completely in focus. A night for romance, indeed. It was a night when she'd better stay alert because James Tenet was a man who'd take advantage of any weakness.

She pulled into the parking lot of the Calypso with her jaw squared and her purse clutched. The saw grass whispered secrets about the moon, and just for a moment she stopped to watch the moonlight glitter silver on the soft waves of Mobile Bay. It was a beautiful evening.

"You walked up, and for a moment it was like a scene from a black-and-white movie." James Tenet stepped out of the shadows of the building. "Moonlight, water, a beautiful woman making an unknown rendezvous. And then I realized I was the lucky man."

His nearness made Jennifer unexpectedly breathless. She was intensely aware of him, of the touch of his wool blazer against the bare skin of her arm. It was suddenly as if every inch of skin had been sensitized to his nearness. The reaction was almost painful.

When she didn't speak—and didn't walk away—James stood beside her, content to listen to the night. "I grew up down the bay a little ways." His voice was as soft and gentle as the water. "Late at night my brother and I would sneak out our bedroom window and go down to the water. Sometimes we'd wade with a flashlight, just looking to see what we could see. Other nights we'd sit on one of the big rocks that had been thrown out to stop erosion. We learned to tell all of the birds by the sounds they made in the dark. We saw nutria and foxes, and sometimes even a passing alligator. One time the animal control people caught a 'gator that was over eighteen feet long. It had been living not a quarter mile from our front yard."

Jennifer felt as if time had stopped. She was in a magic bubble, a time warp where there was nothing but the erotic sounds of the night and James's voice, the smell of water and grass, and the feel of him standing so close behind her that if she drew a deep breath, she'd bump into him. She didn't want to move or speak. She wanted to stand and allow herself the luxury of the experience. James Tenet was a new sensation. She wanted to savor the way he made her feel.

An easy silence stretched between them. "Are you hungry?"

"No." Her voice was low, sensual, and she felt a twinge of embarrassment. "I mean, it's pleasant to stand here."

"I never thought I'd hear you say that it was pleasant to stand anywhere with me." Though Jennifer's words had been carefully chosen, he heard the slightly roughened texture of her voice. The idea that she might actually enjoy his company sent a jolt of pleasure through him.

"I surprise myself sometimes." Jennifer laughed. She was astounded! Here she was, standing in the moonlight with a man who could ignite her fuse like nobody else—and she was actually delighted. "I think Eugene must have cast a spell on me," she added, thinking of the writer and how he'd cackle at her behavior. He wouldn't have to say "I told you so." It would be clear in his eyes.

"He's a remarkable man," James agreed. "I just finished his book. I know it's for children, but I thoroughly enjoyed reading it."

"Eugene says that the best stories for children should also capture an adult's interest."

"He's right. Look, just there." As James pointed to the quick black silhouette of a bird skimming just above the water, his arm brushed her shoulder. "A brown pelican. They were almost extinct, but they're coming back since the chemical companies have been forced to clean up their pollutants."

At the touch of his arm Jennifer felt her heart pounding. She wanted him to kiss her, but it was a wild longing that she certainly shouldn't entertain. No matter what her brain said, her body had its own ideas. Without intending to, she turned slightly. James was at least six inches taller, and she looked up to find the moonlight bronzing the squareness of his chin and his straight nose.

He bent to kiss her, and she lifted her chin. It was a kiss that left both of them startled and breathless.

"We should go inside," Jennifer said. She felt off-balance, and James's hand steadied her as she turned out of his arms and started toward the steps of the restaurant.

For a few seconds James had been surprised by the intensity of the kiss. He was still trying to figure out exactly what had happened between the two of them when he opened the door of the restaurant for her.

Loud reggae music greeted them, and a smiling waiter led them to a table where James ordered two rum specials. He looked across the table at Jennifer, but her eyes were demurely cast at her place setting. For the first time since he'd laid eyes on her, she seemed unsure of herself. He felt a mischievous urge to tease her, but thought better of it. Jennifer Barkley was delightful when she was angered, but he was also developing a real appreciation for the softer side of her. Especially her soft lips.

The waiter returned, and they ordered. Jennifer watched James from beneath her shield of eyelashes. His kiss had surprised her. He was cocky and arrogant and filled with devilment. But his kiss had been tender, and very exciting. It had also been more intimate than she'd ever experienced. There had been a bond formed that frightened her in a way. She'd kissed her share of men, but it had always been carefree and simply sexual. With James, it had been something more.

"I've never seen you so quiet."

Jennifer was too aware that James was watching her. "It's been a long day," she said. "Eugene and I tried to play detective, but we had only minor success." She filled him in on the day's events, glad to put some distance between herself and her unsettled feelings as she talked about her favorite writer.

James leaned forward on his elbows, his interest keen. "That was good work. And the cat really found the hideout?"

Jennifer held up three fingers, then changed to four and finally back to three in an attempt to imitate a scout's pledge of truth. "Honest. Familiar found the place. Eugene says cats have a very sophisticated sense of smell."

James lifted his eyebrows. "Well, when Mimi is found, maybe we can do a story about the cat."

"What do you think has happened to the little girl?" Jennifer respected the fact that James was a lot more attuned to the city than she was. "Have there been other kidnappings lately?"

He shook his head. "Thank goodness, no. But to be honest, I'm worried about the child. I thought at first it was some childish prank, but the evidence you found makes me believe she was taken by force."

"And that's scary," Jennifer said.

The food arrived and they savored the spicy island flavor of jerk shrimp, black beans and yellow rice.

"I had another reason for asking you out tonight." James knew he had to handle the situation just right or Jennifer would think the worst of him. It was tricky business, especially with her hot temper.

Dread washed over her like a breeze from the water. "What?"

"There was a very brief article on the state wire today. It mentioned a 'feud' between Crush Bonbon and Eugene. I wanted to alert you. I think Crush is planting his own stories in the media, hoping for some national attention."

Jennifer lowered her fork to her plate. This was the one thing Maji Call dreaded most—and she, Jennifer Barkley, had never even considered the thought that Crush Bonbon would be smart enough to do it. She wanted to slap her forehead—what a dumbo she'd been not to think of such a thing. It was perfect for Crush—and completely in character. If he could start a real stink, he could promote himself and his sick talk show. It didn't matter that Eugene would suffer. In fact, based on Crush's past behavior, it would make him happy to see Eugene ruined.

"I'm sorry to be the one to tell you, but I thought you should know."

Jennifer saw the concern in his brown eyes and felt a little better. At least he wasn't gloating, or trying to use the story himself. "I should have been prepared for this," she said. Her appetite was completely gone. "It makes perfect sense for Crush. He's found an issue, one that's local but has international implications. I mean, what could be better than tarring and feathering a local writer of children's books, a man who might be involved in bad things happening to local children? It's like the violence on television dilemma. Has Eugene provoked something? Crush is all eager to scream yes and start the hangings."

"It's a tailor-made issue for Crush," James conceded. "I wish there was some way we could stop him."

Jennifer looked down at her plate. That one statement had caught her off guard yet again. James had somehow invested in Eugene's reputation. It was something she'd done automatically—because she loved the writer. James hardly knew him, yet he, too, wanted to protect Eugene.

He read her downward glance with ease. "I happen to think Eugene is one of the greatest writers of this century," he explained. "And Crush is one of the biggest butts. It isn't fair that Crush is going to benefit by harming someone like Eugene."

"My feelings exactly." Jennifer met his gaze. Something was happening between them, something serious. She could feel it in her heart and her mind, and though it frightened her, she would never turn her back on it. Eugene Legander *had* cast a spell on her where James was involved.

"I don't have a way to stop Crush, but I wanted you to know. At least you'll be prepared if the phone calls start coming in."

"Thanks." She sipped her drink. "Thanks a lot, James. You didn't have to do this."

"I sort of owed you." He grinned and his face was boyish again. "I made you lose your temper over at Eugene's, and I wanted you to see that I'm not as bad as you thought."

"I see that." And she saw a lot more. "Don't worry too much. I'll think of something. And the most important thing is to get Mimi home. That would blow out the flame of Crush's big campaign."

They both declined dessert, and fifteen minutes later they were outside the restaurant. James walked her to her car and opened the door.

Though she was tempted to stand and talk, Jennifer got behind the wheel, where she was safe from the temptation of another kiss. Even the thought of it fueled her anticipation and desire. "Thanks for dinner. And a million thanks for the tip." She looked up at him, surprised again by his handsomeness.

"My pleasure, on both counts." He leaned down and quickly kissed her cheek.

It was a brief kiss, but enough to send a sensation of tiny pulses over Jennifer's body.

"I have to cover a political rally in Fairhope tomorrow evening. Would you like to go? We could have dinner afterward, but then I'd have to go to the paper and write the story." He gave her an apologetic smile. "It seems I'm never really off work."

"It sounds wonderful—except for the politicians."

"Look at it as research into the human experience. I'll pick you up at six."

"And I'll see you at the reading." She waved out her open window as she drove away. She had a peculiar mingling of relief and disappointment as she left. The thought of another kiss in the moonlight had been too tempting. With a little encouragement from James, she would have stayed to sample one. But he hadn't encouraged her. Was he feeling as unsettled as she was by the emotions that had been stirred?

She let her mind wander as she drove across the beautiful causeway and was swallowed by Bankhead Tunnel. In a few moments she was deposited in downtown Mobile among the tall, new buildings heralding the downtown area's revitalization.

Mobile was a beautiful city, with a history as long and interesting as that of New Orleans. Spanish, French, British, Confederate and American flags had bannered the city at different times. Before that, Mobile had been a cultural center for many of the local Native American tribes. She'd dreaded her assignment to such a "podunk" little city. But she'd discovered a wealth of hospitality and generosity among the people here. Now she knew she'd never want to leave.

She drove by Eugene's house to make sure that all was settled. It was eleven, and a light was still burning in his front window. For a moment she was tempted to stop and check on him. She slowed the car beneath the willows, wondering if he was asleep. Before she could react, a small figure raced in front of her headlights.

Her foot jammed on the brakes, sending the car into a squealing slide as she swerved to avoid the dark-clad figure. Her seat belt saved her from smashing into the steering wheel, and after fighting for a few seconds, she was able to bring the car under control and stop it.

Legs shaking, she jumped out and turned to confront the person who'd almost ran out in front of the car. She heard footsteps running fast in the darkness, and then she saw a small figure darting beneath a streetlight. The child—and it was a child—dashed into some azaleas and disappeared into the night.

Still shaky from the near accident, Jennifer took a few moments to stop trembling. She'd almost killed someone. That it wouldn't have been her fault meant nothing. If the child had been a split second slower, he or she would have been crushed beneath the wheels.

But what had a child been doing in the shrubs beside Eugene's house?

The creepiest sensation moved swiftly down her spine. What had a child been doing out at eleven o'clock on a school night? At Eugene's? And why had he or she run away so desperately when Jennifer slowed her car?

It didn't bode well at all.

Chapter Five

"'And Giles, his scaly skin crinkling around his neck, turned to cast vertical green eyes at his brother and flicked his forked tongue.'" Eugene settled the manuscript pages on his knee.

"Is Giles going to take his brother into the lizard kingdom?" Tommy Franklin asked. Behind his glasses, his eyes were round with concern.

"What do you think?" Eugene was having fun. The children had spoken not a single word once he'd started his story. Now all fifteen of them were still engrossed in the world he'd woven of boys and girls turning into lizards.

"I think Giles should take his brother Jimmy," Tommy said seriously. "Jimmy is every bit as lazy as Giles. Their parents would probably be glad to see them go."

"I don't think so." Judy Luno shook her head emphatically. "Even when I'm bad, my mother wouldn't want me to turn into a lizard. And sometimes I'm *very, very* bad."

Jennifer stifled a grin. She had no doubt that the dark-haired Judy Luno could be more than a handful. The child had an opinion about everything, and she didn't hesitate to express it with tremendous intelligence. And vehemence.

"But Jimmy sort of wants to be a lizard. I mean, it's gross, but it's neat." Tommy Franklin looked around the group to see if anyone agreed with him.

"I would never want to be a lizard. Lizards are ugly, and I'm beautiful." Stephanie Rogers tossed her dark curls. "I'd hate it if my skin got all creaky and scaly and that red thing ballooned out in my throat."

"You'd never look like that." Chris Estis was smitten with the beautiful Stephanie.

"And lizards can't tap dance." Renee Paul demonstrated a few buffalo steps to prove her point.

"I think you'll have to wait until I finish the book to hear what happens to Giles and Jimmy." Eugene stood. Martha Whipple, the librarian, waved her hand to signal that refreshments for the children were ready. They ran toward her with shouts of laughter as she doled out the punch and cookies and chips and treats.

"It was a wonderful reading." James went up to shake Eugene's hand. "Delightful. I'm sorry I won't get to hear the end of the story." He spoke with sincerity, but his interest was on a big, heavy man standing at the far side of the gathering. Crush Bonbon had attended the reading, but so far he'd remained completely silent. James scanned the room and found Jennifer behind the counter pouring additional cups of punch. She'd kept a wary eye on Crush, and each time she'd looked at him James feared the glare might kill the radio talk show host. Jennifer had a hard eye when her temper was up.

"Don't worry, James. Jennifer won't poison him."

"I think poison is too impersonal. She'd rather choke him to death with her bare hands." James laughed along with Eugene, but both men knew it was true. If looks could kill, Crush Bonbon would be impaled on an ice pick of malice.

"Jennifer is far too defensive of me," Eugene admitted. He sipped the sweet punch, barely touching it to his lips. "I think Mrs. Whipple is trying to kill me with a diabetic attack."

James, too, had set aside his punch cup. It was like syrup, but the kids were swilling it down. "How long have you been doing story hour here?"

"For the past two or three years. Martha Whipple started it twenty-five years ago, though. I can remember bringing Eleanor and several other children up here to listen to her read the classic children's stories. She did a wonderful job."

"She seems to have a way with the children." James was watching them laugh and talk as Martha Whipple bent down to examine a cut or a bruise or to help with a difficult shoelace. "She's been staring at you all morning, Eugene. Is there romance sparking between you?" He owed the old gentleman a good turn, and Mrs. Whipple was an attractive woman with a bright and lively mind.

"Heavens, no." Eugene looked started. "Martha and I have been friends for years. She has no interest in me. Whatever gave you that idea?"

"The fact that the entire time you read, she watched every nuance, every smile, every little thing you did. And she obviously admires your stories." James knew he'd embarrassed Eugene—and good for that. If anyone could appreciate the eccentric life-style of a writer, it would be a librarian.

"Martha is my contemporary. If she's fond of anyone, it's that old reprobate, Allan Juniper, the historian. Now, he's been carrying a torch for her for fifty years." Eugene had recovered and was ready for battle. "I can see you're having difficulty controlling your own yen for Jennifer, but that doesn't mean you have to try and drag me down Lover's Lane behind you."

"Lover's Lane?" Crush Bonbon had moved up rapidly—and silently—for a man with his girth. "Who's sampling the delights of amour?"

"Crush, the mental picture of you mooning after a woman makes me too tired to think." Eugene backed away several steps. "I'm going for a walk and then home. I have some wonderful ideas to finish *The Lizard King,* and I need some exercise to work them out." He walked away without another word.

"Sorry to bust up your tea party, Tenet. Legander wasn't giving you the scoop on the next child he plans to kidnap, was he?"

"He said something about the Lindbergh baby." James glanced up to see Jennifer watching him with interest.

"Very funny," Crush said. He wasn't smiling. "You think you're better than me, don't you?"

"Journalistically, we're not even in the same profession." James normally wasn't so harsh, but Bonbon's personal attacks on Eugene were irresponsible, motivated by jealousy, and potentially damaging—without the first shred of proof. "I know cockroaches with more ethics than you, Bonbon."

Anger touched Crush's small, blue eyes. "You'll be singing a different tune when you have to admit that Eugene Legander is a dangerously deranged man. He *writes* about hurting children. My God, man, did you listen to the story today? A human boy is turned into a lizard because he doesn't mow the grass, or pick up his clothes, or help the old lady down the street. That's a little extreme, isn't it?"

Tenet gave Crush a long, cold look. "I know this is going to be difficult for you to grasp, but try. *The Lizard King* is a story. A made-up story. A fantasy, with magic and wicked princes and good elves. Those things aren't real, Crush. Maybe you should have your doctor check your medication dosage. You can't judge fantasy from reality any longer." He paused long enough to see that Jennifer was now within earshot, and she was grinning so wide it seemed her face would split.

"Yeah, there's magic going on here. Those people have done something to you. Cast a spell to make you forget you're supposed to be objective." Crush's face was red. "Man, you're over the edge. You must be getting some kind of attention from that publicist. She's good-looking, but is she worth your professional judgment?"

James was very angry, but he didn't show it. "Make that charge in public, Bonbon, and I'll sue you so long and hard you won't even own the dirt under your fingernails."

"Is there a problem here?" Jennifer stepped forward. She'd had to bite her bottom lip to get rid of the gloating look on her face. She might be the one hired to protect Eugene Legander, but James Tenet was doing all the work. And he did it from his heart, not because he was drawing a paycheck. That made it a million times more effective, and Crush had to know that.

"No problem." James smiled at her. With a twinkle in his eye, he lifted her hand to his lips. "The reading was wonderful. I told Eugene I can't wait for the end of the story."

"He's actually finished it, but he wanted to get the reaction of his critique group. That's what he calls the children. The questions they ask and the concerns they express are generally what other children want to know. Eugene says adults ask different questions."

"Does he pay them?" Crush wedged his large belly toward them.

"Oh, with his time and his wit and his love for them." Jennifer smiled. "Do you pay the people who call in to your show, Crush? Sometimes I've suspected you did. I find it hard to believe there are actually people that stupid, moronic, asinine and completely uneducated in this area. But you do seem to pull them out of the woodwork."

"Jennifer, Ms. Whipple is signaling you for some help." James pushed her none too gently away from Crush. He was having a hard time holding down his laughter. "Are you sure you don't have pit bull blood? That was some attack."

"He fries me. And most of the food he eats."

James laughed out loud. "Stop it. Now run over and help Ms. Whipple, and I'm running to the paper to file a story. Are we still on for tonight?"

"Yes. I've prepared some questions for the politicians. If I'm going to have to sit and listen to them lie, I'm going to try to pin them to the table."

James shook his head. "And they pay you to be tactful and personable. How did you get your job?"

"I wonder that sometimes myself." She grinned. She thought how delightful it would be to brush a kiss across his cheek, but she didn't. It was the wrong place, the wrong time. But the fact that she would see him later that evening made her very happy.

"Have you seen Tommy?" Ms. Whipple was trying to count heads among the dodging, weaving children.

"He's out on the steps talking with Eugene," Renee Paul said. She did a tap dance slap-ball-change and spun around before she stopped. "You know Tommy. He's all involved in what happened to Jimmy." She rolled her eyes. "He and Mimi were never content to let the story tell itself. They always thought they had to know *before* it happened. Mimi would have liked this story. Can I have some punch? I'm hot."

Jennifer pushed the girl's heavy bangs out of her face and looked around for Ms. Whipple. The librarian had disappeared for a moment and taken the punch container with her. "I wish Mimi could have been here." Jennifer spoke softly. Mimi's absence had been keenly felt by the adults and other children. "I know she really liked to hear a new story."

"She liked to make them up, too." Renee frowned. "I think she's trying to have an adventure. Like the children in Eugene's stories. You know, I think she's hiding because she wants to be brave and exciting. That's what I think."

Jennifer froze. She looked up to see Crush Bonbon; his grin was one of victory. She could see his two-cell brain working furiously. Now a child had leveled an accusation—that Eugene's stories promoted dangerous behavior in children. It was not what she'd hoped to elicit from Renee Paul.

"Except Mimi isn't as smart as the people in Uncle Eugene's books," Renee continued, unaware of the can of worms she'd opened.

"Well, maybe she'll be here next Saturday, for the conclusion of the story." Jennifer was ready to go. She'd offered to give Eugene a ride home. He'd never learned to drive—and never worn blue jeans—two facts of which he was extremely proud.

James was already at the door. He held up six fingers and nodded, indicating that he would pick her up at six. Jennifer smiled and waved him on his way, then turned her attention to the librarian. Martha Whipple was the center of story hour. She made it all happen.

"Thanks, Martha. Everything was wonderful, as always." Parents had begun to arrive to collect their children, and the library was clearing out fast. Jennifer knew most of the mothers and chatted easily for a few moments with each. In ten minutes, though, there was nothing left but paper punch cups, crumpled napkins and a few bites of cookies that had been inadvertently dropped to the floor.

"Do you suppose that little Frost girl is still alive?" Martha asked, pushing her glasses up on her nose. "She was such a frail child. Always a little sad, and determined to grow up to be a writer. I think of all the children, she loved Eugene the most."

Jennifer couldn't show her deep worry. She forced a smile. "I'm sure the police will find her. I have to believe that. It would break Eugene's heart if anything happened to that little girl. As fond as she is of him, he's even fonder of her. He just can't show it, you know."

"Yes, I know Eugene well." Martha smiled. "I've known him for years and years. Since long before he became the acclaimed writer he is today."

Jennifer finished with the cleanup and was ready to leave. The library door swung open and a frazzled Mary Franklin rushed in. "Sorry to be late. I know Tommy is going to be upset. He has a ball game this afternoon, and we're late." She looked around the library. "Where is he?"

Jennifer glanced down several rows of books but didn't spy him. "He was here a moment ago. I thought he'd left with you." She saw the fear rise sudden and thick in Mary Franklin's eyes. "Hold on, now. He's probably looking for a book."

Martha Whipple went to the intercom that was rarely ever used in the silent library. "Tommy Franklin, come to the children's desk. Tommy Franklin, come to the children's desk immediately." She clicked off the microphone and nodded to Mary. "That should rouse him out of wherever he's hiding."

Jennifer checked her watch. They waited three minutes, but it seemed like an eternity. "Maybe he's in the bathroom."

"I'll check." Ms. Whipple had no qualms when it came to rounding up a child, especially when she could see that the boy's mother was getting more and more terrified.

"I'll check outside." Jennifer suddenly remembered that Tommy had been seen sitting on the steps with Eugene. Maybe they were both still there. But surely Mrs. Franklin would have seen them.

She went out, anyway. Maybe they'd gone around the building to look at the plants. Eugene was a master gardener and Tommy was one child who really enjoyed learning about insects and leaves and berries and flowers.

The wide stone steps of the library were empty—except for a stack of three library books. Jennifer picked them up. They were children's stories, and they'd been checked out that morning. She held them against her chest as she walked around. Fluttering on the ground beside a small holly bush was a piece of white paper. Even as Jennifer reached to pick it up she knew it came from the manuscript Eugene had been reading—*The Lizard King*. She scanned it quickly. It was the part where Giles was first taken by the old magician and told he'd be turned into a lizard for his laziness.

She heard her breath in her own ears, a sharp, shallow hissing. Tommy had been kidnapped. Someone had taken the boy and left his library books and Eugene's page behind. Just as had been done when Mimi Frost had been abducted. Except this time the page was from a manuscript Eugene had held in his hands only fifteen minutes before.

She stood in the hot sun holding the page until it glared neon white in the blazing light. What should she do? And where had Eugene disappeared to?

"Jennifer?" Ms. Whipple approached her with rapid, small steps. "What's wrong? Tommy isn't in the library. I've searched everywhere." She touched Jennifer's arm lightly. "What's wrong with you?"

"I think Tommy may have been abducted." She'd tried to say it without letting the dread drag her words away from her.

"He was here not three minutes ago." Martha Whipple walked over to look behind the big azalea that grew right beside the steps. "Tommy will play a prank on you. He's just out here fooling around, not really understanding how worried we are. But I can tell you, Mrs. Franklin is in a state, and when she gets hold of Tommy, he's going to be very sorry he ever thought this trick might be amusing." She walked to the side of the building. "Tommy Franklin, your mother is going to tan your hide, and then when she finishes, I'm going to show you what an angry old woman can do."

Jennifer felt as if all the air had been sucked from her. She heard everything Martha Whipple said. She watched her move about, searching in the places she'd searched a million times before for errant children. She felt the sun beating down on the part in her hair, soaking into her exposed neck where she'd pulled up the long, mahogany tresses. She was alive and functioning, but dread held her paralyzed.

The library door opened and Mrs. Franklin stepped out into the sunlight. "Is he out here?" She looked around before she gave way to her panic and fear. "My God, where has he gone?" She clutched her right fist at chest level, as if she could pound her own heart into not hurting so much. "I should have been here. I was just running late because when I took those clothes back to the store I had to wait in line for half an hour. I should have left and come straight over here, but Tommy is always so good about minding. I told him not to leave the library. Not for any reason. But he didn't listen. He didn't stop and think."

"Where's Eugene?" Martha asked. Her face was white. "You don't think someone took him, too?" As soon as she spoke, she clapped a hand over her mouth. Mary Franklin looked as if she might faint.

"There's no proof someone took Tommy or Eugene," Jennifer said as calmly as she could. She crumpled the manuscript page slowly into a ball in her hand. "We haven't checked the cemetery yet." She gestured behind the library toward a small, well-kept burial ground that dated from long before the Civil War. "You know the kids love to explore in there."

"I'll get Mr. Smith, the caretaker." Mrs. Whipple, her face still splotchy with emotion, was glad of something to do. "Those kids are always getting in there, playing hide-and-seek, reading the tombstones, and generally being kids. I'm sure he's there." She gave Mrs. Franklin a quick, sympathetic look. "We'll find him."

Twenty minutes later the three women and the caretaker had crossed and crisscrossed the two-acre cemetery without turning up a trace of Tommy. They had found a homeless man sleeping on a grave, and a place where a campfire had burned into ashes, but there was no sign of Tommy. Or Eugene.

"I'll run by Eugene's and make sure he's okay." Jennifer wiped the perspiration from her nose. The day was warm, but it was the emotion that made her so hot. This could not be happening—yet it was. She put a steadying hand on Mary Franklin's arm before she spoke. "I think we should call the police. If Tommy were still on the grounds, we would have found him by now. If he's deliberately hiding, I think the police officers can make him understand that this isn't funny."

Unable to do more than swallow, Mary nodded her consent.

"Come on inside, dear. I've got some punch with enough sugar in it to offset any form of shock." Martha Whipple began to lead Tommy's mother inside the cool library.

Standing on the steps, Jennifer saw Mrs. Whipple wave, signaling that she would call the police. For a split second Jennifer started to tell her to hold off, but Tommy's safety was at risk. If he had been abducted, the sooner the police moved to begin the investigation, the better the chances to get him back.

And Mimi.

Jennifer's hands clenched as she realized she'd assumed, without any hesitation, that both children had been abducted by the same person. It was exactly what Mary Franklin was thinking, and Mrs. Whipple. And what everyone else would think.

The library door closed behind the two women and Jennifer stood for a moment in the hot sunshine before she went to her car. The first thing to do was to check to make sure Eugene was safe at home.

It was a short drive to the quiet tree-lined street where Eugene's small cottage snuggled among willow and tallow trees. Azaleas had been allowed to grow thick and tall, denying the traditional term of "shrub" for the plants that had exploded in vibrant pinks, purples, reds, oranges and whites.

As she pulled up at the curb, Jennifer's eye was drawn to the splash of colors in the azaleas and she missed the dark sedan parked just below Eugene's drive. Stepping out of the car, though, she instantly heard a man's voice raised in anger.

"You'd better open this door!"

Jennifer grabbed her purse, which was heavy enough to be used as a lethal weapon, and ran toward Eugene's front porch where a man was pounding on the door.

"Excuse me," she said, slightly out of breath as she stopped at the bottom step. He was vaguely familiar. As soon as he turned around, she recognized him. "Mr. Frost! What are you doing here?"

"I want to talk to the crazy man who writes those books. He was the last person to see Mimi. Why isn't he behind bars? He's done something to my daughter."

Jennifer considered her options—cold water, a slap, or reasoning. The latter seemed the most sensible, and possibly the least effective. Mimi's father looked as if he were about to burst a gasket. His face was red, his eyes almost swollen shut.

"I'm sure Eugene will talk with you, as soon as you calm down," Jennifer said. She walked up the steps and put a restraining hand on his arm. "But if you don't calm down, I will call the police."

"It's my daughter!" His voice was filled with distress, but the anger was fading rapidly from his eyes. "They think I did something to her. I love Mimi. She was the only good thing I had in my life."

Jennifer felt the sting of tears. Charles J. P. Frost was suffering, as any parent would be. He was helpless to protect the very person he loved most in the world.

Jennifer rapped lightly on the door and called Eugene's name. "Maybe some iced tea will do us all a bit of good," she said. "I think it would be a good thing for all of us to sit down and talk." She tried to hide the anxiety she felt. Eugene was not answering the door. Inside, she could hear one of the cats running back and forth.

"Would you excuse me a moment?" she said. There was a chance the writer was in the back garden so engrossed in his work that he hadn't heard the ruckus on the front porch.

"I should have stayed at home with Mimi." J.P. sank to a sitting position on the top step. He hadn't heard a thing Jennifer had said. "I should never have let Sharon push me out of the house. I should have stayed there for Mimi. Now look what's happened."

Jennifer eased down the steps and hurried along the side of the house. As her shoes clicked on the driveway she listened for the sound of Eugene's typewriter. There was nothing. Just the birds and insects that Eugene nurtured.

She slipped her key ring out of her pocket and unlocked the big, old wooden gate that opened on a thicket of trees and vines. In the middle of a suburban area, Eugene had managed to create a small wilderness. His garden was filled with many exotic blooms, yet there was also plenty of space for the native plants and the herbs and weeds that he used for his seasonings.

Jennifer almost screamed as an angry mockingbird let out a raucous cry and fluttered out of a privet hedge. The garden was too quiet. Preternaturally quiet. She had a sudden vision of a giant lizard, a creature who looked at her with the intelligent eyes of someone who had once been a little boy.

"Eugene!" She whispered his name though she'd intended to yell. "Eugene!" This time she was louder. Still, only the woodland creatures answered. "Thank goodness it's broad daylight," she muttered to herself.

Determined not to be a total idiot, she marched through the garden, checking all of the nooks and crannies where Eugene liked to sit and think. At last she had to accept the fact that the garden was empty—Eugene was gone. And J. P. Frost was sitting on the front porch waiting for some word of his child. What would he do when he discovered that Eugene and Tommy Franklin were now missing? What was she going to do?

The idea that Eugene might be in danger spurred her forward. She entered the house through the back door and checked to make sure all of the cats were safe. All were accounted for except Familiar. There was no sign of the black cat.

With her concern growing with each step, Jennifer opened the front door. "Mr. Frost, Eugene isn't home."

"I'll bet." He glared at her.

"Come in and look for yourself." She sighed.

A flush crept up the man's face. "I'm sorry. It's just that there's nothing I can do. Nothing. I thought if I talked with this writer, he might remember something that would help us find Mimi."

"Eugene has talked with the police. He told them everything he knew, and he's been hunting for Mimi, too. We're both very concerned." Jennifer couldn't begin to tell him how worried she was.

"Tell me honestly, Ms. Barkley. Would Mr. Legander hurt my child?"

"No." Jennifer closed the door behind her as she stepped out onto the porch. She put her hand on the man's shoulder. "Eugene would never deliberately hurt anyone, especially not a child or an animal. I swear that to you. Whatever has happened to Mimi, Eugene has nothing to do with it."

J. P. Frost stared at her for a long moment. "I believe *you* sincerely believe that. I just wish I could believe it, too." He turned, walked down the steps, and got into his car without looking back.

Chapter Six

Eugene has no idea he's being tailed. Here he comes, sauntering down the street and taking time to smell the roses, and the wisteria, and the dogwoods, which don't smell, and the azaleas, and the honeysuckle and every other bloom that happens to catch his fancy. Jeez! He's eating one of the honeysuckle blossoms. The man knows his botany, but I just hope he doesn't pick up the wrong bit of flora.

Of more immediate concern than poisoning is the car idling after him. With the glare on the windshield, I can't get a good view of the driver, but I have no doubt he's following Eugene. The question is, why?

I made a stop at the library this morning, but the sight of a dozen little heathens, eyes agoggle with anticipation to hear a story, made me decide to come straight home. I'm from the old school—children should be seen and not heard. Now my sixth feline sense tells me I should have stayed around and watched. Eugene looks happy, but that car makes me wonder. And by the by, where has our author been? It's almost noon and the reading was over an hour ago.

I guess I'll have to sniff out the answer to that one after I ID the driver of this car. Oh, my goodness, it's a woman, and she's crying! And she drove away as soon as Eugene turned to walk up the steps to his house.

"FAMILIAR, my handsome, black friend." Eugene stopped to scratch the cat. "Beautiful day. What an exciting reading. The children were exceptional. And that little Tommy Franklin. He asks the most exquisite questions! What a unique mind he has. My mind is slipping, though. I left without telling Jennifer."

The cat purred but kept his attention on the road where a little red car hit the curb and careered around the corner, as if the driver were drunk.

"My, my, that car almost wrecked." Eugene turned to tickle Familiar under the chin. "I took a stroll through Dr. Ambrose's backyard. Of course, if he'd caught me, he would have shot me. He isn't all that fond of me, especially since I introduced that crate of field mice into the tree stump in his backyard. He simply didn't understand that the mice would live in the tree stump while they destroyed it. He would have eventually gotten rid of the stump, which was his goal, and until that time the mice would have had a cozy home." Eugene sat down on the step beside the cat and stroked his sleek, black fur. "Why is it that people can't seem to grasp that all rodents aren't their enemy? We can live together. Even help each other out. That's the grand design."

"Meow." The cat turned bright golden green eyes on him.

"You understand, don't you? I think my children do, too. That's the wonderful thing about children. They know intuitively. Until society manages to bully it out of them and turn them into *humans*."

"Meow!" Familiar put his paw on Eugene's leg.

"How about a stroll over to the fish shop? I have a yen for some broiled flounder today."

Familiar got up and walked to the end of the sidewalk.

"Impatient rogue, aren't you?" With a spry step, the writer took off, with the black cat leading the way.

JENNIFER SAT DOWN on the steps at the library and buried her head in her hands. There was no sign of Tommy Franklin. None of Eugene. The police had searched the library from top to bottom without a trace of the young boy. Reluctantly, the police chief had called in the FBI. A two-man team was on the way to "interview" Eugene at this moment. They had left Jennifer in the care of the tall, lean agent who now lounged in the doorway at her back. He seemed content to prop against the cool marble pillar, but she knew he was waiting for her to make a move. Whatever she did, he would follow. Including going to a political rally with James Tenet at six o'clock. Jennifer groaned into her hands.

The mess was going to hit the fan, and very soon. There was nothing she could do, either. Worry about the missing children was uppermost in her mind, but she couldn't help but acknowledge the troubles that were now looming for Eugene. He was strongly implicated in the disappearance of Tommy Franklin. Two children were missing, and Eugene had been the last one to talk with each of them. She groaned again as she saw the imaginary headlines. The only bright spot was that Crush Bonbon had left the library before Tommy had gone amiss.

But James would surely have heard of the child's disappearance. She glanced at her watch. He was due to pick her up in two hours. If she canceled, it would only make things look worse than they really were. She wouldn't cancel her date unless—

"I hope you feel guilty. You're an accomplice, you know. If you'd listened to me when I'd tried to tell you about that old man, Tommy Franklin would be safely at home."

She dropped her hands and swung around. Her worst nightmare had sprung to life in front of her. Crush Bonbon stood in the open doorway and he was pointing a finger at her.

"They should charge you with a crime. You set him loose on this town. You aided and abetted him while he plotted to injure those innocent children."

Jennifer stood, looking from Crush to the FBI agent, who gave her no more than a bored glance. There was a hint of a smile at the corner of his mouth. He would be of no use.

"Be careful what you say, Crush. I'll slap a slander suit on you so fast you'll pop your girdle." She resisted the urge to poke at his big belly.

"Truth is my defense." His small eyes sparked with the challenge.

"Truth! You wouldn't know the truth if it bit you on the butt. Eugene has nothing to do with the disappearance of these children. As soon as he returns home, he'll tell the authorities that, and everything will be cleared up."

"Care to lay a small wager on that?"

"Of course!" Jennifer didn't really want to bet, but he'd thrown down the gauntlet.

"How about you give me thirty minutes on my show if Eugene is charged? Thirty minutes where I can ask you any questions about Eugene, children's stories, or how much money your publisher makes off Eugene and how important it is for you to protect his reputation—no matter what."

"Fine, if you'll give me thirty minutes—without interruption—if he isn't charged. Thirty minutes where I get to have my say and you get to answer my questions."

Crush's eyes squinted with delight. "Lovely."

"Check the docket book this afternoon. Eugene Legander won't be charged with a single thing. You want to know how I know?" She stepped forward, so close that she could smell his Old Spice cologne. "Because he's innocent!"

She turned on her heel and sat back down on the step, ignoring him. "Old Spice," she muttered to herself. "The people who make it should sue him for wearing it!"

She heard the library door close and she rubbed her forehead with the heel of one palm. It had been a long, long day and it wasn't getting any shorter.

"Jennifer!"

At the sound of her name she turned around to find Mrs. Whipple at the half-open door. "It's the telephone. Eugene for you. He's very concerned for you."

Jennifer sprang to her feet and almost ran over the FBI agent as she hurried inside. Before she could even get the receiver to her mouth she was talking.

"Where have you been? I've been frantic. Have they told you about Tommy?"

"Hold on, dearest. I've been to the fish market. Familiar and I selected the most superb flounder. Caught only this morning. I've put it on to marinate with some lemon and spices and—"

"Eugene!" Jennifer felt her control snap. "I don't want to hear about a dead fish!"

"That's exactly what those two FBI agents said."

She heard the caution in his voice and was instantly calmer. The two agents were probably standing right beside him. Eugene had a method to his madness. "What about Tommy?" She couldn't help the feeling of dread that came over her every time she spoke the young boy's name.

"I'm terribly worried about him." Eugene paused to clear his throat and gather his emotions. "I left him on the steps, reading a book about a boy in India. He was perfectly content and happy when I decided to walk home."

"You said you would wait for me." Jennifer knew she sounded petulant, but she was so worried she could hardly breathe. Now that Eugene was in good health, all of her concerns centered on Tommy and Mimi. She couldn't allow herself to imagine what might have happened to the children.

"I did wait. But then I decided it was a perfect day for a stroll. The flowers are magnificent." The sound of two male voices could be heard in the background and for a moment Eugene was interrupted.

"I told you the route I took," Eugene said. There was a note of false patience in his voice. "I've told you at least six times. Are you incapable of remembering, or is this some tactic where you think I'll forget what I said and slip up because I'm lying? Well forget that. It's a waste of your time. I'll tell the same story every time because it's the truth."

"Put one of the agents on the telephone," Jennifer directed through gritted teeth. If they were badgering Eugene, she'd give them something to digest until she could get over there and give them the main course.

"Everything is fine, darling. The gentlemen have asked their questions, and I believe they're ready to leave?" There was the sound of chairs scraping on the hardwood floor. "Yes, they're going. They wanted to take me down to the FBI headquarters, but I think they realize that's unnecessary. I've agreed to go down to see Chief Bixley in the morning." There was the sound of the front door closing. "Thank goodness they're gone." Eugene's voice was heavy with relief, but it grew shaky. "I'm so worried about little Mimi, and now Tommy. What do you suppose is happening to those children?"

With the agents out of his house, Eugene could express his concern. Jennifer knew exactly how he felt. The thought of the children made her sick. "We have to believe that they're still okay."

"That's why I agreed to talk with Bixley in the morning. He's got a lot at stake here, finding those children. And if there is some small detail that I've forgotten or overlooked, maybe he can ask the right questions. I've answered everything the FBI asked, and now I have to think."

Sometimes it was difficult for Jennifer to remember that Eugene was not a man of forty. He was always so full of energy and ideas, but his concern over the children was wearing on him, grinding him down.

"Rest, Eugene. I'll do what I can. Maybe James will know more details when I see him."

"What exactly happened to Tommy? Those agents were not very helpful, and of course, I haven't a clue."

Jennifer gripped the telephone and a sympathetic Mrs. Whipple handed her a cup of fresh black coffee. "In the time that you left and his mother arrived to get him, something happened to him. He simply disappeared. Just like Mimi."

"Tommy is a very self-reliant young man." Eugene sighed.

The defeat in that one sigh made Jennifer stand up. "I'm coming over to check on you."

"No."

"What?" Jennifer was astounded. Eugene had never told her not to come over.

"This is terrible. I need some time alone to think. Time to remember. I want to write down everything that transpired between Tommy and me before I walked away. I want to make notes about every car that was parked at the library. Anyone I passed as I walked away. I need to do this and I need utter quiet so I can think."

There was wisdom in Eugene's plan, but Jennifer also felt a creeping suspicion that he was too upset for company. That troubled her.

"I'm supposed to go to a political rally tonight. May I stop by after the rally?" She waited for his answer.

"Of course, and bring James with you. He might have some new ideas about this business. And don't ask—I've never heard you mention politics, so you must be going with that reporter. I may be old, but I'm not senile. Yet."

That tiny bit of feistiness in Eugene's tone took a burden of worry off Jennifer's shoulders. "We'll be by about ten or so. James has to go to the paper and write the story, so we won't be able to stay long."

"By that time, maybe Tommy and Mimi will be home."

"Maybe they will." She knew the words were empty as she spoke them.

JENNIFER SHIFTED her weight in the hard metal chair that made up the spectator area at the Fairhope rally. She'd listened to more than a dozen boring speeches by politicians running for everything from local to state office. The entire evening would have been entirely boring had it not been for James's acute powers of observation and humorous asides.

"Who's up next?" she asked. The woman who had walked to the podium looked familiar, but Jennifer hadn't bothered much with Alabama politics since moving to Mobile.

"Anna Green for the state legislature. She's a school board member, famous—or infamous as the case may be—for her mudslinging in public meetings." James inched forward in his chair.

Around them the crowd stilled as Anna cleared her throat and looked over the gathering. "The future of our children is at stake here, and that's why I've decided to take my campaign from the school board to the state house! We can no longer sit back and let the moguls of television, rock music and publishing destroy our children and our society. They are the enemy and we must attack." Anna Green lifted a clenched fist at the roar of applause from the audience of two thousand at the city park.

"I can't believe this," Jennifer whispered to James as she watched the faces of the crowd. "These people are buying into that propaganda. Anna Green can't possibly make children safe by attacking movie moguls."

"But she can make these adults think that she can. She's tapped into a real fear. These people are worried about their children and grandchildren. They want to believe that someone more powerful than they are can promise safety." James made a few notes on his pad as Anna Green continued her speech.

"Our world has turned violent. Television, movies, rock videos, even books, have portrayed violence as the answer to all problems. Our children are victims of molesters, abductors and perverts. They are even victims of other children who have been taught to shoot, beat or murder by example. I say we must act now. Violence on television must be stopped. Books must be burned. Instigators of violence and cruelty must be punished."

Jennifer felt her skin shiver with the raw power that Anna Green generated. She spoke with fervor and passion, and the crowd was swayed by her emotion as much as by her words. A chill settled over Jennifer as she listened.

"Burn the books!" someone in the audience yelled out.

"Burn the movies!" a woman cried.

"This is scary," Jennifer whispered. "It's mob mentality."

"And carefully orchestrated." James held his pen poised. "I heard Anna Green speak two weeks ago, and there wasn't a mention of her campaign against movies and books. She's playing on the fears brought about by Mimi's and Tommy's disappearance."

"Doesn't she realize she can push this crowd in the wrong direction. These people are truly frightened for their children."

James's jaw was clenched. "If she does realize it, I don't know that she cares. She's found a hot button, and it's irresistible."

The crowd roared approval again and the woman stood at the podium, her smile wide and welcoming. "We can fight this together," she said. "We must make a world where our children are safe."

"And the government controls everything we read, watch and think," James added under his breath.

Jennifer cast him a quick glance. She'd been so busy thinking of Eugene and his books that she'd failed to realize that in this issue, James Tenet and the newspaper stood to lose as much, or more. Freedom of the press was the first principle of democracy, and though Anna Green hadn't proposed muzzling the press, it wouldn't be far behind in an attempt to control the air waves and the publishing business.

"Let's go," James said.

"Where?" Jennifer asked, startled by his sudden decision to leave.

"I want to be backstage as soon as Anna Green steps down. I have a few questions for her."

Jennifer scrambled to her feet and followed James through the rows of chairs and then among the groups of men and women who were standing in the back.

Another speaker had taken the microphone, but Lester Havens did not have the issue or emotion that Anna Green had stirred. The audience milled and talked among itself, completely ignoring the quiet voice that proposed tax increases for school programs and reform of government programs.

James and Jennifer arrived to find Anna Green already swarmed by reporters. Several of the major dailies and television stations in the South had sent photographers and reporters. "Someone must have tipped them off that Anna was going to start a new thrust to her campaign," James whispered to Jennifer as he pointed out the men and women he knew by name and who they worked for. "This is an impressive turnout."

As they drew closer they could see that Anna was using the limelight to full advantage. Television cameras were whirring as the lights focused hot and white on her. "We have a local writer in town who's been linked to the disappearance of two children. I'm not accusing Eugene Legander of foul play, but I do think this is a perfect opportunity to examine the link between books, movies and the violence that follows."

Jennifer started to barrel forward, but James grabbed her arm. "Wait," he whispered.

"But—"

"Jumping in there will only make you and Eugene look worse. Just wait."

A tall, thin reporter with a microphone stepped out of the crowd. "I've read Mr. Legander's books. They seem more fantasy and lively imagination than dangerous dogma. In fact, my two children love his books. I find it hard to believe that Eugene Legander's books have prompted anyone to acts of violence."

"The world is full of unstable kooks, Mr. Grisham. Not everyone is able to discern between fiction and day-to-day life."

"If that's the case, surely Mr. Legander can't be held responsible for the irrational acts of defective personalities."

"He can, and he will." Anna Green's square chin lifted. "We are all responsible for the children of this country. No one, not even a writer, should have carte blanche to act and write with impunity."

"There was another politician with that viewpoint," the reporter said, holding his ground. "His name was Hitler."

Only James's strong hand on her arm kept Jennifer from rushing forward to hug the reporter. "Stay back," he whispered, drawing her closer to him. "That's Gary Grisham. I know him well, and he can handle himself."

Jennifer settled down, all too aware that James kept his hand just above her elbow. His grip was more supportive than restraining, and she felt a touch of anticipation nip along her skin. In the midst of complete turmoil, she was vitally aware of the man who stood beside her.

"This is supposed to be a press conference, Mr. Grisham, not a platform for you to express your views of history." Anna Green was angry but composed. "I'm giving up a secure seat on the City-County Board of Education to run for legislative office because I believe I have some solutions to problems. If you don't like my solutions, don't vote for me." She pointed to another reporter. "Yes, Gloria, what is your question?"

"Are you proposing a statewide ban on certain television programs and authors? If so, who are those authors and what are the programs?"

"I haven't prepared a comprehensive list, but my staff is working along those lines."

James listened to the question-and-answer session until Anna Green left.

"She's a dangerous woman," he said, turning Jennifer out of the crowd toward his car.

"What about the other speakers?"

"I think I should write this story." He checked his watch. "Anna took the sting out of the night. There's not a politician there who will try to upstage that act. This rally's over." His light touch on her waist grew firmer. "Jennifer?"

She turned to face him, surprised at how close he was. Looking into his eyes, she forgot for a moment her concern for Eugene and the problems Anna Green's speech would start. There was only James, his brown eyes caught between longing and determination.

"I need to go to the office. Now."

She stared up at him, watching the way his lips shaped the words. She'd kissed him once, and the memory made her flush. She also realized that she hadn't listened to anything he'd said. "I'm sorry, what?"

"Rain check. On dinner?" He looked at her.

"Of course." She understood. He had to go to the office. The Anna Green story was bigger than he'd anticipated. "Certainly."

"I'm terribly sorry, but this book burning business will have major repercussions. Once again, Alabama will be the laughingstock."

Jennifer shook her head, her dark mahogany hair gleaming in the fading light of the day. "I need to see about Eugene. It's been a terrible day." They'd discussed Tommy Franklin's disappearance, but James hadn't had any new information to add. The newspaper had assigned another reporter to cover the story.

"How is he?" James slid his arm around her waist, expertly maneuvering her through the people who laughed and talked as the political rally continued.

"He's very upset about the children."

"Tough break that he was the last one seen with Tommy."

Jennifer stopped. "How did you know that?" She'd told James everything about Tommy's disappearance. Everything except that.

James looked down at the ground, then back up at her. "You didn't know that Crush did a special show? At five. I heard it on the radio as I went to pick you up."

Jennifer felt the rush of blood to her face, and then the deadly cooling that indicated she was beyond angry. "I'll shove that microphone down his throat. I'll boil him in oil until the meat falls off his bones. I'll—"

"Hush, darling," James said as he pulled her into his arms. "Hush," he whispered. Several passersby had stopped to listen to her vile threats with amazement and then wariness.

"That despicable, cretinous, waddle-mouthed viper."

James pressed her tighter, conscious of the way her firm back narrowed at her tiny waist and then flared into generous hips. She was all woman—even if she talked like a sailor. His body responded to his thoughts and suddenly Jennifer was silent.

At the first pressure against her side, Jennifer lost all train of thought. She'd been enjoying the simple pleasure of dog-cussing Crush Bonbon. The act of saying how she felt about Crush out loud had been very gratifying. And then she'd found herself talking against the clean, starched front of James's shirt—not at all a bad position in which to vent her anger. But now? She eased back and he made no effort to hold her.

"Sorry," she mumbled, unable to meet his gaze.

He lifted her chin with a gentle finger until their eyes met. "You should be," he said, not bothering to hide his grin. "You should have your mouth washed out with soap."

"And *you* should have your mind washed out," she responded.

"A much more complicated process." He chuckled at the outraged expression on her face. "You do have an interesting vocabulary, not to mention your effect on me."

"I've noticed." She squared her shoulders. "Now, I believe you were going to take me home." She couldn't let him see that the brief exchange had affected her in exactly the same way. She could still feel the ironed stiffness of his shirt beneath her cheek, and the swell of muscle beneath it. His chest was lean and hard and it felt wonderful.

"To the car, milady." He gave a formal bow, still mocking her.

"You are the most infuriating man," she rasped. "Just when I think you're nice, you turn into a devil."

"Just when I think you're a lady, you open your mouth and the most outrageous words fly out."

The urge to kick him in the shins was strong, but Jennifer refused to lower her standard of behavior any more. How had the evening gone from one of partnership in horror over Anna Green's speech to sparring? It was almost as if he'd deliberately... She swung around to face him. "You manipulated me into saying those things, didn't you?"

His smile had changed from one of torment to one of appreciation. "It's easier to see you fiesty than worried half to death. Besides, you have to admit, you're easy to goad into an argument."

"You toad-poking Neanderthal." She advanced toward him. "You want to fight? Well, I'm ready."

James saw the fire of battle in her eyes and took a step back in mock horror. As he watched, the expression on her face shifted from grim to disbelieving and then to worry. "What?" He turned around to see Crush Bonbon hurrying away from Anna Green's campaign bus. Right behind him were Anna Green, Chief Craig Bixley, and two police officers.

Chapter Seven

Jennifer, James and Familiar stood on the front porch of Eugene's house at the direct order of Chief Craig Bixley, who stood inside with Eugene. Jennifer held the black cat, knowing that if she put him down and Familiar attacked the police chief again they might well shoot him.

"Take it easy," she whispered to the growling cat. "We'll get him out."

Familiar caught sight of the chief and spat at him.

"That cat may be rabid," Bixley said, tugging his hat tighter on his head. Long streaks of blood had dried on his right hand—the hand that had reached to handcuff Eugene Legander.

"Cats are an excellent judge of character," Eugene said, his dignity unruffled by the prospect of spending the night in jail. "Familiar has determined that you have no character," he said to Bixley. "Please be advised that if you continue with this charade of justice I will sue the pants off you and the city."

"Grand Street Press will see to it that all legal avenues are pursued," Jennifer said through the screen door. She moved to open it, but James restrained her.

"Don't give them any grounds to arrest you," he cautioned in a quiet voice, his large hand warm on her shoulder. "Eugene needs you out here."

Caution had never been her strong suit, but Jennifer heeded his words. "You're right, and I know you need to get to the newspaper."

"True, but now I need to see if they're actually going to charge Eugene. And on what grounds."

"Right." Jennifer slumped against the wall, still holding on to an unhappy Familiar. The reality of James's presence hit her with full force. For a time she'd deluded herself that he was there to support her, to help her, and because he might care just a little about Eugene. "Another story for the paper."

The expression on her face cut James deeply. "Eugene Legander's arrest is news." He didn't have to defend his profession. He hadn't orchestrated the turn of events that had brought him to Eugene's door on the tail of the local authorities and Anna Green. Jennifer had asked him to follow the car containing Bixley and Green. Crush had been right behind the police chief. One glance at Jennifer's face and James had sighed. Lucky for Crush Bonbon, he'd left the cavalcade, or Jennifer would have physically attacked him. Not to mention what Familiar might have done. He gave the angry feline a wary glance. The cat could do some serious damage if he took a mind.

Back pressed against the wall, Jennifer knew she owed James an apology. He'd taken her to Eugene's—at her request. He was here because of her. And he was a reporter. She'd known that about him from the beginning. Her real anger was at Chief Bixley and Anna Green, who was hiding out in the chief's car. How had she managed to persuade Bixley to make an arrest? Bixley wasn't brilliant, but he wasn't completely brain-dead.

And Crush Bonbon. He was definitely cruising for a bruising. She closed her eyes and tried not to think of him.

The screen door swung open and Eugene descended the steps between the two police officers. Bixley brought up the rear.

"I promise you, Bixley, this is going to be the most expensive mistake you've ever made," Jennifer said. "Anna Green is using you. She can use Eugene's arrest in her campaign and claim credit for it, which she will do unless it backfires. Then you can be certain she's going to stick you with the blame." Jennifer struggled to keep Familiar in her arms. He was growling at the chief.

James stepped out of the shadow of a porch column. "Mighty coincidental that Anna Green was plugging her campaign into the antiviolence movement and now you're here making an arrest."

"Remove yourself," Bixley said, puffing out his chest.

"Let me introduce myself, Chief. I'm James Tenet, reporter for the newspaper."

Bixley blanched. "What are you doing here?"

"I was covering Mrs. Green's speech and followed her here. Mighty big coincidence, wouldn't you say?"

"I don't know, Tenet. I'm not involved in politics. I'm paid to uphold the law and protect the innocent citizens of this town."

"And Mr. Legander isn't a citizen?" James knew he was stepping over the line of professional objectivity, but it was so clearly a case of politics that he couldn't let it go without pointing it out.

"Look, Eugene Legander may be involved in the disappearance of two children. You know, those little people who can't drive or defend themselves."

"*May,* Chief. May. That's the key word. You have no proof. You've let yourself be bullied by a woman seeking public office. She's using you to make herself look good. Now let me ask you one question. If all of this blows up in your face, who will pay the price? Will Anna Green be around to pick up the tab for a gigantic lawsuit, which I'm sure Ms. Barkley will file on behalf of her client. Grand Street Press will also sue for damages. That could run into the millions. And the city will have to pay. Right?"

"Well, that's not going to happen," Bixley blustered. "We're not really arresting Mr. Legander." He looked down the street to the car where Anna Green waited for him. "We're just going to take him in for questioning."

"Now that's a horse of a different color." James winked at Jennifer, gratified by the look of glee on her face. He might have stepped outside journalistic objectivity, but he had also prevented an expensive lawsuit that the city could not afford, and Eugene would be spared the humiliation of an unwarranted arrest.

"Then I'll come along with Eugene to give him a ride home," Jennifer said. She stepped to the front door and put Familiar inside. "Wait here, Familiar. We'll be right back. Entertain yourself with AnnaLoulou." She slammed the door before the cat could make a break for freedom.

Bixley's look told her what he thought of someone who talked to a cat. She eyed him back with one arched brow. "Ready? I'm sure Eugene wants to get back in time to watch the reruns of 'Dynasty.' He likes it with the sound off so he can make up his own dialogue." She sailed past Bixley and stopped at the sidewalk to wait for James.

"I can't thank you enough," she whispered as she took his hand. "You saved Eugene a lot of embarrassment, not to mention some time in a holding cell."

"Eugene doesn't need to go to jail. It's wrong that they're taking him in for questioning. This could wait until morning. He's answered all the questions put to him by local authorities and the FBI." James's voice was harsh. "This is a miscarriage of justice."

"And it ain't over until the fat lady sings," Jennifer vowed. She pressed his hand hard. "I'll take care of Eugene."

"I know you will." He took her small hand in his large one and brought it to his chest. "I have to write the story."

She smiled up at him. "I know. It is your job, like protecting Eugene is mine."

"Then let's go. I'll drop you by your house so you can pick up your car."

Impulsively Jennifer rose up on her tiptoes and placed a kiss on his cheek. "Thank you, James."

Before she could step back, his hands circled her waist and held her. The kiss he gave her was not chaste or sedate, his hands moving up her back to cradle her. His hungry mouth held hers, claiming her with an intensity that made her dizzy. But not too dizzy to kiss him back. Her arms twined around his neck and her fingers caught his thick, dark hair as she gave herself to the feel of his lips on hers, his body against hers.

At last they broke apart, both slightly unsettled by the power of the emotions they'd unleashed. He touched her lips lightly with his finger, a devilish smile lighting his face. "You're more than welcome."

ANNALOULOU, what an aristocrat! She's sprawled along the mantel pretending that I don't exist. Eyes closed, tail flicking seductively, she is totally alert. Ah, the quiver of a whisker as I change my position on the sofa. She's aware of me. Extremely aware. And I shall sit here on the green suede sofa and enjoy her beauty and charm—while I wait for Jennifer to return with Eugene.

I have a bone to pick with Jennifer. She may be smart and beautiful, but she has to learn that I do not appreciate being locked in a house. That dimwit Bixley would never have taken Eugene had I been left in charge. The absurdity of it!

And so far, not a single clue has been turned up to find those missing children. The human brain is simply not capable of logical deduction. Therefore, I have taken on the task. I will find little Mimi and that rambunctious Tommy.

Mimi was abducted from the woods. She put up something of a fight, and though no one else has bothered to check, I've ascertained that Eugene Legander has no scratch marks on him, except for a few on one arm made by a rose-

bush in his garden. Tommy Franklin is something of a little scrapper, too. I don't believe he was taken without a fight.

As soon as I get out of here, I'm going to take a gander at Crush Bonbon. I expect to find some flesh missing from his neck or his arms. That would be a basic piece of evidence.

Crush could easily have been at the park when Mimi was snatched, and he was at the library just before Tommy disappeared. What better alibi than to have been there and left! He's probably smarter than the average bear.

But in all fairness, Crush isn't the only suspect. I see that Charles J. P. Frost has something to gain—his daughter. And, also, as hard as it is to believe, Mrs. Frost could be behind all of this. Both are in a terrible child custody battle. If the father took her, he could make the mother look like a neglectful parent. If the mother took her, she could be planning on hiding her out in case the custody battle goes against her. It might sound farfetched, but I read those magazines at the newsstand on the corner of Jefferson and Ninth. There's a lot of craziness in families that break apart. And as we all know, humanoids aren't the most rational species in the universe.

The one thing that bothers me with the parents' scenario is the pages of Eugene's work left behind. Jennifer could be in serious trouble for taking that manuscript page from the library. I found it crumpled in her jacket pocket. If Bixley and that crowd ever finds out she tampered with evidence, she's going to a jail cell faster than you can say boo.

I could be off on the wrong track here, but Trained Observer that I am, I did notice something interesting about that manuscript page. Jennifer realizes it is an abduction scene, of sorts, but the page number at the top was also x-ed out and a new number written in. The original number was ninety-five. The new number, written in a very unstable hand, I might add, is ninety-eight. Since I've been confined in this house like a common prisoner, I did manage to check

Eugene's original manuscript pages. They are perfectly paginated, something any editor would appreciate. And the page should have been ninety-five. So that leads me to believe that ninety-eight is a significant numeral. But how or why, I haven't any idea. This gives me a very creepy sensation, as if the kidnapper is someone who considers himself very smart. Much smarter than Eugene or Jennifer or the cops or anyone else who might be looking for these kids. It's as if the kidnapper is playing with us—deliberately tossing clues at us that we're too dense to pick up on. Or, at least, the humanoids aren't exactly setting the woods on fire with brilliant leaps of deduction.

As interesting as the puzzle is, I can't help but wonder where the children have been stashed. My feline instincts tell me that they're being held against their will, but that they haven't been injured. At least, not physically. I don't imagine being abducted and held is good for any kid's emotional development. But at least Mimi isn't alone now. Or that's what I feel. And Tommy seemed like a kid with a lot on the stick.

The other interesting point is that a ransom note hasn't been received. If I had to make a kitty prediction, I'd say another child will disappear. And in the not too distant future.

Hey! What's that noise outside the back screen porch? Someone is prowling around Eugene's garden! Drat! The door is locked and the windows are bolted down. I know I could pry one up—if I had the time and some tools. But I'll have to settle for pulling down the blinds.

Ah, a satisfying crash, but I fear it frightened away whoever was out there. Yes, they climbed the back gate and I hear their footsteps on the drive! Blast my clumsiness! I didn't even get a glance at them!

"LOOK! Someone's running down the street!" For the second time Jennifer had discovered someone skulking around

Eugene's house. The dark shadow disappeared among the shrubs of the Johnson house just as she jumped out of the car.

"Don't go." Eugene's soft command made her turn quickly back to him.

"Are you okay?"

"Perfectly. But you aren't exactly armed to take down an intruder." Eugene's observation was made with a dry tone. "Let's have a glass of port instead. I have the feeling we're overlooking something very important, and very simple."

The intruder was long gone, and Jennifer gave up any thoughts of chasing after him. The foliage along Eugene's street was dense and healthy. There were a million places to hide.

They hurried up the walk to the front porch and in a moment Eugene ushered her inside.

"Ouch!" Jennifer felt the swat of an angry cat paw. "Familiar!" She shook her leg but he only dug his claws in deeper.

"Now, now." Eugene bent down and lifted the cat with ease. "He's paying you back for locking him in the house. Familiar is a free agent. He likes to make his own decisions." He stroked the cat. "He deeply resents the fact that you imprisoned him."

"Meow!" Familiar nuzzled under Eugene's chin, his motor running like an outboard.

"Disgusting." Jennifer flopped down on the sofa. "If you can tear yourself away from that manipulative cat, I'd like a glass of brandy, or maybe some Drambuie. Even better, do you have any Baileys?" She let her head fall back against the overstuffed sofa. "I can't believe this day. And I haven't even begun to deal with Crush Bonbon."

Eugene appeared at her elbow with a cut-crystal glass of the rich chocolaty liquor. "To your health, my dear." He produced his own glass of ruby red liquid, lifted in a toast.

Jennifer sat up, clinked glasses, and savored the taste of the liqueur.

To her astonishment, Familiar leapt from the sofa and attacked the stacked manuscript pages of Eugene's book. With two swats, he had the four hundred pages scattered across the floor.

"Now, Familiar." Disapproval made Eugene's voice harsher than normal. "If you're angry with Jennifer, take it out on her. Not on my book." He bent to gather up the pages and Familiar made another dive, pushing them completely out of order. Clapping his hands together, Eugene scatted the cat. "He is a torment tonight."

Jennifer got down to help put the manuscript together. For several moments they worked in silence, until Eugene held up a fistful of pages. "One's missing," he said. "Page ninety-five."

A guilty flush crept up Jennifer's neck. Tilting her face down, she hid behind the curtain of thick, dark hair.

"It was in the manuscript when I was at the library." Eugene stood, his face perplexed. "I read that page, came home and put the manuscript down right on this table and it hasn't been moved since." Awareness made him arch his brows. "Except for the few moments that I left it on the steps at the library when Tommy and I went around the building to examine the black hawthorns in the cemetery." He cast a glance at Jennifer. "There was a page of my manuscript at the library, where Tommy disappeared, wasn't there?"

Jennifer nodded, then finally met his gaze. "I took it. I found it and I took it, before anyone else saw it."

"That's tampering with evidence." Forgetting the manuscript at his feet, Eugene took a seat on his favorite chair beside the bay window and a fireplace. "You could be in serious trouble, my dear."

"It was an instinctive action." She wasn't trying to apologize, not really. "It was there, I saw the implications, so I took it. I knew you were innocent and I knew that page would make you look guilty."

Eugene sipped his port, his fingers stroking the brocaded arm of his chair as he thought. "Only trouble is, there might be a clue to Tommy's whereabouts in the manuscript."

"Meow!" Familiar leapt from under the coffee table onto Eugene's lap. "Meow!" he insisted.

"Familiar agrees," Eugene said, completely unperturbed by the cat's behavior. "In fact, that's why he knocked the manuscript over, to let us know about the clue."

"I think he was tattling on me." Jennifer gave the cat a dark look.

"Well, someone has to keep you honest." Eugene looked directly at her. "Stealing evidence."

"Protecting you," she countered.

"But I've done nothing wrong. I don't need protecting."

Jennifer started to speak, then stopped. There were times when Eugene Legander had too much trust in the basic goodness of humankind. He couldn't really believe that someone would set him up, out of jealousy, hatred, or whatever base motivation. It was just difficult for him to accept that some people were rotten.

"You're going to have to tell the police what you did." There was no arguing with Eugene's tone.

"Not in this lifetime." Jennifer put her glass on the table. "I acted out of an honest impulse to protect you. If I so much as hint that I disturbed evidence, it will only make you look twice as guilty, and possibly me, too."

"Jennifer, there might be something on that page that would help the police find Tommy. Whatever risk of embarrassment we run, it's certainly worth Tommy's and Mimi's lives."

It was exactly the thing that nagged at her. There was nothing on the page that would lead to the children. She'd read it over several times. Not a single thing. All it would do was implicate Eugene, and now her.

"There might be fingerprints." The writer had stood up and was pacing the floor.

She cowered at the thought. She'd crumpled the paper up and stuck it in her jacket pocket, never thinking it might contain some valuable evidence. No, she hadn't thought of that until much later.

"Where is it?" Eugene asked.

"In my jacket, in the car." She got up, also. It would be better to get this over with. She went out and fished around in her pocket until she found the ball of paper. Back inside, she held it out to Eugene.

"Oh, dear," he said, seeing the condition. He sat down and started to smooth it out on the sleek surface of the coffee table.

Before he could get it unwadded, Familiar was on the table patting it with a paw. "This isn't a toy," Eugene said.

"Maybe he's trying to show you the important part," Jennifer said, giving Familiar a look. "He's a rat fink."

His only response was a flick of his tail that caught her just under her nose.

"Wait a minute." Eugene held the page down and watched in fascination as Familiar slapped the top right hand corner. "Did you change the page number?" He shot a look across the room.

"I didn't change a thing. I just wadded it up." Despite her determination to keep a safe distance from Familiar, Jennifer leaned over to look. "Why would someone change the page number?"

"It's a clue."

"Meow!" Familiar leapt off the table and headed into the kitchen yowling a loud complaint.

"He's hungry." Jennifer shook her head. "He's finally got us stupid humans to understand the clue and now he's ready to chow down."

At the doorway of the kitchen, Familiar twitched his tail twice and licked his whiskers.

"Remarkable," Eugene said, getting up and following Familiar's disappearing tail.

"Don't give him anything except dry cat food." Jennifer was rewarded with an indignant meow from the cat, and she leaned back against the sofa and sipped her liqueur. The blasted cat was something special. But she had a major problem. If the page number was a clue to the whereabouts of the children, she was going to have to tell the authorities. And to do so, she'd have to admit she took the page, which would cast even more shadow on Eugene.

"Maybe Martha Whipple could *find* the page?" Eugene was standing ten feet away, staring at her.

"I hate to involve her."

"Just put the page in the library. She could find it there. I wouldn't enlist her in any deception. That wouldn't be fair, but she could discover the page and report it, which would serve the same purpose as you turning it in."

Jennifer sat up. "That might work. Except I'm not certain anyone would understand the importance unless they knew the page was left at the time and place Tommy was taken."

"Or you could give it to James, explain what happened and hope that he could explain it in the press." Eugene chuckled as he took his favorite chair. "Your enthusiasm is overwhelming. There's no easy way to do this."

She felt her newfound resolve evaporate. "That might work, too." She put her glass down and leaned forward, elbows on her knees. "Who do you think took the manuscript page?"

Eugene's brows drew together. "I was thinking about that in the kitchen when I was giving *le chat* a sampler of cheeses. He seems fond of the Brie. I did put the manuscript down for several minutes while I was helping some of the youngsters with their lizard lessons."

"I don't know if I want to hear this."

"I was demonstrating how still the lizard can be, and how they blend into the foliage. There were several chameleons outside the library, and I put them on different greenery, admonishing the children not to injure them. I was only out there a minute."

"And your manuscript was left unattended?"

"On one of the chairs."

"With Crush Bonbon right in the room." Jennifer didn't know if she was excited by the discovery or upset.

"Mr. Bonbon and a number of other people. I have to point that out, in all fairness."

"Parents. The library staff. Me. James. Who else?"

"Anyone could have been in the library. It is a public facility, and someone could have been in the stacks hiding, waiting for an opportunity."

"Was Tommy selected, or was he just convenient?" Jennifer felt her muscles involuntarily tense. Every time she really concentrated on the children, she felt so helpless.

"Deliberate. Both Mimi and Tommy were the would-be writers. They're the children who spent the most time with me."

Jennifer felt her apprehension grow. "Then if that's accurate, who's next?"

"Judith. Maybe Renee. Or it could be Stephanie."

"My God. We have to stop this. Listen to us, we're sitting here planning this out as if there's nothing we can do to stop this monster." She went to Eugene and sat on the arm of his chair. "We have to stop this, Eugene."

"I don't know if we can," he said, for the first time showing the desperation and despair he felt for the loss of the children. "God help us, I don't know what we can do."

Chapter Eight

James Tenet sat on Eugene's sofa and let his fingers stroke Familiar's silken hair. Jennifer, dressed in a soft peach suit complete with hose and heels, sat with her hands clasped in her lap, her features a study in contrition. The midmorning sun filtering through the semiclosed blinds seemed to bathe her in a celestial light, an image heightened by her pose.

"I wasn't thinking clearly. I just took the page from the steps and crammed it into my pocket." She spoke to her hands as if she were too timid to address James or Eugene.

Eugene produced the rumpled page and spread it out on the coffee table before James could say anything.

James glanced down at the paper but instantly looked back up at Jennifer. "This is serious," he said. He made no effort to write anything in his notebook.

"It was an act of innocence," Eugene insisted loudly. "She saw the page, thought I'd dropped it, and picked it up."

James never took his gaze from Jennifer. "Is that true?"

She swallowed, then lifted her crystal blue gaze to meet his. "No. I saw the page, thought it looked terribly incriminating, so I jammed it into my pocket to hide it. That's the truth."

She looked as sweet as an angel, and that made him deeply concerned. He paused for a long moment before he spoke. "Incredibly stupid." James made the pronouncement and waited again. "I said it was stupid." He leaned forward, trying to catch her elusive gaze. She wouldn't look up at him. The sheet of silky hair covered everything except her nose, casting even her full lips in shadow.

When he failed to get any reaction, he gave Eugene a worried look. "I've never seen her so docile."

Eugene shrugged. "She's been like this since she came over this morning and insisted that I call you. She wants you to go with us to the police when we turn the page in."

"Me?" James swiveled his head to look at Jennifer. For one split second he caught a lively blue gaze peeking out from under the hair. "Aha! You're up to something! I should have known that this demure, modest creature who sat before me, so contrite, was a fake, a cheap imitation of the real Jennifer Barkley."

"Oh, give it a rest," Jennifer snapped as her head came up. "I'm practicing for the benefit of the police chief. I took the page and I want to give it to them now. We think there's a clue in it." She picked it up and showed him the page number that had been changed.

"Ninety-eight. What could that mean?" James studied the page but his gaze slipped over the top to find Jennifer. Her blue eyes were crackling with determination, and he found that he much preferred her alive, every cell hopping with energy and mischief—rather than slunk down like a kicked dog.

"If we knew what it meant, I wouldn't have to go turn myself in," she said, getting up to pace the room. The pale silk suit shimmered like molten peach light along the contour of each muscle as she strode to the door, turned and came back like a tiger in a cage.

"This is going to look terrible." James studied the page, reading it several times before he spoke again. "Even if you can pull off acting like a saint, Anna Green will buy television time for this, and Crush Bonbon will do a week-long show."

"I know." Jennifer twisted her hands in an uncharacteristic gesture of sheer anxiety. "But we have to give the police the information. What if it leads to the children? Even knowing how terrible this is going to be for me, and especially for Eugene now that I've mucked it up, I'm still going to have to do it."

James picked up the paper. "Maybe not." One expressive eyebrow lifted over his dark eye. The hint of his ancestry showed in the inscrutability of his eyes, suddenly shuttered.

"What's cooking in that brain of yours?" Jennifer asked. "What are you thinking?"

"That I can turn the page in. I can say it was sent to the newspaper, and I didn't realize the importance so I threw it away, had second thoughts, and then decided to give it to the police."

Jennifer exhaled her breath. "You'd do that. For me?"

His smile was slow to arrive, lifting one corner of a mouth that had taken on a very sensual cast. "Of course, it's going to cost you."

"How much?" Jennifer swallowed. She didn't necessarily dislike the look in his eyes. In fact, it sent her blood rushing, tingling along the most intimate stretches of flesh. It was one payment she might look forward to making.

"You aren't in a position to negotiate," James observed.

His enjoyment was too much. It was one thing to tease, but he was getting far too much satisfaction over her predicament. She leaned forward, her eyes boring into his. "You think this is funny, don't you, you sick, demented word hustler. This is just a chance for you to flex your power. Neanderthal! Cretin! Low-life blood-sucking—"

"Jennifer!" Eugene was laughing. "Wherever did you learn such colorful descriptive words. I do believe *you* should be writing a book."

"I'm going to tear his heart out and eat it with a spoon!"

"That one you stole from a movie," James said calmly. "*Robin Hood,* the Sheriff of Nottingham."

"Then I'll carve your liver with a fish scaler!"

James couldn't help himself, but just to be on the safe side, he firmly grasped her wrists before he answered. "That sounds very original. Except fish scalers aren't very sharp."

"I know." Jennifer tried to tug free but couldn't break his grip.

"Calm down now. I just wanted to be sure you weren't sick. You were so biddable, so tractable, so *ladylike* when I first came in, I was afraid you might be terminal."

"I'll show you ladylike!" Jennifer tugged harder. "I'm worried sick, and your idea of help is to taunt me. Especially when I'm trying to keep my temper under control." She jerked so hard her hair shimmered in a curtain of mahogany lights.

"Eugene?" James looked to the writer for help. "If I let her go, she might kill me."

"Do whatever you think is necessary." Eugene gave a courtly bow to them both. "I shall retire to the garden to finish a scene. Please don't yell. It upsets the cats terribly when humans act savagely. Other than that, have a go at it. Do whatever is necessary, James."

"Eugene!" Jennifer tried to break free. "Don't leave me with this devil."

With a wave over his shoulder, Eugene went into the kitchen, closing the door behind him. In the silence that followed, Jennifer clearly heard the back door slam.

"Now you're mine, to do with as I choose." James's grin was wicked.

"Familiar!" Jennifer made an appeal to the black cat.

Familiar stood, stretched, and then curled into a ball on the wing chair with his back to Jennifer.

"I think he's telling you that this is a lesson you've been needing for a long time."

Jennifer ceased struggling. Her heart was pounding and every inch of skin was wickedly alive. Holding her with his gaze, he drew her hands slowly toward his chest, forcing her to lean toward him.

"What shall I do with you," he asked rhetorically. "Such a spitfire. And one that specializes in destruction of vital organs."

"James." She swallowed again as she saw his gaze linger on the pulse at her neck. She could almost feel his lips, and the idea made her want to run from him and surrender in his arms at the same time. Once he started, it would no longer be a game. "You know I talk with... some exaggeration."

"Indeed?" He lifted that single eyebrow and grinned. "I've noticed that you're very bold, on verbal assault."

"Then you also know that I don't really mean all of those things that I say." She could feel the heat of his body through his slacks where her arms rested on his thighs.

"I'm not so certain." He drew her another inch closer.

"I wouldn't really hurt you." She felt the whisper of his breath against her neck where he'd leaned toward her. The first brush of his lips made her want to moan, but she held it in her throat.

Very gently, he released her wrists and placed his hands on her shoulders, offering support rather than restraint. "There are many things I want to do with you, but injury certainly isn't one of them," he whispered, the words like soft kisses on the heated skin below her ear.

He lifted her face up with one hand, eyes asking her permission, and leaned down to kiss her.

Jennifer met the kiss with soft, willing lips. She'd dreamed about the kiss they'd shared outside the Calypso, wondering if her memory could possibly be accurate. As she yielded to his exploration, she knew it had been no fantasy. Her hands lifted to his chest, feeling the drumming of his heart and knowing that it matched the pulse of her own blood.

Strong arms lifted her into his lap and tilted her back, exposing her throat and the excitable places along her neck. His lips, warm and hungry, moved to her ears, and her right hand tightened in his straight black hair.

"You're so soft," he whispered, and was rewarded with a delicate shiver.

Using his shoulder as a brace, Jennifer lifted herself to return the attention. The collar of his shirt was crisp against her lips and her searching fingers found the buttons. Undoing two, she slipped her hand inside, pushing back the material so her fingers had free reign. The musky scent of after-shave lingered on his bronzed skin and she kissed a trail to his ear.

Exploring the contours of his body, she drew a moan of excitement from him. "Ah," she whispered, making him groan again. Her hand played inside his shirt, searching the taut muscles of his upper chest, the skin sleek and smooth, finding the hard nubs of his nipples, tense with desire.

James captured her hand and held it still with his own. With a slight shift, he tilted her back and resumed his soft kisses as he nuzzled her dark, clean hair. "You smell like rain," he said. "It's wonderful."

A heavy wanting made her languid, and she savored the slow path of his lips, moving back to her mouth where he claimed her with sudden passion and need.

Reluctantly he lifted his lips and stared at her. "Somehow, I don't think this is exactly the cure for your tart tongue."

"Oh, I think I may need a lot of this medicine," she said, her blue eyes brimming with desire and amusement. "Stop now and I'll cut out your gizzard and cook it with rice."

His kiss was so hungry that Jennifer's heart lurched. Her arms wound around him, holding him tight as his hands moved up her back, touching, teasing, tantalizing, until one circled her breast, feeling the full softness.

She opened her eyes to look at James and caught the green gaze of Familiar staring at her from the back of the sofa. The cat was perched, his whiskers puckered in disapproval. His tail twitched three times in a rapid, whipping motion.

This time Jennifer broke the kiss, her breathing ragged. "What are we going to do?"

He looked around the room and eased her up slightly. "Nothing more, at least not here." His eyes were no longer inscrutable, and passion blazed in them. He lifted a hand to touch her lips. "So sweet," he said, "to produce such dire threats."

Her own fingers traced his jaw, aware of the softness of his skin. He was a handsome man, a man of intelligence and integrity. A man she wanted. "If I'm not in jail tonight, let me make dinner for you. I promise, I can cook."

"The menu is not really my biggest concern." His gaze slipped to her breast where the first button of her jacket had come undone, revealing the tiniest edge of peach-colored lace. He bent swiftly and kissed it. "Dinner tonight," he said, finally looking into her eyes. "I'll bring the wine."

She nodded, excitement tickling her throat. "And now?"

"We have to figure out what to do to keep you from being put in jail. And we have to find the person responsible for taking those children. It's been two days for Mimi. Two days of terror, I'm sure."

Jennifer eased onto the sofa beside him, buttoning her jacket with quick, sure fingers. "What could ninety-eight possibly mean?" she asked.

"I don't know." He picked up the manuscript page again and studied it. "But I have to take this to Bixley right away. They may be able to figure this out, and time is crucial."

"I know." Jennifer ducked her head at the rush of guilt. When he started to rise, she reached out and stopped him. "James, you could get into a lot of trouble if anyone finds out about this. It could be your career."

He didn't look away, but held her gaze for several seconds. "I know. But I also know that Eugene Legander is innocent of having anything to do with the disappearance of those children. He'll be crucified if you take this in. And I agree, the police have to have it. They can't conduct an investigation if we withhold evidence. This way, they get the evidence, and Eugene isn't tarred with guilt."

"But what about you? It could mean your job, your reputation, everything."

"Let me worry about that." He gave her a wink. "Somehow, I think maybe I've found something that's worth the risk." He picked up his jacket from the arm of the sofa. "I'll see you tonight. At seven."

"I'll be waiting for you."

"BOY, do the mighty fall hard. Miss Spitfire was going to die before she would consider going out with Clark Kent. Now she's planning a menu and I think it has more to do with which lacy little teddy to wear than what goes good with asparagus. Ah, humans. I guess they have to work hard at this lovemaking business. Long gestation period, normally one offspring at a time. If they didn't work at it, the race might disappear from the face of the earth. Then felines would rule.

I've given it some thought and if we had a prehensile thumb, humans would never have taken control. There's no solid scientific evidence to prove this, but there's none to disprove it, either, and I'm certain I'm correct.

Enough philosophizing. It's time to find those children. The day is young, and the weather is beautiful. James also left the door open a crack. Miss Spitfire is lost in her own thoughts and it's time for me to make a break for freedom. I want to check outside the windows to see if there's a trace of our late-night visitor.

"FAMILIAR!" Jennifer made a grab for the black cat as he slithered out the door, but he was quicker than greased lightning. "You'd better come back here or I'm make kitty dumplings out of you and I'll serve them trimmed with your tail!"

The black cat slipped off the porch and jumped into the big azalea bushes beside the house.

"Great." Jennifer sighed as she went after him. This was exactly the activity she needed to finish off her silk suit. But Eugene wanted the cat inside. He was afraid the busy roads near his house might be the scene of a disaster for the cat.

"Familiar!" She made sure the door closed behind her. AnnaLoulou was giving the front porch chase an interested look.

Jennifer took the long way around the azalea bushes but wound up beside Familiar as he stood over two footprints in the soft dirt. "Now this time I'll be smart enough not to touch anything," Jennifer said, kneeling but taking care not to disturb anything.

She took off a shoe and held it beside the print. "It's a small person, maybe a woman." That didn't fit in with her theories. "Or maybe a child!" She had a sudden burst of hope. Maybe Mimi and Tommy were playing a practical joke and were spying on Eugene, trying to gauge the best time to come home.

SO FAR Spitfire is right. It's a kid or a woman. Prints aren't deep enough for a man. Well, I guess it could be an eighty-five pound man, but that doesn't seem likely. At least, not one tall enough to see in the window. My guess would be kid. But why?

I've learned from solving past mysteries that once I can answer the why, I'm close to a solution.

I hear Eugene tapping away in the garden on his old manual. And I hear the telephone ringing inside. I wonder who's calling. Eugene refuses to have an answering ma-

chine, though I'm glad to see Jennifer forced one of those caller identification devices on him. So many calls, so many kooks out there who think writers are public property.

Let's see if Miss Spitfire can run in a tight skirt and high heels. My, my. She just lifted up the skirt to reveal some mighty fine gams and ran. Oops! She hurdled right up on the porch! My goodness, if she gets tired of publicity work she might consider the Olympic track team. That woman can hustle!

"HELLO?" Jennifer tried to control her breathing.

"Help me."

"Hello? Who is this?" Jennifer held her breath. The voice on the other end of the line was so soft, so far away, she thought she heard someone ask for help.

"Please, help me."

The words froze her heart. Suddenly everything in the room was too loud, the ticking of the clock, the gentle flutter of the venetian blinds where a breeze from the open front door rippled softly against them, the little girl's voice speaking to her from what sounded like far, far away.

"Please, I'm afraid. It's dark here."

"Mimi?"

"Miss Barkley?" Mimi's voice suddenly grew in strength. "Oh, please help me. Tommy and I are afraid. Make Eugene bring us home. We won't be bad again, I swear."

"Mimi, where are you?" There was static on the line. "Mimi?" Jennifer yelled the word. The dull hum of a disconnect was her only reply.

It took three tries for her to hang the telephone up. The receiver slipped from the cradle again and again, and her clumsy finger couldn't seem to make it work correctly. When she turned to close the front door, her feet tangled and she slumped into a chair. She was shocked, and terrified. She was ninety-nine percent certain that the little girl who had called was the missing Mimi Frost. And if the caller was Mimi, she was alive, but terrified, and Tommy Franklin was with her. Mimi also believed that Eugene was her abductor. It was almost too much information to assimilate.

The black cat's paw, firmly pressed against her knee, brought her back to the moment. Familiar's large golden eyes watched her, then he turned and went to the small device beside the phone. He patted it twice.

"Caller ID!" Jennifer was across the room in three strides. It had been a terrible battle to force Eugene into having the "nasty little bit of intrusive, modern technology," but Jennifer had prevailed. It had been four months ago, when he'd been getting a series of crank calls late in the night that turned out to be an ex-wife thinking she was calling her ex-husband's new girl. But once installed, the device had remained, and now it contained the digital number that could provide a major lead in finding Mimi and Tommy. If the caller had actually been Mimi. Jennifer had to keep that thought firmly entrenched in her mind. The call could have been a prank—someone intending to torment Eugene.

Fear that somehow the number would disappear made her grab the pen and pad beside the phone and take down the number: 555-4343. She repeated it several times, memorizing it just in case something happened to the notepad.

Her fingers itched to call the number back, but sudden fear for Mimi's safety prevented her. If the child had somehow managed to get to a telephone and make the call, Jennifer didn't want to call back and alert her captor.

At least not until she could find out where the call had originated.

Snatching up the telephone, Jennifer dialed the newspaper office. There were directories of numbers, and James, of all the people she knew in town, would have easiest access to them. If she could find the location the call had been made from, then she could scope out the situation and perhaps rescue the children herself. Or at least turn it over to the police when she was certain where they were. Surely Bixley couldn't mess up a rescue if everything else was put in his hands.

The idea of Mimi and Tommy safely home with their families was almost more than she could stand. The possibility galvanized her. As soon as she had James on the line, she told him, and three minutes later he was looking through a phone directory that was listed by numbers.

"It's not here," he said, the sound of the pages flipping as he searched.

"It has to be." Jennifer's stomach knotted. To be so close!

"Ah."

"Ah, what?" She felt her heart kick back into life again. "What is it, James?"

"Let me make a few calls and get back to you." His voice was terse and he didn't wait for a response.

Jennifer held the receiver in her hand, almost not believing that he'd hung up on her so abruptly. A million fears zipped through her head, but she replaced the phone and sank into a chair. The stillness of her body was a total contrast to her thoughts. Two minutes hadn't passed before the phone rang.

"It's a cellular phone..." James hesitated. "Listed to J. P. Frost."

Jennifer let the information sink in. So, J.P. Frost *had* taken his daughter. It was a horrid thing to do, no matter what his reasoning. And poor Mimi had undoubtedly been told that Eugene had taken her. Anger boiled in Jennifer, but she kept her mouth firmly closed.

"Are you there?" James was waiting for the explosion.

"Is there any way to trace *where* the call came from?" She felt her doubts beginning to loom huge and formidable.

"As you know, cellular phones are transportable. The call could have been made from almost anywhere. There's no way I can trace that, and I don't think the operator would, even if she could, without a court order." He gripped the phone, knowing that Jennifer's high hopes of finding the children were sinking lower and lower.

"It wouldn't matter. Frost would simply claim that *he* made the call to Eugene."

"It isn't evidence, Jennifer, but it is a clue. Possibly a damn important clue. But why would Frost take Tommy Franklin, too. I mean I can understand that he might snatch his own kid in some custody battle, but why another child?"

"To put the blame on someone else. Like Eugene." She held the receiver to her ear and sank back against the chair. It was insane. J. P. Frost was a crazy man.

"Well, whoever is behind this, he's one smart son of a gun."

"You mean, you don't think it was Mimi's father?"

"I don't know what to think. There's something cock-eyed about all of this." He said something to someone standing at his desk. "Excuse me, Jennifer, John's waiting on a story here. Listen, let me finish up and then we'll hash this out."

"Sure." Even as she spoke she knew she didn't sound convincing.

"You'll wait for me to get off?"

"I'll be at Eugene's, or at my house." She crossed her fingers behind her back.

"Good. I'll be there as soon as I can."

Jennifer hung up the phone. "Damn!" She hit the table with her fist and then leaned down on her arms. "Double damn!" she whispered against the cool wood of the table.

Chapter Nine

Jennifer forced her body out of the chair and into action. Her muscles weren't tired but her brain wanted only to retreat into the unconsciousness of sleep. There wasn't time for such self-indulgence, though. All of her plans for the evening had been pushed aside. If that call was from Mimi, then she and Tommy were safe—that was what she had to cling to. And if they were safe, then they could be rescued. But time was ticking away.

When her brain finally started functioning, she targeted the one piece of information that might solve the entire case. J. P. Frost. It had been his telephone.

She hurried through the kitchen, each move followed by the curious stares of Eugene's cats. They were so well behaved, so in control, that they lounged around the house and she hardly noticed them until they moved.

Eugene had built perches for them around the entire house and along the screened back porch where they reclined. Taking care that none tried to follow her into the yard, Jennifer entered the maze of blooming shrubs and potted plants that Eugene rooted and nurtured, and listened for the sound of his typewriter clacking away. In the distance the old keys clattered.

"Eugene!" She listened, but he didn't respond.

The garden wasn't large, not over half an acre, but it was so chock-full of plants that it was a small maze. She knew the way to his work area and hurried there, her high heels sinking into the rich loam.

As she rounded the corner, she stopped.

The young girl looked up from the typewriter. "Where's Eugene?" she asked. "I've been waiting here for over half an hour."

Jennifer stared at the girl. She knew her. Judy Luno, one of Eugene's protégées who lived several blocks down the street. "You haven't seen Eugene?" Jennifer asked.

She shook her head. "He was helping me learn to type. He said I could practice on his typewriter here." She slowly stood up. "We were supposed to have a lesson today. At eleven. But I've been here since ten forty-five and he wasn't here. I thought I'd practice till he came out."

Jennifer did the math in her head. Eugene had walked out the back door and left immediately. The entire time she'd been talking with James, Eugene had been gone. The sound of the typing had been Judy practicing. Where could Eugene have gone?

"He never breaks an appointment," Judy said. Her dark eyebrows drew together and she flipped her hair back over her shoulder. "It's rude to break an appointment."

"I'm sure he didn't intend to do it." Jennifer stumbled over the words. Where could Eugene have gone, without a word?

Judy shrugged as she sat down again in front of the typewriter. "It's okay. The heat's really been on him, huh? Some folks think he took Mimi and Tommy and hurt them." She rolled her eyes. "What doofos. Eugene wouldn't hurt a fly."

"Yes, I know." Jennifer watched the young girl. She was quick, and Eugene had often remarked how observant she was. "Where do you think he went?"

"Well, his bicycle is gone." Judy nodded toward the garden wall where an old Schwinn had once stood, covered with honeysuckle vines.

"But he hasn't ridden in years!"

Judy smiled. "That's what he tells you because he says you try to mother hen him to death. He rides a lot, and when he puts the bicycle up, we pull the vines over it again. He rides me on the handlebars!"

Jennifer wanted to sit down, but the child had the only chair. "He shouldn't do that. He could hurt himself. And you."

"Oh, he's great. We go all over the place. Especially Thrill Hill. I scream the entire way down!"

The hill under discussion was a very steep drop that was part of a new subdivision. There was little traffic on the road and the hill was fast, curvy, and a roller coaster ride even in a car. It would be the ultimate bicycle thrill. And Eugene was in his seventies with a child on the handlebars! The mental picture made her cringe.

"It's okay. We've never had a wreck yet."

"I'm going to let the air out of his tires and then tie him up with the bicycle chain when I find him." Jennifer saw the laughter in the young girl's eyes. Apparently Eugene had told her plenty about his publicist.

"Eugene says you make up terrible threats but don't follow through on any of them."

"This time I might actually do it!"

Judy stood. "Have you found Mimi and Tommy yet? Eugene said you'd find them. He said you were the smartest woman he'd ever known and that you'd figure it out."

Jennifer sighed. "I only wish he was right. First I have to find him, though. Any ideas where he'd go on his bicycle?"

She shook her head. "No. But that black cat took off toward Donovan Street. He was sniffing the ground like a dog, so maybe he knows where Eugene went."

"Familiar. He's gone, too?" Jennifer wanted to lie down. Eugene and the cat were both missing. If anything happened to that black feline, Eleanor Curry would skin her *and* Eugene alive. The issues of who's kidnapped whom would be moot.

"What can I do to help?" Judy asked.

"Shoot me," Jennifer answered, then saw the look of worry on the child's face.

"It's just a figure of speech."

"I didn't think you meant it," the child replied indignantly. "I don't have a gun."

"Right." Jennifer gathered herself. "Judy, do you know where Mimi lives?"

"Sure, right by the park."

Jennifer did another take. "No. I meant, where her father lives?"

Brows drawn together, Judy thought. "I've never been there before, but I think Mimi said he had an apartment over on the west side of town." Her brows tightened. "Glendale Woods!" She looked up. "That's it. I remember because Mimi said she wanted to move out to the country and her daddy said if she came to live with him they'd buy this farmhouse that was for sale right beside the apartments. That's the old Glendale place. It's haunted."

Jennifer wanted to hug the child. "Wonderful."

"Are you going there?" Judy looked around. "I want to go."

"I think it would be better if you waited here for Eugene and Familiar to come back. And promise me, Judy, if either one of them shows up you'll drag them into the house and make them stay there."

"I'd rather go with you." There was a stubborn set to her jaw.

"You could help me more here. And Eugene."

She kicked a stick with the toe of her shoe. "Aw, darn! Okay. I'll stay here."

Jennifer gave her a hug. "Thanks, Judy. This is really important. You're being a big help."

J. P. FROST'S APARTMENT, according to the manager, was on the bottom floor in the last unit. Jennifer hoped the manager was right—about several things. One being that J. P. Frost had gone out of town for two days and wasn't due back until tomorrow.

The small backyard had been artfully landscaped, complete with a gas grill, patio and a privacy fence. Jennifer knew the fence was pine. The splinter in her palm proved it. The gas grill hadn't been used. Jennifer crouched beside it, noting the unspattered racks and clean dials.

The grass was cut, the shrubs neatly trimmed, but there was not a sign of personal care about the yard. Easing up to the sliding-glass door, she peered inside. Thank goodness J. P. Frost didn't have a dog! At least, the manager had volunteered the information that tenants weren't allowed to have dogs.

She pulled the screwdriver from the back pocket of her jeans. Even though it had cost valuable time, she'd gone home to change. And she'd also picked up a few items she thought she might need. A camera. The screwdriver. A can of Mace—just in case she miscalculated.

Back in high school her best friend's boyfriend had been a kid with a passion for snooping. He'd taught Jennifer some tricks of the trade, and popping open a sliding-glass door was one of the easiest ways to get into a house. At the memory, Jennifer shuddered. Nick wasn't a thief, but he had been extremely strange. Thank goodness Jessie had broken up with him before they'd all gotten into serious trouble. But now, his lectures on break and entry would do her some good.

The door popped and she eased it carefully along the track. She gave another silent thank-you that there was no burglar alarm system.

Inside the door, she stopped. The house was silent. There wasn't even the sound of a fan or a clock. It was as if no one lived there. In the light from the doorway she noted the Formica-topped kitchen table and four chairs. The counters were devoid of canisters or the small electrical appliances that made a place home. J. P. Frost might sleep here and collect his mail, but he didn't live here. She felt a moment of compassion for him. His divorce had been hard on him—hard enough to push him over the edge to kidnap his child?

Standing in the spotless kitchen she felt a sudden rush of disappointment. At that moment she realized she'd hoped to find Mimi. But there wasn't any sign of a child in the house.

Just to be sure, she started toward the bedrooms. That was her last hope. The apartment had only two bedrooms, and one was obviously a bachelor's dwelling and the other was filled with unopened moving boxes. The things he'd salvaged from his marriage that might make his apartment more homey were still packed away. J. P. Frost had not yet begun to put his life back on track.

It wasn't a sign that he'd kidnapped his daughter, but it also wasn't an indication that he was adjusting smoothly.

"I'm clutching at straws," she whispered, a sudden headache striking her between the eyes. She'd risked bodily harm and discovery to break into a shell of an apartment. And to make matters worse, her conscience was kicking at her. She'd invaded a man's privacy and seen a bleak side of his soul.

She returned to the kitchen and paused a moment to decide whether to risk the front door or to climb back over the privacy fence. There wasn't a bit of warning when the front door flew open and J. P. Frost returned.

Jennifer made a dash for the sliding door, but he heard the sound of her footsteps and gave instant pursuit. She'd made it onto the brick patio when he tackled her.

She went down hard, the breath going from her lungs in a painful explosion. Sand and small rocks ground into her palms where she'd tried to break her fall, and worst of all, J. P. Frost was tugging at the collar of her jacket. The canister of Mace skittered, useless, across the bricks.

"Get up!" he ordered, trying to drag her to her feet. "What the hell were you doing in my house?"

Gasping, she held up her hands in a sign of surrender. "Wait!" she managed to rasp, her lungs screaming for oxygen.

When he saw she was in no condition for fight or flight, J.P. backed off slightly. "You're the woman who works for that crazy old writer." Anger tightened his features. "Lady, you're in big trouble."

"Wait." She held up one hand and concentrated on getting her breath. Her palms were burning and she looked at one. It wasn't worthy of a doctor, but it hurt like the dickens.

"You've got thirty seconds. Then I'm calling the cops."

In twenty seconds Jennifer could manage to talk in short sentences. Sitting on the patio, she told him about the phone call. At his repeated questions, she assured him that she thought it was Mimi and that the child sounded afraid but unharmed.

He sank to the bricks beside her. "Did she say where she was? Did she say anything?"

At that moment Jennifer knew J. P. Frost wasn't party to his daughter's disappearance. "I'm sorry, no. She didn't say anything. In fact, I had the call traced and it came from your cellular phone. That's why I came here. I thought..."

"You thought I had her."

She nodded. "I don't know you. It was a possibility."

"And you risked coming here? What if I'd had a gun?"

Jennifer looked down at her hands. That thought had crossed her mind—more than once. But she'd been willing to take the risk to find Mimi and Tommy. "I had to do it, anyway."

Taking her elbow, he helped her to her feet. "Let's clean up those hands. It's a bad scrape, but not serious."

Together they went to the kitchen. As she washed her hands, she talked. When she'd told him everything except Mimi's assertion that Eugene had kidnapped her, she asked him about the phone.

He held out the tube of antibiotic salve. "You're not going to believe this, but my telephone was stolen two days ago. From my car. They broke the windshield and took the phone. Not the stereo, but the phone."

"Where?"

"Outside the apartment. It was a clean job. No one heard them. There's security here at the apartments, and they didn't have anything else reported stolen. It was as if the person came in here to get the phone and nothing else."

Jennifer met his worried gaze. "You may have hit the nail on the head, Mr. Frost."

"THE PRODIGALS RETURN." Jennifer gave Eugene and Familiar an angry glance. For Judy, she produced a frozen yogurt cone.

"Hey, thanks." Judy took the cone and sat down out of the line of fire. "I told them you were going to be pissed."

"Judith!" Eugene looked at her. "Your mother would have a fit if she heard you talk like that."

"Right. She thinks I'm going to grow up to be a lady." Judy laughed. "I'm not missing all the fun."

Jennifer ignored the youngster for the moment. "So where have you been?"

"Spying." Eugene answered without missing a beat. "I thought I was pretty good at it until Familiar found me." He gave the cat an affectionate pat. "Lucky he did. Crush was pulling into the drive and if Familiar hadn't beaten him there by several minutes, I might have been caught red-handed."

"You were at Crush Bonbon's house?" Jennifer didn't doubt it. Eugene was capable of many, many things.

"I wanted to see if the children might be there."

"And were they?" Jennifer knew if they'd been there Eugene would have risked everything to get them out.

"I didn't see them. The house is too old, too big, too tall and too dark. I tried to climb a magnolia tree, but I just don't have the strength anymore. Maybe James will give it a try later this evening."

"Maybe we should get the cops to get a warrant," Judy said. She licked a swirl of boysenberry from the side of the sugar cone. "This is great. The perks on a spy job are terrific."

"No cops," Jennifer and Eugene said in unison.

"You act guilty," Judy pointed out. "In the movies that's always the mistake the heroine makes. She doesn't go to the authorities. Of course, in the movies, if she went, they'd lock her up because they think she's the one who. . ." She looked up at Jennifer. "I see the problem. Forget that I ever said anything."

"Don't fret, Judith. We'll figure out a way to check out Crush." Eugene spoke softly to the young girl.

"Want me to go look at Crush's house?" Judy was suddenly on the edge of the sofa, the last few bites of her cone forgotten. "I could do it. I'm really good at sneaking around."

"Absolutely not," Jennifer said firmly. She nudged Eugene.

"Of course that wouldn't be appropriate behavior, Judith. You might be injured, and then you'd be in a fine pickle. Leave this to us adults, who can afford legal counsel."

"That's not exactly the reason why she shouldn't break into someone's house," Jennifer whispered to Eugene. "It's wrong."

"Judith has enough sense to know right from wrong. But it isn't right that they're trying to frame me, either," Eugene said loud enough for the child to hear. "If anyone breaks into Crush's house, it's in an effort to get the truth." He gave Judith a long, contemplative look. "But it has to be an adult, Judith. For a lot of reasons. Children aren't considered reliable witnesses, though God knows why. They're far more observant than most adults. And you're an exceptionally bright young lady."

"I've studied subversive tactics, too." Judy looked around. "I've read all the Nancy Drew mysteries, and I've been practicing."

"But not at Crush Bonbon's house." Jennifer saw pending disaster. "Please, Judy, promise me that you'll leave this to us. If anything happened to you, it could go very badly for Eugene."

Judy's mouth flattened into a thin line as she thought it over. "Okay." She held out her hand. "You have my word I won't go near Crush Bonbon's house tonight."

Jennifer's hands shook with relief. One disaster averted. Now for plans for the night.

METHINKS MISS SPITFIRE has all of her brain cells in high gear and churning. That look in her eyes is enough to call to mind the great strategists of the world. Hannibal to be specific. And that makes my kitty fur twitch. I see trouble abrewin', and it ain't no mild afternoon blend.

This is going to take some fine maneuvers, but I've got to get in the car with her and make sure she doesn't get herself in trouble. I know she won't take me voluntarily. Let me think...

Ah, there's the morning newspaper. Let me push it toward Eugene's lap. A gentle nudge and there it goes, off the arm of the sofa and right into his lap. He looks surprised. Eugene is a student of feline behavior, and he knows whenever a cat knocks something off, it's deliberate. Yes, he's picking up the paper and looking at it. Scanning the headlines now, looking to see what might have caught my interest.

Eureka! He's found the byline by James. Light is dawning. He understands. I can tell by that little smile of his that he'll call James as soon as Jennifer and I are out the door.

Yes, he's up and giving her a goodbye kiss. He's standing in the doorway—against all the rules—with the door open and he's letting me through.

God bless a human with a fully developed brain! I may have to adopt this man.

But for now, I've got to make it to the back seat of the car before Jennifer slams the door on my lovely... tail.

Piece of cake! I'm in. The car is moving. And Spitfire drives like a bat out of hell. Ah, one of the finest things in life is to be chauffeured through an interesting old city by a beautiful woman. I'll just kick back and enjoy this until she discovers I'm here.

JENNIFER STOPPED in her driveway and reached into the back seat for her purse. When her hand encountered the warm furry obstacle, she hesitated, felt it again, and then knelt on her seat so she could get a better look into the back seat of her car.

"Familiar! How did you get there?"

The cat yawned.

"So I'm boring you with all of this? Eugene is going to be worried sick about you." She watched as Familiar stretched slowly and then got up. "Or did he put you up to this?" She had the strangest sensation that the cat and the writer were in cahoots. "Well, you can stay at my house, but you aren't going to follow me around like a dog."

Ignoring her completely, the cat leapt out of the car and landed on the ground. Acting as if he'd grown up in her house, he went to the front door.

"Meow!"

Jennifer let him in and watched in amazement as he went directly to her refrigerator.

"Don't you ever get enough to eat?" She pulled out a grilled chicken breast and cut up a handful for him. "Occupy yourself. I've got to make some calls."

She took the portable kitchen phone onto the small deck off her back porch and sat down with a pad and pen. The only sign of her emotions was the muscle in her jaw clenching and unclenching as she dialed. At the back of her conscience was a nagging concern—she should call the police and report the telephone call from Mimi. But if she did that, she might lose her chances of finding the cellular telephone in Crush Bonbon's possession. It was a dilemma that made her twitch with guilt. Her mental hand-wringing was interrupted when someone answered her call.

"Hello, Crush? This is Jennifer Barkley. I'm ready to call in my bet." There was a pause. "Yes, he was taken in for questioning, but he wasn't charged. That was our deal, remember. He had to be charged." Her fingers on the telephone tightened. "That's not the agreement. You said if I won the bet I'd get a half hour to give my side of this issue."

There was another long silence as she held the telephone to her ear. Hot color ran up her cheeks. "You wouldn't know the meaning of honoring your word. In fact, your word isn't worth much at all, Bonbon. I don't know why I ever expected more from you."

She slammed the telephone back into the cradle and looked up to see the cat in the doorway watching her. He walked forward slowly and without a by-your-leave jumped up into her lap. He rubbed his whiskers against her chin and in a moment she felt the strange roughness of his tongue licking the tear that had tracked down her cheek.

"It's okay, Familiar. I'm not upset. Not really." She started to pick up the phone, then hesitated. "Maji is going to hog-tie me and roast me over an open spit. It's my job to prevent this kind of thing from happening."

The cat licked another tear, then gently nipped the fingers of her right hand.

"You're right. I have to make this call." She picked up the phone and dialed the long-distance number. After a few rings, she heard the nasal twang of Maji Call.

"I have some bad news," Jennifer said without bothering to sugarcoat it. "A second child has disappeared and Crush Bonbon is planning on launching a public crusade on his show this evening to begin gathering Eugene's books for a bonfire."

Chapter Ten

Jennifer's hand hovered on the radio dial. Her tears of the afternoon had been replaced by a cold anger as she listened to Crush Bonbon and his series of "guests."

They were all guests with a political agenda, and anyone with half a brain would be able to see right through the entire show. It was a very pitiful attempt to focus public emotion against Eugene so that Anna Green could benefit from the surge of fear and anger.

James had called her house once, leaving a message to call him at the paper. But Jennifer had other plans for the evening, and it would be best for both of them if he didn't know what she was up to. Crush's pompous voice caught her ear.

"And before I give Anna Green time for her closing remarks, I'd like to say that our country has been ruined by a warped view of personal freedoms. Words are dangerous in the hands of dangerous people. Freedom of speech should be reserved for those who think through their actions, who understand the consequences. Publishers, television networks and magazines that are willing to destroy the fabric of this great country so that they can reap huge profits should not be allowed to do so."

Jennifer checked her watch. It was ten o'clock, and Crush was scheduled to continue with his show until eleven. She had an hour to break into his house and find the goods on him. An hour.

She'd chosen black jeans and a black T-shirt, even though she felt slightly covert just looking at herself in the mirror. Maybe she needed some of that black stuff under her eyes. She caught Familiar's reflection behind her, and he was giving her a speculative look.

"Don't even think about it," she warned him. "I'll be lucky to escape alive, and I refuse to have to worry about you. You're staying here."

The black feline twitched his tail and yawned.

He'd eaten half a pound of fresh shrimp sautéed in butter and wine, and Jennifer grinned at her own deviousness. She'd deliberately fed him well in the hopes of fostering the need for a nap. Heck, it worked for her. She picked him up and put him on the green velvet sofa he seemed to prefer. His purr was a buzz saw as she stroked and scratched him until he curled into a snugly ball and closed his eyes. Just to be on the safe side, she sat down with a magazine in her hand. Not ten minutes later, the cat was sound asleep.

Carefully putting the magazine on the floor, Jennifer crept from the room. At the doorway she turned back. The cat was still snoozing. She'd taken the precaution of leaving her keys in the car so they wouldn't rattle. Based on his past actions, Familiar was not a cat to be underestimated.

With a sigh, she eased out the back door and crept along the drive to her car. She failed to notice the dark shadow that clung to her right leg and popped into the back seat as she slid behind the wheel.

Crush's home was in an older section of town. The houses were neatly painted clapboard with big porches, enormous screened windows and yards at least an acre or two in size. They were from a time when people sat on the front porch and visited with neighbors strolling by or watched children safely riding their bicycles along the sidewalk. It wasn't a neighborhood of brick homes, or tennis courts or hidden swimming pools. Even better, there were basketball backboards nailed to tall pines and huge old shrubs that made perfect hiding places for games of hide-and-seek and cops and robbers.

Jennifer parked a block from his house, pocketing her keys but leaving the car unlocked and a window down. As she got out she caught a sudden movement from behind a large oak.

For a split second it seemed as if her heart had stopped beating. She tasted acid and knew it was fear. Someone was hiding behind the large oak on the corner, watching her.

She tried to calm herself with the idea that J. P. Frost had gone back on his word and was following her. She'd finally convinced Mimi's father to give her a chance to do a little detective work before he took any rash actions. The poor man was distraught with worry over his little girl, and he wasn't exactly rational.

Turning away from the tree, she forced herself to pretend to look in her car for something. Maybe she'd imagined the watching stranger. She had to see if she could trick him. Whirling around, she caught a glimpse of the figure again, this time ten yards closer and darting behind a big azalea.

Panic pulsed through her veins, her heart trip-hammering in her ears. The man, and it was a man, was too tall to be Frost. This was a large, lithe man who moved with the grace of a cat. And he was stalking her!

The Mace canister was on the back seat. Moving as swiftly as her trembling body would allow, she opened the door, reaching inside and caught it, at the same time encountering a purring Familiar.

"You!" she breathed, barely able to stop the scream. "How did you get here?"

Familiar hopped into the front seat and leapt to the ground. With a cat's keen vision he stared directly at the place the man had disappeared.

Holding the can of Mace at the ready, Jennifer edged around the car. There was no sign of anyone. It could have been someone out walking. Or someone planning on burglarizing a house. That wasn't comforting, except she'd probably frightened him away. But where was his vehicle? It was hard to steal enough stuff without a car to haul it off in.

Her mind whirred in circles as she started walking down the street. Time was ticking away. If she was going to make it into Crush's house and out again, she had to move. She had only this night, this one chance, before Mimi's father called the cops. And the truth was, if J. P. Frost didn't call them, she'd have to.

Familiar was like a moving ink spot beside her feet, and he'd completely lost interest in the area where the stalker had last disappeared.

"Maybe he went on about his business," Jennifer said, hoping that her own voice would give her some comfort. "I'm just being paranoid because I know I'm getting ready to break the law."

"Indeed."

The voice came out of the bushes to her left. Jennifer screamed and jumped sideways into the gutter of the street. Her foot slipped off the curb and she felt herself falling.

Two very strong hands grabbed her flailing arms and pulled her upright—against a chest that ignited a thousand small memories.

"James!" She knew it was him instantly, even though she couldn't see any of his features behind the ski mask.

"Jennifer!" He was trying hard not to laugh. "Guilty conscience? You act like you're up to some mischief."

"You low-life heathen. You pond scum, mud-licking gar. You ambushing, yellow-bellied muckraker. I'm going to split you and toast you until your toenails turn black and curl!"

Unable to stop laughing, James pulled her closer to him and held on tight.

"Unhand me, you villain!"

That provoked even more laughter, though he did a good job of muffling it in her hair. "Stop, please. You're killing me with those wild threats. Even the ones that date back to the silent movies."

Jennifer pressed both elbows out with all of her strength. She didn't break free, but it did allow her enough space to draw back her foot and put all of her energy into a healthy kick.

James dodged, catching her beneath the knee and pulling up so that she fell backward into his waiting arm. "Any more dire threats, milady?"

Jennifer snatched the dark ski mask off his face to reveal a mouth crooked in amusement, and desire.

"Why did you feel it necessary to scare the daylights out of me?" she said through clenched teeth.

"I didn't actually mean to frighten you. I knew you'd seen me. I thought you were trying to ignore me, hoping I would go away, since you tried so hard to avoid me."

As he held her with his right hand, his left moved provocatively up her rib cage to rest just below the weight of her breast. Jennifer's gasp made his smile widen and a ray of light from a street lamp touched the hunger in his eyes. Before she could think, he kissed her.

The adrenaline of fear evaporated, replaced by the intense pleasure his lips aroused. Jennifer's anger was gone as quickly, and she felt her body begin to respond to his hungry kiss with a hot desire of her own. Her arms moved around his neck and she felt that he was the only stable thing in her world as she gave herself to the intensity of her feelings for him. She'd never known such irrational, unreasonable, completely glorious hunger.

With a muffled exclamation of pain, James straightened abruptly, pulling Jennifer to her feet.

"What?" She looked down the street, expecting car lights or the footsteps of someone approaching. James had straightened as if he'd been scalded.

James bent to rub his leg. "Familiar. He was reminding us that we're neglecting our business, and time is wasting." The cat took a swat at Jennifer's jeans-clad leg in a fit of frustration.

"Of course." Jennifer cleared her throat, trying to hide the sudden embarrassment she felt. Familiar was right. They'd been necking on the sidewalk in the middle of a break and entry. They were behaving like teenagers—especially in view of the fact that James had scared ten years off her life with his jumping out of the bushes. But the anger was gone, and she didn't really want to resurrect it. She tugged her T-shirt back into place and confronted the question of exactly how James had come to be stalking her right at the corner of Crush Bonbon's home.

"Eugene called and told you, didn't he?" She felt a spark of irritation—and then gratitude. She'd specifically told Eugene not to involve James, but the writer had a definite mind of his own.

"He did. He was worried about you. He said he wanted someone with a level head..."

"Level head! You? The man who's risking his career in this little gambit? What if you're caught? You'll be fired and never get another job at a newspaper."

"True." James directed her along the bushes and closer to Crush's side yard. "All of that is true. But I don't intend to get caught, and if we do find the goods on Crush, I'll have the scoop of the year in this town. Crush has pushed this into a national media story, and I can finish it for him."

Jennifer felt herself stiffen. Was it the story for James? Or concern for her and Eugene? The doubt passed in the split second that it arrived, but it still left her feeling strangely upset.

Unaware of the cause of her sudden silence, James led her to a picket fence. With a deft twist of his wrist, he removed two pickets and made a space for her to climb over without danger from the sharp wooden spikes. His long legs put him right over, and Familiar crept through the crack.

"We'll put the pickets back on the way out," he assured her.

There was no night-light in the back of Crush's lawn, and the trees were simply denser blacks against the smooth black of the lawn. Jennifer tripped over a garden hose but James caught her elbow before she fell. "Spend a lot of time in charm school?" he asked.

"You are infuriating. I can't see, you myopic microbe." She jerked free of him, determined not to do another thing where he could come to her rescue.

James's only response was a warm chuckle.

The house loomed in front of them, an older building with a warm glow of light in three of the windows.

"Crush will be here in just over half an hour." All teasing was gone from his voice as he went to work. His quick hands checked first one screen and then another. They were all latched at the bottom with hook-and-eye locks. All of the windows were up, allowing the cool April breeze redolent with magnolias, wisteria and a million other sweet Southern smells to blow through the house.

James pulled a small pocketknife from his trousers and slit the screen just enough to work a finger inside and pop the latch. Five seconds later he'd lifted the screen from the high hooks on the side of the house and set it on the ground. The house was open.

Motioning Jennifer forward, he cupped his hands to boost her up. "Hurry," he whispered. "Get in, take the first floor, and I'll search the second floor and the attic. Find the cellular phone, and meet me back here at the window."

"What—"

Before she could ask her question he'd boosted her up to the window and she was wiggling through. Her hands found a smooth, highly polished wooden floor and she pulled her legs in behind her and rolled into a crouch. Familiar dropped beside her, another victim of James's muscle. Standing perfectly still, he sniffed the air beside her. Familiar stepped out of the way just as James pulled himself up and into the house.

It took a few seconds to get their bearings, but the weak light from another part of the house gave them the vague outline of heavy, overstuffed furniture and Jennifer realized they were in a denlike room with a big-screen television.

A small flashlight was hanging from a cord around her neck and she pulled it out and began a methodical search of the room. There was a telephone, but it was conventional.

James waved her toward the kitchen as he crept to the staircase. One of the old steps creaked loudly as he began to make his way slowly up into what appeared to be a half story on the upper floor.

Jennifer moved through the brightly lighted, immaculate kitchen, taking care to duck below the windows just in case a neighbor should be watching. She negotiated the darkened, more formal living room and hall and entered the master bedroom. The bed was neatly made, no clothes tossed around like many bachelors were wont to do. In fact, the entire house was suspiciously clean.

A quick check of the dresser drawers and closet showed carefully folded and hung clothes, shoes arranged side by side in order of black to brown to white. The total organization made Jennifer's search a snap.

Jennifer had a bitter thought—clean house, clean mind. Or in Crush's case, empty mind. She hurried into the next bedroom and caught her breath.

The room was filled with stuffed animals. They hung from shelves on the walls and curled along the canopy of the beautiful bed. They clung to the bedstead and doorknobs, blending perfectly with the sunflower wallpaper. An entire bookshelf was filled with the stories of childhood. Fascinated, Jennifer stepped into the room and went straight to the bookshelf. Eugene's books were there, dominating the top row.

Jennifer's fingers closed around a copy of *Tribe of the Monkey Children.* She could hear her own breathing as she opened the book. Page 123 was missing—the exact page that had been left beside Mimi Frost's things when she was kidnapped.

"Holy cow." Jennifer hastily replaced the book, regretting now that she'd touched it and disturbed any fingerprints. To be on the safe side, she wiped the binding clean, cursing herself for such a stupid, careless mistake. She'd removed traces of her own prints, but she'd also taken anyone else's with them.

"Double damn!" She had to be more careful. Swinging the light around the room, she saw a telephone on the bedside table. It was designed like a red racing car, but it was conventional. With a sweep of the flashlight beam, she checked under the bed—nothing.

Throughout the search of the entire house there'd been no sign of a cellular phone. That disappointment was receding as Jennifer found more and more peculiarities that clearly implicated Crush in the disappearance of the two children.

The roof overhead creaked and Jennifer caught her breath. It was James, investigating the rooms above her, but it was still scary. The child's bedroom where she stood was eerie, filled with the dolls and stuffed animals that seemed to stare at her, waiting, watching, wanting a little girl or boy to play with them. A child that had never belonged to Crush Bonbon. "Creepy," Jennifer whispered, then looked down to discover that Familiar had abandoned her.

With each beat of her heart she knew her time was running out and she had to get out of the house before Crush returned. She checked her watch—ten forty-eight. Twelve minutes before Crush went off the air, and then maybe another ten minutes for him to drive home. There was time to go through the room, but she had to hurry.

She checked the drawers and found them as empty as the closet. No child had ever lived in the room. A closer inspection of some of the stuffed animals showed they still had their tags on them, and Crush had spent a pretty penny on some of them.

The bookshelf gave up no clues—except for the nearly complete collection of Eugene's books. It took her a moment to realize that Eugene's second book, *If Frogs Could Fly,* was the missing title. It was a delightful frolic about a redheaded boy whose classmates tormented him endlessly about his carrot top—until a wizard garbed in the disguise of a cardinal gives the young boy his wish, to be able to fly.

Jennifer had not worked at Grand Street Press when the book was originally published, but she knew every one of Eugene's works by heart, and she felt a surge of fear. In the book, the main character flew far from home to seek out adventure and to find friends who wouldn't make fun of his red hair. It was a harrowing adventure story filled with near tragedies, not to mention the fact that the boy's parents were hysterical with worry.

Jennifer's heart drummed in her ears as she thought through the possibilities of the missing book, coupled with the missing page in the other book. The evidence was circumstantial, but it certainly marked Crush as a prime suspect in the kidnappings—at least, in her opinion.

She forced herself to continue her search. If she could find one solid bit of evidence that Mimi or Tommy had been in the house, then she could call the authorities and demand action. Maybe there was even a clue as to where he was holding the children. She remembered Mimi's frightened voice and gritted her teeth in determination. If there was any way possible, she wanted to see those kids safe in their own beds before another night came around.

She went through the rest of the bookshelf. There were the standard childhood stories, from fairy tales to the more modern Dr. Seuss classics. Her flashlight beam returned to the top row of Eugene's works—all first editions, none of them signed. Jennifer's eye for detail noted that they'd been well read. Unlike most of the toys in the room, Eugene's books had seen a lot of use.

She had an impulse to take them, but knew it would be foolish. She crept out of the room to explore the bathroom.

Obviously decorated for a child's pleasure, the bath had cartoon-figure puppets over the water knobs and a host of floats ready for bathtime. It was all perfect, except for the fact that Crush had never married, had never owned up to being the father of anyone's child, and didn't even have nieces or nephews as far as Jennifer had been able to deduce.

She opened the medicine cabinet and found a variety of neatly boxed first-aid salves and sprays. There was also a new box of cartoon-character bandages and a prescription. Using a washcloth to touch the bottle, she saw that it was nearly empty and she recognized the name of the drug. It was a well-known antidepressant written out for Crush.

The drug was powerful, and sometimes had side effects of irrationality. Dr. Kyle Fontana was the physician who'd prescribed them, a name Jennifer wasn't familiar with. She committed his name to memory for further use. Replacing the bottle exactly as it had been on the shelf, she went into the hallway and paused to listen for James.

It was five minutes short of the time for their rendezvous and her findings had made her nervous as a cat. She looked around for Familiar, but there was no sign of him. She knew it was her imagination, but there was the sense that someone was watching her. Someone hiding just around a darkened corner. Someone who did not belong in the house any more than she and James did. Someone who'd seen the evidence of Crush's obsession with the *idea* of a child. She couldn't suppress a shudder. It was all too sick.

Lingering at the base of the stairs Jennifer waited for James—and the black cat who'd slipped so stealthily away.

In the stillness of the night something heavy dropped against the floor and Jennifer held her breath. Had James broken something? Maybe that was what Familiar had gone to investigate.

She listened intently for some sound from above. The seconds ticked away, the old house as silent as a tomb. Dread crept along her skin, inching deeper into her heart as she heard no sound of James above her. Had something happened to him?

"James." She went to the foot of the stairs and called his name softly. He didn't answer.

"James!" she whispered louder.

There wasn't a sound from above, but just down the hallway a door hinge creaked.

Jennifer gripped the stair banister so hard she thought she'd leave her finger imprints in the beautifully carved wood. Someone was in the house. Maybe it was James. But why hadn't he answered her? Maybe it was someone trying to hide the children!

The old floors creaked under Jennifer's weight as she moved down the enormous central hallway and back toward the living room. She checked the den to make sure James wasn't waiting for her at the window. A frilly cluster of azalea blossoms bobbed gently on a breeze, but the window was empty. James was not there.

The door hinges moaned softly.

It could have been the wind blowing a screen door, or the settling of an old house, but Jennifer knew it wasn't. Someone was creeping around Crush Bonbon's house.

Jennifer checked her watch. There were five minutes left before they absolutely had to clear out of the house. Five minutes, and there was a door that she'd failed to open. A smaller door that looked as if it led to storage, or a cellar, or a prison.

Pushing her imagination along to gruesome images was the sound of something moving around in the darkness behind the door. Jennifer tried to convince herself that she'd imagined the soft, scuttling sound, but even as she tried to deny it, she heard it again.

The door was slightly ajar when she got there and she felt her nerve begin to give out. What if someone was down there? Someone waiting for her. A trap. It had been an assumption that Crush lived alone. A logical assumption. He was single. He'd never been married. He'd certainly been hatched, so he wouldn't have a mother. She tried to play to her own sense of humor because she was so afraid. Every corpuscle of her body screamed for her to leave, to get out of the house. Not to open the door to see what was in the room.

She could wait for James. He'd be down momentarily. Or she could wait for Familiar. The cat had to be somewhere in the house. But waiting wasn't part of her nature.

Before she could think of all the dire things that could happen to her, she pushed the door open and saw a narrow flight of steps descending into what seemed to be a basement.

"Oh, brother." She took a breath and went down.

It was a tiny room, damp and claustrophobic. A string dangled in the beam of her light and Jennifer pulled it, flooding the tiny basement with the glare of an overhead bulb. She didn't know if she was relieved or disappointed to find a washer and dryer—and Familiar perched on the washer.

"Meow." He patted the lid of the washing machine with one paw.

"Sorry, I don't do laundry or windows," Jennifer answered as she arched the light around the room. It was a creepy place with enough cobwebs hanging from the corners and eaves to catch every mosquito in lower Alabama. But it was empty. Completely devoid of other human habitation. And it was obvious that it had been Familiar who'd made the door creak when he'd slipped inside. "I could skin you and wear your hide for a winter hat," she said as she walked toward the cat.

Familiar slapped the washing machine again, demanding her attention. "Meow."

"Where's James?" She stepped closer to the cat. His whiskers were covered with cobwebs. "So you've been exploring, too."

"Meow." He slapped the lid so hard the machine gave an empty echo.

"Okay, already." Jennifer moved him aside and lifted the lid. At first she couldn't make out what was inside, and then she reached both hands in. The telephone was lighter than she'd expected. She lifted it out and clutched it to her chest, unwilling to believe that she'd actually found what she'd broken into the house to search for. The instrument she held was a cellular phone—one without a battery, she discovered as she examined it. Now she only had to find out if it was the phone stolen from J. P. Frost's car.

Combined with all of the other evidence she'd discovered this evening, she could nail Crush Bonbon. To the wall. And rescue Mimi and Tommy.

"Good work, Familiar," she said. In a million years she'd never have thought to look in the washing machine. Never. With her free hand she scratched the cat's chin. Instead of a purr, he snagged her hand with his claw in a gentle but unrelenting grip.

"Hey." She felt her delicate skin begin to prickle, but the cat didn't let her go. "What is it?"

"Meow!" He jumped to the ground and ran up the stairs. Halfway up, he turned to look at her and cried again, this time with a note of panic in his voice.

"If you're hungry, I can't feed you here," she said, closing the washing machine lid and reaching for the string to turn out the light. She wanted to return everything to normal. She didn't want to tip Crush off to the fact that someone had been in his home. If he knew the phone was gone, he might make a run for it, and there'd be no telling what would become of Mimi and Tommy.

"Meow!" There was a sharp reprimand in the cat's tone, as if he clearly told her to do something very unladylike.

As soon as she pulled the light string, Jennifer regretted that she hadn't turned her flashlight on. With the telephone clutched against her chest, she fumbled for the flashlight that still hung around her neck.

There was the sound of footsteps scuttling through the kitchen and she knew instinctively that something terrible had gone wrong. The footsteps were quick, furtive.

And they didn't belong to James.

Before she could open her mouth or even think to try to hide, she heard Familiar's angry hiss and growl and the sound of the door at the top of the stairs slamming shut.

The lock slid into place with a final click.

Chapter Eleven

Jennifer's only comfort in the damp darkness of the small cellar room was the big black cat who sat beside her on the steps and licked her elbow. "We were stupid, Familiar." She had been locked in for only a few minutes, but it was long enough to ascertain that the door had been firmly secured with a thumb bolt, and that no amount of pounding or prying with the limited tools in the basement could free her. She would be set free only when someone came home and released her. A someone she didn't want to confront face-to-face—Crush Bonbon, most likely.

Getting caught was the least of her worries, though. Given her current circumstances, she now knew what the sound of something heavy dropping on the second floor had been.

James. Hitting the floor because he'd been knocked out.

And she'd failed to go check on him. He could be seriously injured.

Or worse.

"Meow." Familiar nuzzled her side as if he'd read her mind and wanted to offer the only solace he could. In the pitch blackness, his whiskers tickled her tender skin.

"We have to get out of here." She spoke calmly, forcing her mind past the panic and anguish she felt. If she was going to help James, she had to keep a clear head.

Someone knew she was locked in the cellar—the same someone who'd latched the door. But it couldn't have been Crush. He was still on the air!

So who was it? Did he have a cohort? Anna Green? She buried her head in her hands and squinched her eyes tight against the blackness. The total lack of light and the smallness of the room made her feel as if she might faint. She hated small, dark places.

The cat beside her tensed and sprang up to the door. Putting all of his fifteen pounds into it, Familiar slammed the door and cried as loudly as he could.

"Hush!" Jennifer crawled up on her hands and knees after him. She hadn't gotten far with her next plan, except to hide under the steps to try to trip whoever came down after her. That way she'd stand a chance of making it to the second floor to check on James. But Familiar was scratching at the door like a mad creature, and if there was any element of surprise, he'd give it away.

"Familiar!" Just as she reached for him, the door sprang wide open and a shaft of bright light blinded Jennifer. She dropped to her stomach and tried to roll against the wall, cellular phone hugged to her chest, in a blind maneuver of self-defense.

"Ms. Barkley!" The voice was shocked. "Are you hurt?"

Jennifer's eyes adjusted to the bright light and she saw the silhouette of a young girl standing at the top of the steps.

"Judy?"

"Are you hurt?" The girl bounded down the steps. "We have to get out of here. Crush went off the air half an hour early. I was listening but I had to wait until my parents went to sleep before I could come over here to warn you. What are you doing in the basement? Where's Mr. Tenet? What's going on here?"

The volley of questions was more than Jennifer could manage. She scrabbled to her feet and ran up the steps with Judy on her heels. There were several questions she had to ask the young girl, but they would have to wait—until she could find out about James.

"Where are you going?" Judy stood at the open window, ready to flee. "We've got to get out of here. He could come back any minute. You could go to jail. Then what would Eugene do?"

Jennifer ignored her as she rushed up the stairs to the second floor. There were two identical bedrooms on either side of the landing. She chose the left one, the one that would have been above the "children's room," and went inside. Judy had not had any compunction about turning on the lights downstairs, and Jennifer followed suit. She hit the switch and then gasped.

Behind her, Judy stopped dead in her tracks. "Holy cow. Is he dead?" she asked.

Jennifer took in the blood that had spread from the gash on James's head to the way his body was sprawled on the floor and the pallor of his normally glowing skin.

He looked dead.

She hurried to his side and knelt beside him, forcing back the flood of strong emotions that threatened to choke her. She touched his cheek and found it warm, and his chest moved shallowly with his breathing.

"He's alive." The relief was almost debilitating.

"James." She touched his cheek softly and looked up to see Judy exiting the room as if her feet were on fire.

There was no time to worry what the young girl was up to. "James." She checked his head. He'd been struck with something very heavy and blunt. There was a gash and a lot of swelling, but the bleeding had stopped. She had no idea how serious the damage might be, but at least it hadn't crushed his skull.

"Here." Judy returned with a glass of water.

"He can't drink water."

"I know." Without hesitation, Judy poured the cold water on James's face.

His body jerked and flailed, and he swung out wildly with his fists, narrowly missing Jennifer's face. "W-what the hell?" he sputtered as he pushed himself to a sitting position.

"James." She put both hands on his chest and pressed him back to the floor and held him with all of her weight until she could determine that his vision was slowly clearing. Fear that he might be horribly injured and that the sudden return to consciousness would aggravate his injuries gave her strength. "James, it's me, Jennifer."

"Somebody coldcocked me," he said. "From behind."

"I know." She eased the pressure off his shoulders and gently touched his face. He seemed rational. But she knew by the heart-tripping response she'd felt when she'd seen him injured that perhaps she was not. She had too many feelings for this man. "Are you okay?" She felt such a tide of tenderness that she had to look away from him for fear he'd too clearly read it in her eyes.

"I have no idea. My head is throbbing, and you tried to drown me." His eyes narrowed as he looked at her. She looked as if she were about to cry. This was not the Jennifer Barkley he'd come to know...and care deeply about. He touched her hair.

"Give me a break," Judy said, sighing and rolling her eyes. "We've got to get out of here."

"I didn't provide the cold water." Jennifer eased to the left so he could see a grinning Judy Luno standing behind her.

Arms akimbo, Judy was ready with an explanation. "It's what they do in all the cowboy movies when someone's been knocked unconscious. We don't have time to fool around here. Crush could be back any minute. That's why I came to warn you guys. He went off the air half an hour early when Mrs. Franklin went to pieces and they couldn't get her to quit crying. It was terrible. She was begging whoever took Tommy to bring him back. She said she'd sell her house to pay them. Then Mrs. Frost got all wired about Mimi and she started crying. It was awesome."

Under the constant flow of Judy's words, James eased himself to a sitting position.

"Then Mrs. Franklin had some kind of medical fit and they had to call 9-1-1 and the ambulance came. You could hear the siren and all of that on the radio. My folks were, like, glued to the radio, and they hardly ever listen all the way through one of Crush's shows." She took a deep breath. "So when the ambulance came for Mrs. Franklin, Crush was telling everyone how she looked with her hands clenched together and all of that, and Mr. Frost arrived and said if Crush didn't stop using the agony and distress of others for self-promotion he was going to mop the floor with him and wring him out like a dirty rag!"

"Wait!" Jennifer held up a hand. "You heard all of this on the air?"

"Right. And Mrs. Franklin came to when the ambulance men gave her something and she was wailing and moaning. She thinks Tommy is dead, and Crush said Uncle Eugene ought to be arrested. Then there was a big argument, and Mr. Frost said something very nasty, and there was the sound of something breaking and a scream and they started playing music."

"It's a talk radio station," Jennifer said.

"I know. And the music was awful. It was some old group from the dinosaur age. Devoe, or something like that." Judy rolled her eyes. "My dad said it was some tape one of the deejays had left in his car too long and it had warped. But you guys had better get up, get your butts in gear and get out of here."

"Meow!" Familiar stood in the doorway and cried.

"I think he's trying to tell us something," Jennifer said, gathering the telephone into her arms. The cat was too smart by far.

Strange shadows danced across the far wall of the room as a car's headlights swept the house. Someone, most likely Crush, had turned toward the house and had started up the long, winding driveway.

"It's time to go." James jumped to his feet, ignoring the fury of his pounding head. He hit the light switch, casting the room in darkness. "Run for it," he said, nudging Judy first and following hot on the heels of Jennifer and Familiar.

They sprinted down the stairs in the darkness, heedless of the amount of noise they made. Judy was the first to the window and she tumbled through it with the agility of the very young. Jennifer sat on the sill, phone clutched tightly to her chest, and threw herself down into the scratchy branches of the azalea beneath. James followed with less regard for his own bones. With the grace of thousands of generations of perfect balance, Familiar sailed out to the ground and landed in a crouch.

When Judy started to run to the west, he snagged her foot and held on.

"Follow the cat," Jennifer ordered, glad for the bit of moonlight that gave them limited vision but also aware that it could give them away.

There was no time to replace the screen. They ran across the yard, fleeing figures that moved in and out among the shadows of the trees. They just made it to the safety of the thick line of oaks and azaleas when the car lights swung across the yard and pulled up to the front door.

In the light of the moon a heavyset man got out from behind the wheel and went to the front door. He went in, opening the door without even unlocking it, flipping on the entrance lights as he went.

"It's Crush," Judy whispered. "The front door was open. We didn't even have to crawl through the window."

Jennifer felt James's strong fingers close over hers, a touch that was meant to steady both of them. She knew he was still unsettled from the blow to the head—and the hundreds of questions that had to be answered.

"Meow!" Familiar brushed beneath their hands, reminding them of his presence and the need to get farther away if they didn't want to get caught.

"Let's move it." James backed into the denser bushes and led the way out to the fence. They arrived at a point fifty yards from where they'd entered, and James helped Jennifer and Judy over the picket fence.

"I suppose it's futile to go back and repair the fence. We left the screen off the window. It won't be long before he realizes someone was in his house."

"If he doesn't already know it. Someone had to knock you out and lock me in the basement," Jennifer said darkly.

"And he was off the air," Judy added. "It's possible he might have done it. He had motive and opportunity."

"Good grief," James said under his breath. "I have to work with the princess of slander and now a junior Sam Spade."

"Instead of making fun of me, you should thank me," Judy said quickly as she bent to scoop Familiar up into her arms. "Me and the cat. If I hadn't heard him at the door, I might have given up the search for you two and thought you'd gone home. I mean, I did risk my flawless reputation to break in there and get you out before Crush returned. If my parents knew what I was doing they'd ground me forever. They'd probably nail my feet to the bedroom floor."

"My God, she's even beginning to talk like you," James whispered as he put his arm around Jennifer and squeezed her shoulders tightly before he directed a shallow bow to Judy. "Thank you, Miss Luno. You did a wonderful job of saving us doddering, old adults."

"Eugene said someone had better keep an eye on you. He said not even Familiar could keep you two out of Dutch for long. But at least y'all found something to steal." Without waiting for a reply, Judy skipped ahead with the cat in her arms.

"So much for Eugene's opinion of us," James whispered in Jennifer's ear. "Where *did* you find the phone?"

Jennifer still clutched the instrument. "Familiar found it, sans battery, in the washing machine, *before* we got locked in the basement. Judy let us out—it's a good thing she doesn't take her promises to stay away seriously. But let's get out of here. Someone was in that house, and they may still be watching us."

James set the pace with a long stride that covered the distance quickly. They'd put a block between them and the scene of the crime, and his headache had settled into a dull pain. He didn't feel great, but at least he knew he wasn't going to die.

They had circled the three blocks around Crush's house and were moving back in the direction of Jennifer's car when James suddenly stopped. "Don't you think Crush has had time to discover someone was in his house by now?"

Jennifer shrugged, a gesture lost in the darkness. "Maybe. Let's just get in the car and get out of here before a cruiser happens along. I mean, it *is* nearly midnight. We've got a minor child who is supposed to be in bed, and a cat who lives in Washington, D.C. If Crush does call the cops, we aren't exactly the most innocent people on the street and we're the only people on the street."

"But if he has discovered the break-in and hasn't called the police, what does that tell us?"

Jennifer had momentarily put the peculiarity of Crush's decor out of her mind. "That he has something to hide—from the cops." As soon as she said it, she felt a rush of certainty.

"Exactly. What did you find at his house?" James asked. His headache was easing and he had begun to formulate the questions of his trade.

"The phone. Nothing much." Jennifer nudged him and nodded toward Judy, who walked ahead.

He nodded that he understood she didn't want to talk in front of the child. "Good. Let's get home."

The car was parked under a leafy crepe myrtle and they shifted through the shadows. When they were all ready, Jennifer checked the back seat to make sure Familiar had gotten in—and stayed there.

"Just let me out about a block from the house. I can sneak through Mrs. Evan's backyard and get back in my window."

"Maybe we should just knock on the door and explain," Jennifer said. She had a real hesitation about leaving the young girl out in the night—especially to sneak back into her own house.

"I do it all the time." Judy was exasperated with their foolishness. "You grown-ups must never have done anything fun. My folks sleep like logs. They work all day and then sleep. What a boring life. They have no idea what goes on once they close the bedroom door. They'll never catch me. But if you wake them up, I'll be in big trouble." An edge of worry had crept into her voice.

"I'll go with her," James assured Jennifer.

At Judy's instructions, Jennifer parked and waited as Judy and James crept through another yard. In ten minutes James was back. "Safe and sound. Now let's go someplace nice and quiet. I think we have a lot to talk about."

"Meow!" Familiar put his paws on the back of the seat and tucked his head between them.

I HAVEN'T HEARD the logic Madame Spitfire and Clark Kent are going to apply to the events of this night, but I can tell you, there are a lot of things that trouble me.

For instance, the placement of that darn phone in the washing machine. During the few weeks after Jordan Lindsey's birth, Eleanor wasn't exactly in the most coherent frame of mind. It was a joke around the house that she would pick up an item, put it down, and then it would be gone forever—until it turned up in some bizarre place. The perfect example was the rack of ribs she'd bought for a dinner party. She'd put it out on the counter, but when she'd started to prepare it, she'd discovered there was no garlic in the house.

Ah, tragedy! A trip to the grocery with baby in tow meant at least an hour, so she'd packed up the little urchin and taken off. As it so happened, I'd decided to take a nap in the middle of her preparations, so I'd missed the departure. When she'd returned, the ribs had disappeared.

The Dame must have spent twenty minutes standing in front of the open refrigerator door looking for the rack of ribs because she'd been sure she'd put it in the refrigerator. Needless to say, I discovered it some ten hours later—in the washing machine.

This is a long, rambling story to make a point. Peter would never have put the roast in the washing machine. The trash compactor, perhaps. The toolbox, maybe. But not the washing machine. Few men, based on my trained observations, understand that a washing machine is an empty metal container.

Now, it's difficult for me to lower myself to human standards of behavior, but I believe the person who put the phone in the washing machine was a woman.

First, the tread was light—and second, there was a teensy bit of foundation makeup smeared on the phone. Although my thoughts are brilliant, my eyes and nose are keener. The phone was smudged with traces of makeup. The phone belongs to J. P. Frost, who does not wear makeup. Thus my "woman" theory.

It pains me to have to admit this, but I allowed smugness to interfere with my work tonight. I was so delighted to have discovered the phone that I wasn't paying attention. I should have heard someone else in the house. I should have been alert.

If it had been Crush Bonbon prancing about the house, I would have heard him. He weighs a ton. I insist that the person who locked the cellar door was a woman. Someone about the size of Anna Green. Or Mrs. Frost.

I'll see if I can't get this point across to Jennifer and James. Along with the fact that whoever it was had some upper body strength to be able to whack James in the head and knock him completely out. It was a well-directed blow—as if whoever struck him knew what they were doing. Well-directed and well-executed. That implies knowledge of martial arts, or at least some form of self-defense. A woman with training.

We're getting closer to some answers, but I have a terrible, nagging feeling that something else awful is about to happen. And though Eugene doesn't make a big deal about his concerns, this is having a grave impact on him. My worry is that even if the children are safely returned, this could affect his writing.

And it's my job to see that it doesn't.

JENNIFER DROVE to her house without asking James's opinion. As they pulled into the driveway he gave her a curious look.

"I have an ice pack, aspirin, a thermometer and all of the other things to make sure you aren't permanently brain damaged." She tried to sound tough, but her voice cracked and she knew she couldn't hide her true feelings much longer.

James got out of the car and went around to her side, pulling her into his arms. "I'm okay," he said. "Better than okay."

He was solid against her, his heartbeat regular, steady, his arms strong and supporting, and Jennifer allowed the last dregs of her fears for him to slowly slip away. He had been injured, but not seriously.

Without a word James led her to the door, took her keys and opened the house. Familiar darted in ahead of them, making a beeline for the kitchen.

"I think he wants a reward for saving all of our hides tonight," James said, following Jennifer to the kitchen.

"And he shall have it." Jennifer opened a tin of sardines. "This isn't gourmet, kiddo, but I've never seen a cat turn it down. Just don't breathe on me for at least an hour."

For James and herself she put on some coffee and found the aspirin. Their gazes met and held as they each took two. "I know I wasn't hit in the head, but the tension from this night is more than I can take," she explained, motioning him into a chair. "I have to tell you what I found, James. And we have to think of something to do. I believe I know the next kidnap victim."

At her words James eased into the chair she'd indicated, his arms on the table. He instantly picked up the pen and pad of paper she kept beside her phone. "Okay, shoot," he said. "I'll make notes."

Jennifer began her description of the room she'd found in Crush's house, concluding with the missing page from Eugene's book, and the missing book from the bookshelf.

James's pen stilled in midair as he took a deep breath. "And the book is about a redheaded boy?"

Jennifer found her anxiety had increased—she'd hoped James would discount her theory. But he seemed as certain as she was. She nodded. "Eugene knows at least two redheaded children. I can't think of their names, but I've seen them at story hour, and I know they've visited his home at least once."

The tip of the pen tapped on the pad. "I wish we'd been able to get that screen back on the window."

"Not to mention, cleaning up the blood on the upstairs bedroom floor," Jennifer added. "There's no doubt that

Crush knows someone was in his home." She felt a sudden defeat. "What has he done with Mimi and Tommy?" She had so hoped to find the children, to rescue them and deliver them safely home. "There wasn't a trace that they'd been there."

"Just the phone, and the clues about the books. Not to mention the... peculiarity evidenced in that room. But it does give me hope, Jennifer."

"Hope?" She looked out from her own misery.

"Hope that the children haven't been harmed. That room sounds as if it were created by someone who cares for children. Maybe not in a normal way, but everything there was for the child's pleasure. The toys, the wallpaper, everything. If Crush has Mimi and Tommy, it may be because he wants them to be his. And this attack on Eugene may be because he feels the children will care for him if they no longer care for Eugene."

The words James spoke gave Jennifer a measure of comfort, but they also made her sad. "How awful," she said. "Never in a million years did I ever think I'd feel sorry for Crush Bonbon. And yet... I do." She looked up, her blue eyes unaccountably filmed with tears. "How terrible to want to be loved, to want to love someone that much."

For all of Jennifer's appeal when she was shooting fire with her eyes and mouth, the tears were James's undoing. He put down the pen and stood. With two steps he was beside her, drawing her into his arms. "It's been a long, long week for you." He kissed the top of her head. "There's nothing we can do now, except wait to see if Crush files a report with the police that his home was broken into. That in itself will tell us a lot." His lips brushed her temple, lingering at the edge of her hair.

Tired did not begin to describe Jennifer's emotional state. She was weary—and exhilarated. The touch of James's hand, his lips, sent pulses of need throughout her, and this time there was no hesitation as she lifted her lips to his.

All of her life she'd used her wit and caustic tongue to drive back suitors. But James was amused by her verbal attacks. In fact, he enjoyed and provoked them. Yet he was also moved by her tenderness. Even as she kissed him, she smiled at a sudden thought. He also had a rapier wit and a quick tongue, and yet he could be gentle and tender. Perhaps, at long last, she'd met a worthy adversary.

"What's so amusing?" James asked, his breath warm against her cheek.

"You. Me." She kissed the stubble of his jawline. "Us."

"Is this a lesson in pronouns?" he queried. God, she was beautiful with that glint of devilment in her eyes. It took all of his willpower not to crush her against him.

"Personal pronouns." Jennifer let her teeth nibble his bottom lip. "Very personal."

"Any chance there might be some verbs attached to those pronouns?"

She chuckled softly against his neck, a sensation that made him groan. "If this is your idea of foreplay..."

Before she could finish, she felt his arm sweep beneath her knees as he lifted her up. His dark eyes looked into hers.

"Yes or no, Jennifer?"

She had never been so certain of an answer in her life. "Yes," she answered clearly.

Chapter Twelve

The lovebirds were a little too much for me last night, so I took an exit through the back door and decided I'd check out the action at Crush's pad. Humans are a definite drawback on a stakeout. They're big. They can't hide. They make noise, and they can't run. Or jump. Or climb. Very unwieldy species. I'll have a lot better chance of success on my own, though I do miss the way Miss Spitfire strokes my back. She's a woman with talented fingers.

This is a great town. Traffic is almost nonexistent in these nicer old neighborhoods. I can't say for certain what's dragging me back to Crush's, but I have this compulsion to spy on him. While the dynamic duo were noticing the lack of a child in his house, I also observed that there wasn't any evidence of a pet. Of course, no self-respecting cat would voluntarily live with a guy like him. But what kind of man is this? No children, no wife, no pet. What does he do with his spare time? That's what I want to discover. And, also, to see if he remains at home. If he has those kids, then someone has to be taking them food and water. Then perhaps I can get Jennifer and James to come up for air long enough to follow him. That is if they live through the night. I must say, they seem to have an abundant supply of energy and ardor. Ah, the combination of youth and love. I remember back in my salad days when I was hanging out be-

hind that palace of Southern cuisine, The Okra Pod. There was a young feline who'd been partially adopted by one of the cooks. He'd bring her out a fried liver delicacy, which she gladly shared with me, and then our thoughts turned romantic. Yes, those were the days. When I was unattached and carefree.

Though I may admire the set of AnnaLoulou's delicious little ears and the way her tail makes a question mark whenever Eugene strokes her back, I am true to Clotilde. True to my commitment.

Ah, but a short trip back in time can stir the blood to a pounding thunder. James and Jennifer are making their own moments to hold and savor in the future. They may not realize it yet, but this kitty could get a job on the psychic hotline when it comes to predicting the future of Miss Spitfire and Clark Kent. It's a done deal—someone should rent the chapel—unless something tragic happens.

Enough of this mushy foolishness. I want to see what Crush is doing. He's up in one of the bedrooms. Not the one where we found James, but the other. Lucky for me magnolias have smooth, tough bark. I've learned a valuable lesson while hanging out in the coastal plains—don't climb pines. That sap is something else and hard on a kitty's fur.

What's that noise I hear? Typing? A soft clack-clack sort of noise. Not like Eugene's old typewriter. It couldn't possibly be. It's too... erratic. It sounds like Dr. Doolittle trying to type a report before the Dame takes pity on him and puts it into the computer. I'll just climb another limb or two and I'll be able to stare him eye to beady little eye—a terrifying thought for me.

Yep, it's Crush! At a keyboard! And he's going to town as fast as his little pea-size brain will let him. Man, he's concentrating like his life depends on it. It's nearly one o'clock in the morning. What could he possibly have to type now?

Maybe a ransom note!

I have to get inside to read what he's done, but I have to wait until he gets up. He'll have to go to the bathroom eventually. Or get something to eat.

Look! There he goes. But, damn it, he's blanked the screen and *unplugged the machine. May a thousand mice invade his basement. I'm not as good as Jennifer with the invectives, but I'm learning. Now I'll never be able to figure out what he was working on. Even if I break in, I don't have the foggiest understanding of what he was doing on that computer. Whatever happened to the good old days of pens and pads?*

Now there's nothing left but careful surveillance. Down the tree and a little walkabout along the edge of the yard. The entire house is dark. Crush's car is still in the drive. There's no sign that he's expecting company or that he intends to leave. I'll just curl up in this little nest of pine straw beside the door and sleep. If anyone or anything stirs, I'll wake up.

JENNIFER'S BLUE EYES opened to dangerous slits as she reached out from beneath the teal sheet and snatched up the clamoring telephone. The weak light that drifted through the wooden blinds showed early morning—and a delightful profile of James Tenet lying beside her still sound asleep. She checked her bedside clock—it was not even seven—and mentally formed a bleak prediction for the person on the other end of the line.

With her teeth clamped together, she picked up the receiver before the phone could ring again. Before she could utter a word, Maji Call started talking.

"I don't know what you think you're doing down there in the decadent South, but it isn't taking care of Eugene Legander's reputation. There's a story on the network news this morning about some brouhaha down there in that backwater town. It seems that radio person has called for Eugene's arrest in the disappearance of two children."

Jennifer held the telephone away from her ear, then, remembering that James was still sleeping, pushed it under her pillow. Even through the layers of feathers she could hear Maji Call's hysterical voice.

"Hold on a minute, Maji," she mumbled into the phone. Burying the receiver deeper beneath the pillow, she slipped out of the room and went to pick up the extension in the kitchen.

"I have no control over Crush Bonbon," she tried to explain, but Maji had worked up a head of steam and she was going to let it off.

Holding the receiver on her shoulder, Jennifer listened as she put on a pot of coffee. As soon as Maji was winded, she'd have a chance to talk. There were times when Maji Call could be a real pain, but she eventually wore herself down into a state of rationality.

Jennifer had finished half a cup of coffee before she got her chance. In five succinct minutes, she'd updated her boss on what had occurred.

"Well, I can see that you've been doing your best." It was as close as Maji could come to an apology.

"There are a lot of things I can't go into," Jennifer said. One of them was the break-in. Her boss would die if she knew Jennifer was sneaking around at night performing illegal acts. "Just trust me. I'm doing everything under the sun to find out who's behind all of this."

"What about those kids?" Maji's concern was real. "Do you think they're okay?"

"I don't know." That was the truth. "But I have to believe that they haven't been seriously harmed. Each day that passes, though, makes it worse. You know that. And I feel so sorry for their parents. And for Eugene. He hides it well, but he's terribly distraught."

"He has a book due, Jennifer. Keep that in mind. He has to be able to work. We're going to have to resolve this. How about if Grand Street Press hires a detective? Hey, that may be a great public relations move. We could get a big name, someone who could create a—"

"No." Jennifer's voice was sharper than she'd intended. "This place is enough of a circus without our side adding to it. Putting fuel on the fire would be the worst thing we could do."

Maji sighed. "You're right. I just got carried away."

For the first time that morning, Jennifer smiled. Maji frequently got carried away. And about fifty percent of the time her ideas were brilliant. The other fifty percent... well, not quite brilliant.

"Call me this afternoon. I want updates every four hours."

"Maji—"

"No, darling. I mean it. I have to stay on top of this. We have an editorial board meeting at four today, and Eugene is a top concern. He must be protected, and I have to have the most current information to present. Jennifer, you're out of New York now. Perhaps you've forgotten how *intense* these editorial meetings can be. I mean, you are living in the land of the siesta."

"Can the sarcasm, Maji. I haven't forgotten. It's been something of a pressure cooker down here, too." Jennifer refilled her coffee cup. "I'm doing everything that can be done, and I'll call you this afternoon."

"Good girl. You have my full confidence. Ta-ta." Maji hung up before Jennifer could reply.

"That woman is slicker than a greased pig in the July sun," Jennifer said to herself as she replaced the phone.

"I see you haven't lost your gift for description. But there's a definite drawl developing in your voice."

Jennifer whirled around to find James standing in the kitchen doorway, his dark hair wet from the shower and a towel around his waist. The faint stubble of his beard gave his skin a darker cast along his jawline. He was so handsome, she stopped and stared.

"At a loss for words?" he teased. "Did you forget where you left me?"

"Coffee?" Her ability for witty repartee was severely hampered by the sudden rush of desire she felt for him. Quick images of the night before flashed in her mind and she felt a blush rise to her cheeks.

"A modest maiden?" He stepped up beside her and slowly took the coffeepot and cup from her hand, returning them to the counter. "It wasn't really a desire for coffee that brought me in here." His fingers traced a feathery touch beneath her chin. "I wanted a look at you. To make sure I wasn't dreaming."

She knew he could hear her heart pounding. She placed her hand on his chest, still damp from the shower, and felt a corresponding beat. Her gaze never left his, and she thought she'd faint if he actually touched her again. She saw the hunger in his eyes, and the delight, and knew she was seeing a reflection of her own emotions.

"James, what time do you have to be at work?" She smiled.

The jarring ring of the telephone made her freeze. "Don't answer it," she said when she saw him look at it. "I've already had a call from my boss in New York."

A frown touched James's brow. "It could be Eugene," he reminded her. "Besides, no journalist worth his salt can ignore a ringing telephone. It's like ink in the blood."

"Damn, damn, double damn. I'm going to find out who this is, sell them to pirates and then make them walk the plank. Into a vat filled with hungry sharks." She turned away from him and went to the phone. "Hello?"

"Miss Barkley, this is Tommy Franklin's mother. Can we talk?" Jennifer sat down at the table in defeat. The moment with James was lost. She could hear the terror and fear in Mrs. Franklin's voice. "Of course, Mrs. Franklin, what can I do for you?"

James went to the counter, poured her another coffee, and a cup for himself, and retreated to the bedroom.

"I wanted to talk with you before I did anything. An officer was at my house this morning. They believe Mr. Legander is responsible for kidnapping Tommy and Mimi. They want me to go down to the police station and sign papers against Mr. Legander. They say if I sign the papers, along with Mrs. Frost, they can take Mr. Legander into custody and question him."

Jennifer's fingers clutched the telephone. "Do you believe Eugene could harm Tommy?"

Mrs. Franklin started to cry. "No. No, I don't. But he may know something that could help them find my boy. They say they just really want a chance to talk to him, at length."

Jennifer waited a few seconds. "Mrs. Franklin, if Eugene knew anything, he'd willingly tell the police. He's cooperated in every way."

"They said he might remember something. You know, being at the jail and all. They said sometimes people remember things they've forgotten."

"Does that sound like intimidation to you?"

"Tommy is a good boy. He's never harmed anyone. He even looks out for all the birds and animals in the yard. Why would someone do this to him?" She sobbed, completely out of control.

"Mrs. Franklin, Eugene and I are looking for Tommy. I promise you that we're doing everything we can. And I believe the clues to these missing children may lie in Eugene's books. But it isn't because he's taken them. It's someone else." She took a breath. "But if you believe that signing papers against Eugene will help, then you have to do that. You have to do whatever you believe it takes to find your son."

Mrs. Franklin's tears slowed considerably. "I won't sign those papers. I can't do that to Mr. Legander. If I did,

Tommy would never forgive me. I'm sorry I disturbed you." Her voice caught on a sob and she hung up the phone.

"Bad news?" James, now fully dressed, went to the counter to pour himself another cup of coffee. He refilled Jennifer's mug before taking the seat across from her at the table. "By the way, that black cat is gone. There's not a trace of him in the house, and I found the back door pushed open. I'll bet he went back to Eugene's. Now, what's going on?"

"Someone's pulling strings at the police department."

"Anna Green?"

"That's my best guess."

"I'm going down right now to check the docket to see if Crush reported that break and entry." James checked his watch. "I'll give you a call in about thirty minutes, after I check in at the newspaper. Then I think we need to make a trip to the library."

"For what?"

"If anyone can give us a list of redheaded children, it'll be Martha Whipple. That way we won't have to upset Eugene with our suspicions."

Jennifer's face broke into a smile. "You're a genius, James Tenet."

He smiled at her as he set his coffee cup down and stood to leave. "You know, it scares me when you start handing out compliments." He picked up the cellular phone. "And I'll run by the phone company with this to find out exactly who it belongs to."

WHEN SHE GOT OUT of James's car at the library, Jennifer was still mulling over the significance of the fact that the telephone they'd discovered was actually the property of J. P. Frost, *and* that Crush had failed to report the blood in his house, or the illegal entry. The trouble was that not one single piece of evidence against Crush was strong enough to force law officers to act against him. The telephone could have been put in Crush's home. They'd broken in to find it, so someone else could just as easily have broken in to put it there. And after the terrible row that had occurred during Crush's show, even such a publicity hound might shy away from calling the police to examine an unexplained bloodstain.

There was also the little matter that they *had* broken in. Not exactly a position of strength when they were making accusations about someone else.

On the other hand, Crush Bonbon's possession of the telephone and lack of action in calling the police was extremely suspicious. Especially if he had the children.

Side by side, James and Jennifer climbed the white stone steps that marked the entrance to the graceful old building from which Tommy Franklin had disappeared. On either side of the steps, two plaster lions seemed to gaze into the distance, as if they had seen plenty but were unwilling to speak.

"Ready?" James's question was more one of mental preparedness than physical ability.

"As I'll ever be. I've thought of one child, Charlie McNair. He's quite a carrot top. I'm sure Ms. Whipple can supply the entire list. You can tell she adores those children."

"And she's more than a little fond of Eugene, I'd say." James grinned at her. "I was watching her during his reading. She absolutely hung on his every word."

Martha Whipple looked up over her glasses as James and Jennifer approached the children's desk. "How is Eugene?" she asked, her eyes darkening with concern. "I know how hard this is on him. I've been worried to death, but I didn't want to call him for fear I'd interrupt his work." An expression of dismay crossed her face. "He is working on that wonderful book, isn't he?"

Jennifer felt a current of guilt. She really didn't know if Eugene was working. Lately, they'd both been so caught up in the disappearance of the children that they hadn't discussed his book. "I'm sure it's coming along fine."

"Good." Relief swept her face and she lowered her gaze for a moment to compose herself. "What can I do for you and Mr...?"

"Tenet. James Tenet." Jennifer made the introductions, but she didn't mention that James was a reporter. "We're interested in a list of all the redheaded children who attend story hour here."

Martha Whipple's eyebrows lifted above the dark rim of her glasses. "Now that's a strange one, if I do say so myself. Is this some research for Eugene?"

"Yes."

"No."

James and Jennifer spoke in unison.

"What we mean is that—" Jennifer looked helplessly at James.

"It's for the cover of his book," James said. He pinched Jennifer's hip lightly.

"Right." She started forward, bumping her knee into the counter. "The art department is thinking about a cover with a redheaded child, and we thought it might be fun to feature a local boy or girl."

"Some lucky Mobile child may be featured on the cover of a book?" Martha Whipple was beaming. "How wonderful. Let me get the list."

From the shelf beneath her chair she pulled out a folder and flipped to the last page. "Let's see here. These are the boys and girls who attend story hour. And—" her finger traced down the page "—there's Charlie McNair. Yes, and his sister, Patti. Did you want boys and girls or just one gender?"

"Both." They spoke together again, and this time they all three grinned.

"Okay. And then there's Julie Ralston. She's strawberry blond, but she could be considered a redhead, I suppose.

Her brother, Rick, is so very blond, you know." Her finger traced slowly down the list. "And that's it. Charlie and Patti are the true redheads of the lot. But Julie is a possibility."

"Could we have their addresses?"

"You aren't going to stir them up by telling them this and then disappointing them, are you?" She gave Jennifer a stern look. "I've heard from Eugene how fickle the publishing industry can be and you know how easily a child's heart is broken."

"I won't disappoint them," Jennifer promised.

"Then have fun." She waved them away. "I've got to write a letter to the children. There's been some talk about canceling story hour until Mimi and Tommy are found, but I think that's a serious mistake. The children are frightened enough about what's happened to their playmates. Canceling story hour isn't a good idea."

Jennifer was ready to leave the library but she hesitated. "Miss Whipple, would you mind reading the story this week? Eugene has an appointment that he has to keep."

"An appointment?" Mrs. Whipple gave her a look steeped in curiosity. "Eugene never misses story hour."

"This time it can't be helped. If you can't fill in, I'll find someone to take his place to read."

"Love to do it, Miss Barkley. Don't trouble yourself about it at all."

"Thanks. You've been a wonderful friend to Eugene."

James had walked on to the door, but he'd heard the entire exchange. "What appointment does Eugene have?"

"He doesn't have one," Jennifer whispered. "But at this point, I think it best that Eugene doesn't engage in public appearances, especially not with a group of children. I mean what if something happened again. He'd be tarred and feathered and set on fire. They wouldn't wait for an explanation. He'd never leave the library alive."

James guided her through the door with his hand on the small of her back. "I get your drift."

Out in the warm April sunshine Jennifer hesitated. "I need to see Eugene and find that ornery black cat. I'm sure he went back to Eugene's, but I have to be certain."

"He's not ornery, he's just extremely bright." James hefted his car keys. "And I've got to go to work. We have a lot of latitude to work on a story, but I have things stacked up on my desk that have to be taken care of. Why don't we meet for lunch and then go and talk to the parents of those children? We also need to come to some decisions about what we're going to do with that telephone. We're withholding evidence."

Jennifer's look was scornful. "They'll figure out some way to say we were planting it, I'm sure." But her lip caught between her teeth was a truer reflection of her worry.

"We'll figure it out. I'll be by Eugene's for you at noon. Then we'll talk to the McNairs and Ralstons. Together."

Jennifer wanted to kiss him. "You'll go with me?"

"Someone with a clear head and stable personality should go along." He grinned, rewarded with a glint of surprised anger in her eyes.

"Of all the toadlike things to say. Just when I thought you were going to be nice to me, you imply that I'm a mental midget, that my behavior is questionable, that the parents of these children won't believe anything I say."

"Jennifer, I'd love to stand here and listen to you reel off more amusing little verbal daggers, but we should get going." He ducked down and kissed her. "You're the most remarkable woman I've ever known. Put down your battle sword, I was only teasing. But I will go with you, because this could be difficult."

"Thanks." She shook her head at him. "It's funny. I go from wanting to punch you to wanting to kiss you."

"We'll do some of the latter as soon as we're sure these children are safe. Now, let me drop you off at Eugene's."

JAMES AND JENNIFER stood at the curb and watched as a big black cat trotted along the sidewalk toward them. "I hope you haven't been out tom-catting around," Jennifer said sharply.

Familiar didn't dignify her remark with a look. He went past her to the front door and rattled it a few times with his paw.

Spying James, Jennifer, and the cat on the porch, Eugene called out, "Come in, children. I've made a wonderful cheese grits soufflé and fresh-fried mullet. There are days when I simply must return to my childhood diet."

For all of his joviality, Jennifer saw the dark circles under his eyes, which meant he wasn't sleeping. If he wasn't sleeping, then he wasn't working. He was worrying.

"That black rascal has been up to something," Eugene said as he followed Familiar into the kitchen. "He's worked up an appetite. Just as Judy Luno did last night. She was by here earlier, about to pop with some secret information. And as hungry as a tigress." He cut a look first at Jennifer and then at James. "Is there anything you want to tell me?"

"Not a thing," Jennifer assured him. "We have a few theories, Eugene, but the less you know, the better. Especially since the police are doing their level best to find some excuse to make an arrest."

"That's not unexpected, after last evening's Crush Bonbon show." Eugene served up two plates of steaming food and put them on the table with flatware. "Dig in, you two. I'm going to make Familiar a plate."

James bent down to stroke the cat. "Yes, I'm sure Familiar has earned some chow."

Eugene sat down at the table with them. "Jennifer, I don't want you to be shocked or dismayed, but I'm withdrawing *The Lizard King* from publication."

Jennifer almost choked on a piece of the crisply fried fish that was known along the Gulf Coast as Biloxi bacon. "What?"

"I have my own theories about what's going on with these children, and I believe the only way that they'll ever be returned is if I retire from writing." He got up and paced to the front door, where he stood and composed himself. "I've decided to do that."

"Eugene! You can't let this maniac drive you from the thing you love the most."

Eugene's smile was sad. "No. I love my work. But I don't love it more than these children. I've spent the last few days and nights trying to figure out what I have that this person might want. Not the cats. As fine as they are, there are plenty of cats to be had. Not my home. My garden is lovely, but anyone who loves plants can have one as fine or better. Not my savings. As handsomely as I've been paid in some cases, I've been as extravagant in others." He shrugged. "It has to be my writing. That's all I have that anyone could covet at all."

James put down his fork and stilled Jennifer's protest with one hand. "Wait," he said.

"Wait, my foot. This is the stupidest thing I've ever heard. Eugene is a *writer.* He can't quit being what he is. It would kill him. And we can't let this low-life, conniving, sneak-thief, child-snatching, roach-kissing, vermin-infested coward force Eugene into retirement."

"I couldn't have said it better myself," James said. He watched her face go from red anger to white-hot fury.

"This isn't the time to mock me," she warned. "I'll cut off your tongue and serve it to you on a bed of watercress."

James held his laughter, but just barely. "Hear me out, oh, violent one."

Eugene had come closer to the table, intrigued by the expression of delight on James's face. "What is it?" he asked. "What are you thinking?"

"A retirement *announcement.*"

"Like a fake press stunt?" Jennifer's temper evaporated. She was immediately caught with the possibilities.

"Exactly. We do a big story in the newspaper, with a picture, and how sad it all is, but that some health problem has forced you into retirement. We'll draw the son of a gun out of the woodwork if it's your talent that he's trying to destroy."

"You think maybe he'll give the children back?" Eugene asked. For the first time in a week there was a burning light in his blue eyes.

"It might work." Jennifer was trying to hold her enthusiasm down. But the idea seemed brilliant. If Eugene's logic was correct, and the attacks on the children were directed at him, then it might be that his retirement would push the kidnapper into releasing Mimi and Tommy. "It's worth a try." She stood, too excited to finish eating. "I'll have to call Maji and prepare her. If she reads this without warning, she'll probably have a heart attack. As long as she understands this is a hoax, she'll be fine."

Eugene smiled at her. "The truth is, darling, I can't write as long as I'm worried about those children. I've tried and tried. Everything I've done to *The Lizard King* since Tommy was taken is pure drivel. Worthless." He shrugged one shoulder as he looked out his back door. "So you see, it doesn't matter if I retire or not. I simply don't have what it takes to create until those children are safe and sound."

Chapter Thirteen

Jennifer tapped on the beveled glass door of the McNair residence and held her breath. James stood a discreet four steps behind her, there but not intrusively so. Footsteps echoed on the hardwood floor and then the door opened.

Zelda McNair gave Jennifer a warm smile before a look of perplexity touched her face. "Is something wrong with Mr. Legander?" she asked before Jennifer could say a word.

"This is going to be more difficult than I thought," Jennifer said as she cast a despairing look at James. "We may be crazy, Mrs. McNair, but we believe that either Charlie or Patti may be in danger."

She knew instantly that her words were too brash. Mrs. McNair's fair skin flushed with emotion. "How? They're in the backyard. They're—" She broke off as she turned from the door and started to run through the house.

Jennifer and James followed, knowing that it would do no good to try to calm her until she was certain her children were safe. Zelda stopped at the back door and looked out. Charlie and Patti were industriously setting up toy soldiers in what looked to be a battle zone. They never even bothered to glance up at the adults who watched them.

"I've kept them in the backyard ever since Mimi Frost disappeared," Zelda said, relief making her face go red, then white.

"We didn't mean to upset you, and we have no concrete proof." Jennifer realized how foolish she sounded. Only the slight pressure of James's hand on the small of her back gave her the courage to go on. "We have a hunch—"

"We have reason to believe that the kidnappings of the children are directed at Eugene Legander," James deftly overrode Jennifer's halting attempts to explain. "Jennifer and I have stumbled on what we think may be a clue. And we believe the next child scheduled to be kidnapped will be redheaded."

"How in the world did you ever come to that conclusion?" Mrs. McNair, now that she knew her children were safe, was curious, and a little dubious of her guests. "How could you know that, unless you know who's taken those children?" Her voice sharpened.

"We don't know the kidnapper," James assured her. "This is a guess. But if it's true, we wanted to warn you, and we're on the way to the Ralstons to warn them. I understand they have a girl—"

"Julie." Mrs. McNair nodded. "Strawberry blond. Lovely child. So unusual. She makes things from paper. Beautiful things." She looked out the back door again, making certain her children were safe. "This has been a nightmare for all of us parents. I don't know how Mrs. Frost is surviving. And now Mrs. Franklin." She clutched her hands together. "It's horrible, but I keep thinking that it could be my children, and I'm so glad that it was someone else's. That's unforgivable of me, I know, but I can't help it."

Jennifer put her hand on the woman's arm. "Not terrible, just very human. All of the mothers feel the same way, I'm sure. But just keep Charlie and Patti safe. In fact, if I had relatives I could visit, I think I might take a trip."

"They're both A students. It wouldn't hurt them to miss a few days of school, and I've been promising my sister that we'd come for a visit." She went to the sink and began to run dishwater. "I'll just clean up this kitchen, pack a few things, and we'll load up and go to Jackson."

James nodded at Jennifer, indicating they should leave. "Thanks for your time," Jennifer said. "We'd better check in with the Ralstons."

"Thank you for coming by." Mrs. McNair wiped her hands on a towel and walked with them to the door. "There's so much to do to get ready for a trip. But it would do us all a world of good. The children are sick of my watching them like a hawk, and I'm sick of the worry." She stood in the doorway. "I hope they catch whoever is doing this and make them pay a heavy price."

"Thanks."

James took Jennifer's elbow as they hurried down the drive. "She was pretty shaken, but I think getting out of town is an excellent idea. At first I thought she was going to call the cops, but thank goodness she didn't."

"What about the Ralstons?" Jennifer knew the risk James was taking. He needed to be at work, and he had no business being caught in the middle of her big, boiling pot of troubles.

"Let's do it, and then I have to get to the office."

"And I have a retirement announcement to write and a press conference to put together. I want Eugene to go out with some style, even if it is a fake retirement."

Bonnie Ralston reacted in much the same manner as Zelda McNair. She gathered her two children close and decided to leave town. The pressure had become too much, and she thanked James and Jennifer for their warning.

On the short drive to Jennifer's house, James reached across the seat and picked up her hand. It was cool, fragile-looking. He wrapped his fingers around it. "We'll get through this," he said, kissing the tips of her fingers as he drove. "I promise."

"I just hope it's before something terrible happens to Mimi and Tommy."

"If we've thwarted Crush's plans, we may have bought them more time." He shook his head. "It just doesn't make sense. Why would a radio personality on the brink of going into national syndication do such a crazy thing?"

"I've been thinking about that myself," Jennifer said. "Why does he hate Eugene so much? I can't seem to find an answer, but maybe I haven't asked Eugene in the right way." There was an edge of steel in her voice.

"I don't think you can threaten Eugene into telling you a single thing."

"Maybe not, but Familiar may be able to help me out."

James pulled the car to the curb and stopped. "I don't even want to hear a plan that involves you and that cat. The fur will fly, is all I can say."

"I'll call you and let you know when I schedule the press conference."

"Make it early afternoon," he said. "Better for my deadline." He grinned, and blew her a kiss as he drove away.

Two hours later Jennifer examined the printed copy of her release. It was brief, simple, to the point, stating that due to health reasons Eugene Legander was hanging up his pen. It stated that no future Legander books would be issued by Grand Street Press. Due to Eugene's illness, there would be no retirement party at this time. The writer was going into seclusion.

On the one hand, it made Eugene look as guilty as sin. On the other, it added an element of sympathy to his side—if the reader believed that his worry about the children had driven him to retire. That was what Jennifer was hoping without being able to state it clearly. The idea was to manipulate the public. Not always the easiest thing to do.

She tapped her pen against her coffee cup and read it again. She wanted it to be perfect before she faxed a copy to Maji—after she called and told her of the plan.

But first she'd have to call Eugene, to check it out with him. She continued to tap a staccato beat on the coffee cup with her pen as the phone rang and rang. Jennifer's forehead wrinkled in thought. Why didn't Eugene answer? Where could he have gone? It was a small, niggling worry, but one that she knew would bother her until she spoke with him. He was so adventurous—and unpredictable. And he was also very worried about his young friends.

Jennifer replaced the receiver and dialed J. P. Frost. It was time to tell him what she'd found. She didn't completely trust the man, but it was his daughter, and his telephone. And with a little bit of luck, Frost might be the perfect foil for a scheme she was hatching. One that not even James knew about yet.

EUGENE'S HOUSE is a pack rat's haven. I mean there's stuff here that probably belongs in King Tut's tomb! The most amazing assortment of odds and ends, art and tinsel, expensive and junky. It's heaven! There's something to tickle any cat's curiosity, not to mention those wonderful peacock feathers that he uses to make AnnaLoulou dance and leap. What a gazelle she is. I do believe that I could abandon my heart to her if it were not already given to another.

Speaking of Clotilde, that brings to mind the Washington scene and the trials and tribulations of The Dame. Eugene got a call from her this morning with good news. Peter is out of jail and he has videotape on the atrocities of one of those canned hunts that should put several of those butchers in jail for a long time. Eugene was near tears as he spoke to Eleanor, so it must be some pretty gruesome stuff. I'm glad I didn't have to hear it. I just want to be in Texas so I can show those fake big game murderers what a small fifteen-pound feline with full claws and teeth can do.

Enough of that! My blood pressure is at the boiling point and I have my own set of troubles here in Mobile.

I've been looking at Eugene's manuscript, and the more I look at it, the more certain I am that the numeral 98 is significant. I'm certain Jennifer figured out the redheaded child angle, so that's one clue that was left and used. This is one smart kidnapper, and one that likes to play with us. It's almost as if he were deliberately tweaking our noses with the clues. He's telling us every step he's going to take before he takes it.

In Crush's house there were stuffed dolls and toys, and a computer. And in the backyard, an impressive swing set. It has occurred to me that perhaps Crush is not establishing a kingdom for a child, but a place to imagine things like a child—i.e., a writer of children's stories. That would give him a reason to hate Eugene. It's only a theory, but it seems to work better than the one where he hates the books that Eugene writes. Even a human has more sense than that—what's to hate about wonderful stories? Even someone with the literary IQ of a Bonbon should be able to appreciate a well told tale. But I forget, you can't really generalize about such an undeveloped species.

For certain, though, Crush is not stupid. Not by a long shot. He's annoying and malicious and conniving, but he isn't dumb.

So if he wants to write children's books, maybe he views Uncle Eugene as too much competition. If the great Uncle Eugene were to step down as an author, it would leave a void that Crush would be only too glad to fill. It's a hypothesis, but one that has some substance.

Well, I need to get back inside the Bonbon house to see if there are some diaries, or some records of how to get that computer up and running. I don't think Miss Spitfire has any computer talent, and I know Eugene can't even use an electric typewriter. So maybe James?

Or even better—Mademoiselle Luno. Now she's the kind of kid who could turn a computer inside out. And I don't think she'd object to an evening of scampering around the Bonbon estate. No, I think that would be right up her alley.

First a snack, then a nap, and then some very serious cat-astrophic breaking and entering!

SUNLIGHT WARMED the lavender azaleas around Eugene's house to a vibrant glow as Jennifer pulled up and stopped at the front of his house. She'd called him seven times in the last hour—to no avail. If he was home, he was dodging the telephone.

She used her key to open the front door, and the silence of the house told her that she was alone with the cats.

Outside she heard a cheery whistle and went back to the porch. Eugene was coming down the sidewalk, two large bags clutched in his arms and a forced smile on his face.

"Welcome, darling. What are you doing in my neck of the woods?"

She gave him a critical inspection, noting the haggard look and the fake cheerfulness. "Checking on you. I have your retirement announcement. Want to take a look at it?"

"Excellent. Let me put these things away." He went into the kitchen. "I had the most delightful chat with little Bobby Fornaro in the parking lot at the grocery store. That child is a whirlwind of mischief."

Jennifer couldn't immediately place the youngster. There were at least fifty kids that Eugene knew well.

"His mother was buying groceries and left him in the car to play with one of those hideous video game things. She had warned him against talking to strangers, and what was Bobby doing but sneaking out of the car and using the tip of an umbrella to tickle women on their rumps when they bent over to put their groceries in the trunk." Eugene laughed. "That youngster is going to end up in prison."

"If some woman doesn't kill him before he has a chance to make it to puberty." Jennifer had a memory flash of the child. He was a devil, but he was also pretty funny. No matter what trouble he got into, he often got out of it unscathed because he could make people laugh. "He may be a comedian."

"Well, I caught him good and proper and put him back in the car before he gave poor old Mrs. Edison a heart attack. She thought something was in her pants." Eugene started laughing and stopped with a can of soup in his hand. "It *was* funny. Every time she bent over to try to straighten the groceries in the trunk, Bobby would lean out from behind the tail of the car and goose her with the umbrella."

Jennifer laughed, too. "Well, I hope you made him apologize."

"Of course, and she forgave him and gave him a cookie."

Jennifer rolled her eyes and grinned. Mrs. Edison had been a neighbor of Eugene's for the past thirty years. There was hardly a night when one of her grandchildren wasn't staying over with her. It did Jennifer good to see Eugene laughing at anything, even if it was the antics of a nine-year-old gangster-in-training.

"So what did Mrs. Fornaro say?"

"Oh, darling, I didn't wait and report Bobby. I took him to the car, made him promise to lock the doors, and I came on home. You know how his mother likes to squeeze all of the tomatoes in the store. She would have been in there all morning, and I had business to do." He shook his head. "How a couple with southern Italian backgrounds ever produced a redheaded child is beyond me—Jennifer?" Eugene hurried toward her. "What is it?"

"Bobby is redheaded?"

"Deep auburn. But it shouldn't concern you if it doesn't concern Mr. Fornaro."

"What store?"

"What store what?" Eugene looked at her as if she'd gone mad.

"What store were you shopping at?"

"The Delliwag over on Pinkham Street."

"Let's go." She snatched at his shirtsleeve in an effort to hurry him along. Just in time, she saw Familiar rise from the sofa and stretch, his pink mouth open wide in a yawn. "And you, too." She pointed at the cat. "Now!"

Eugene saw the panic on her face and didn't wait to argue. "Let's go, Familiar. We have our marching orders."

Jennifer was already at the door, car keys in hand. "Hurry, Eugene. I'm afraid Bobby Fornaro may be kidnapped."

"Darling, he was perfectly fine not twenty minutes ago. His mother was on her way to the checkout line. I saw her through the plate glass window. I'm sure they've left Delliwag and gone home by now."

"Hurry!" Jennifer pulled the door closed behind them and made sure it locked. Eugene was too lax in leaving his house open.

Ten minutes later they made the corner by Pinkham Street. The wail of the sirens in the parking lot told Jennifer her worst fears had been realized. In the seat beside her, Eugene's face had gone completely gray.

"How did you know it would be Bobby?" he asked in a monotone.

Familiar leapt into his lap and rubbed his whiskers against Eugene's cheek.

"He's redheaded." Jennifer felt like a fool for not telling Eugene what she'd figured out. Maybe if she'd told him, he could have warned Bobby. But the child's name hadn't been on the list prepared by Ms. Whipple, and Jennifer had forgotten about him.

"Why a redhead?"

Jennifer told him about the missing book at Crush Bonbon's house. "The story was about a redheaded boy. I made the connection, and then I carefully went to the Ralstons and the McNairs and made sure their children were safe. But I didn't remember Bobby Fornaro. I didn't, and Ms. Whipple at the library didn't, either."

"Martha checked her list?" Eugene glanced at Jennifer.

"She did. And his name wasn't on it."

"He hasn't been to story hour since February. His grandmother was sick and they've been going to Anniston every weekend. I guess he got left off the list that Martha updates every month."

Jennifer swallowed. She'd stopped the car some thirty yards from where two police cruisers remained, doors open and lights and sirens whirling. Nikki Fornaro sat on the bumper of her car crying into her hands. At her feet was Bobby's dark green school jacket.

"What should we do?"

"Go over there," Eugene said immediately. "I was here only a few moments ago. Maybe even then the kidnapper was in the parking lot, waiting for his chance." Eugene pinched the bridge of his nose as his eyes filled. "If I had talked with Bobby another fifteen minutes, this wouldn't have happened. But I was in a hurry to get home. I had some new treats for the kitties and I wanted to repot those carnations."

Jennifer put her hand on his arm and gave it a squeeze. "Even if you'd stayed with Bobby, if the kidnapper was determined to get him, he would have, eventually. But I think this puts the finger of suspicion firmly on Crush. It isn't going to be easy, but we're going to have to go to the police. And we're going to have to make them believe us."

"I don't think we're going to have to go anywhere." Eugene pointed through the windshield as two patrolmen started toward Jennifer's car. The looks on their faces said they were coming to deal with a dangerous individual.

They walked to the passenger side, hands hovering near their weapons. "Eugene Legander?"

"Yes." Eugene was unflappable.

"You're under arrest for the kidnapping of Robert Fornaro."

"Don't be ridiculous—" Jennifer shouted.

The officers glared at her. "You stay out of this or we'll take you in on an obstruction charge. Mr. Legander has been identified in the parking lot with the boy. Just as he was with the last two children who have gone missing. This time, he won't get another chance to hurt one of Mobile's youngsters."

The car door was jerked opened, and the officers reached inside, grabbing Eugene.

There was an angry, warning growl from the back seat and the biggest officer reached for his gun.

Just before Familiar made a leap for the policeman's face, Jennifer got her hands on him and pulled him into her arms. "Easy, boy. There's nothing we can do now, and I don't think they'd charge you with assault. These bullies would shoot you on the spot."

"Right." The taller officer gave the cat a wary look as the other snapped handcuffs on Eugene.

"Don't worry, Eugene. We'll get you out in no time."

"Don't you worry, darling," Eugene said over his shoulder as they hustled him away. "I'm always game for an adventure. This episode may even force me out of retirement."

Jennifer felt the tears burn her eyes as she watched, helpless to stop Eugene's arrest. She knew that Eugene wouldn't suffer any mistreatment at the hands of the police. It was just the idea of the humiliation of being dragged off in handcuffs. The process *was* humiliating—and damaging. Only Eugene would consider it an adventure.

The patrol car, with Eugene in the back, pulled out of the parking lot and headed downtown. Jennifer wanted to follow, but she knew it would do no good. She had to figure out a good defense position for the flack that would soon rain down on her head harder than a hail storm.

The Fornaro station wagon was still in the lot, blocked off from the handful of curious spectators by the yellow crime scene tape that Jennifer had grown to dread. She knew better than to touch the car. Good Lord, they had enough troubles without the authorities finding her fingerprints on anything.

She was about to go home when Familiar made an agile leap out of the open passenger window. Darting in front of a black pickup that was traveling far too fast, he scampered across the lot and headed straight for the blue station wagon. The crowd was dispersing, drifting back to work or to finish errands now that the cops and emergency vehicles were gone.

Even so, the parking lot was crowded, and Familiar had disappeared near the station wagon. Jennifer had to get him, and fast.

"Familiar." She got out and stood beside the car, hissing at the cat. "When I get you I'm going to make microwave kitty puffs. Delicious with a glass of milk." She gritted her teeth. The cat could hear her but he was sauntering under the right front wheel of the Fornaro car.

Checking around the lot, Jennifer made sure there were no plainclothes cops hanging around. They'd called for a tow truck to haul the station wagon to the city garage where they could take it apart piece by piece in the hopes of finding some clue.

If they even hunted for one. Jennifer knew they were going to try to pin it on Eugene. And his fingerprints would be on the car. He'd leaned in the window talking with Bobby. All she needed now was for Familiar to do something and get himself impounded. That would be the final straw.

Jennifer hurried across the parking lot. Familiar's black tail disappeared around the back wheel of the station wagon.

"When I get my hands on you, you're going to make a lovely ornament for the rear window of my car. I'm certain I can break your neck so that your head bobs whenever I stop."

"Me-ow." Familiar blinked, golden eyes seeming to tilt with amusement as he looked out from beneath the car.

"You better not be laughing at me." She made a lunge for him, but he darted deeper under the vehicle.

"Drat you." She got down on her hands and knees, doing her best not to allow any part of her body to come in contact with the car.

Just out of reach, Familiar sat on a rectangle of paper. "Kitty, kitty," Jennifer pleaded.

Instead of coming to her, he got off the paper and nudged it toward her with his paw. It took some effort on his part, but he finally marshaled the paper to her outstretched fingers.

"This had better be good," she warned, feeling the shells embedded in the asphalt of the parking lot dig deeper and deeper into her knees.

Even as she touched the page, she recognized what it was. How had the police overlooked it? Perhaps they hadn't looked. Not very hard. They'd believed Eugene was guilty, and they'd looked no farther. So they'd missed the page from his book that had been left by the kidnapper.

Rocking back on her haunches, Jennifer stared at the page. It was about the young redheaded boy who wanted to fly. Familiar came out from under the car and rubbed against her bruised knees.

The words seemed to blur and blend in front of her, yet she stared at the page in the hot sun as if it would tell her secrets.

Familiar's black paw slapping at the page finally brought her back to the present. She looked at the cat's knowing eyes, and then at the spot on the page where he'd slapped.

Ninety-eight.

"What does it mean?" she asked herself softly. "What could it possibly mean?"

The sound of a large truck headed in her direction made her look up. The tow truck, followed by a police cruiser, was headed straight across the parking lot toward them. Still on her haunches, she duck walked around a green Chevy coupe. Three cars later, she got up to a crouch because her legs were burning with pain.

Zigzagging across the lot, she went to her car. Familiar took the back seat and she slid into the driver's seat. For a long moment she stared at the page before she put it on the passenger seat beside her. There was something there, something obvious. If only she could see it!

Jennifer slammed the steering wheel with her hand in complete frustration. "I could do something dire and gruesome—if I knew who to do it to." She slammed the steering wheel again. The glove box of the car popped open and a pile of paper and clutter spilled to the floor. "Well, I'll be a cross-eyed lounge lizard." She reached across the console to grab the mess when Familiar suddenly dropped off the seat into the middle of the clutter.

"Well, my fine feline, since you're so smart, you can clean it up." She started the car and eased out of the parking lot. There was nothing to do but go home and face the music with Maji. She'd driven Eugene right into the arms of an arrest. And no matter that the old writer had gone cheerfully, she still felt as though she'd let him down.

Not to mention the fact that another child was missing.

"Meow!"

Familiar's cry drew her attention to the floorboard. He'd managed to unfold a map of the state of Alabama and was clawing a hole in the portion of the state near the gulf.

"What now?" She looked for a place to pull over before the cat shredded the entire map into a zillion pieces. Eugene was adamantly opposed to having his cats declawed—an abominable act promoted by heathens, he'd said. But as Jennifer watched the pieces of the map fly around her car, she considered its merit.

"Eleanor might prefer you declawed—and lobotomized!"

Familiar didn't dignify her remark with a look, he just kept shredding.

At a side street Jennifer stopped the car. When she reached down to get the map, there was little left, just a small section of the coastline of Alabama, Mississippi, and Florida.

And a highway ran east to west across the entire section. Highway 98.

Chapter Fourteen

"Be still!" Jennifer nudged her big purse with her toe and spoke to it with tightened lips. The bag shifted and finally stopped.

"Did you say something to me?" the receptionist at the newspaper asked. She gave Jennifer a doubtful glance.

"Uh, I said it was still hot outside." Jennifer smiled, but knew it looked as fake as pearls from a Mardi Gras parade.

"Mr. Tenet is on the third floor." She gave Jennifer a badge to indicate she was a visitor.

"Thanks." Jennifer grabbed the bag, staggering slightly under the weight. Ignoring the receptionist's questioning look, she hurried up the stairs.

"You're going on a diet you overfed, underdisciplined feline," she whispered to the bag as she huffed up the three flights of stairs.

James's cubicle was off to the left, and he was busy at his computer, the keys rattling along as he wrote.

"James?" Jennifer stopped three steps behind him. The sight of his broad shoulders and his dark, thick hair, made her lose her train of thought. He was a handsome man. An ethical man. Her feelings for him were growing stronger each day.

He whirled in the chair, a smile touching his eyes and lips. Then his glance fell on the bag Jennifer carried, which was moving.

"You brought me something alive for a snack?" He quirked an eyebrow. "How thoughtful."

"Shut up and help me with this cat." She handed him the bag. "I couldn't leave him in the car in the parking lot. You know how much trouble Familiar can get into, but I had to come here. It's Highway 98. I know it. And Familiar knows it, too."

James looked at her, then the bag, then her. "Let's go into the conference room. I think we need a place where we can talk privately."

He led the way to a room with a long conference table. As soon as he closed the door behind them, Jennifer unzipped her bag. Familiar came out, his fur bristled and a gleam was in his eyes.

"I'm sorry," Jennifer said, stroking his fur back into place. "I said it would be uncomfortable."

"What's going on here?" James motioned Jennifer into a chair but he remained standing.

"Eugene has been arrested. Bobby Fornaro has been kidnapped." She took a breath as she saw the worry on his face. "Familiar found another page from Eugene's book, and we cracked the clue."

James eased into a chair. "I know I can follow this conversation. It's just going to be difficult."

"Ninety-eight. It's a highway. It was the same page number left by the car where Bobby was taken."

"Highway 98." He nodded. "It's possible."

"I'm positive. Now all we have to do is figure out where along the highway the children are being held."

At Jennifer's look of hope, James felt his heart contract. "Jennifer, it's a long highway. It goes through several states." To avoid the look of dismay on her face, he got up and left the room. In a moment he returned with two soft drinks and a map. "See." He spread the map across the table. "Highway 98 runs from Natchez, Mississippi to St.

Petersburg, Florida." He spoke softly, but he knew the words were devastating.

"They could be anywhere." The elation she'd felt was completely gone. What was left was despair.

James lightly rubbed her shoulders. "We need more information. This is a good start, but it isn't enough to find them."

"What am I going to do?" She turned and looked up at him, her blue eyes filling with tears. "We have to find those children, James. We have to."

"We will." For Jennifer's sake, he forced his voice to sound solid and certain. But the disappearance of Bobby Fornaro had added another measure of grave doubt to an already bad situation. It wasn't that James suspected Eugene—he knew the writer was innocent. But the children were gone, and the chances that they would be returned, unharmed, grew slimmer and slimmer with each passing day. What kidnapper would continue to select children without demanding a ransom of some type? Unless...

"What time is Eugene's retirement announcement set for?"

"Tomorrow at three o'clock." Jennifer had gained control of her emotions. "Why?"

"Where?"

"The library."

"Perfect." James smiled for the first time in what seemed like days.

"What's perfect?"

"What if Eugene is right? What if the person taking these children is doing it because of professional jealousy. If Eugene retires, then maybe the children will be freed."

"What's perfect about the library?"

"It's the most significant place to do this. It'll lend credence to the announcement. And, we have Ms. Whipple to help us keep an eye on a few things."

The glint in James's eye was contagious. "What's going on in that clever little mind of yours?" Jennifer asked. Even Familiar was watching him with interest.

"Cameras."

"As in home video or still?"

"Video." James went to a small table and picked up a phone book. He handed it to Jennifer. "Here. Look up some places that rent video equipment. We want enough to set up cameras so that the library is covered from every angle at that retirement announcement."

"So we can study the tapes." Jennifer was right on track. "The person who wants Eugene to quit bad enough to steal children wouldn't dare miss the formal retirement announcement."

"Exactly!"

"And if we can come up with a suspect, then maybe we can find a connection to Highway 98."

James gathered her into his arms and kissed her. His desire for her was constant. Her body felt so right against his. He eased back from her and forced his mind to function. "Yes! We have to find the connection."

"Oh, God, James, I hope this works."

"So do I."

"Meow!" Familiar nudged the phone book toward Jennifer.

"I think he wants me to get busy."

James held her and kissed her again, lightly. "That cat may be right, but he's a real pain in the butt."

"Go." Jennifer pushed him toward the door.

"I'll finish up this story and then we'll go get the equipment and set it up. I'm sure Martha Whipple will help us."

Jennifer nodded, her fingers already walking through the Yellow Pages.

THE FOURTH CAMERA was mounted and loaded with fresh tape. Martha Whipple showed James the closet where the library ladder was stored.

"You two are very thorough." She nodded at all of the equipment, and the control center that they'd located beneath the library desk. There were dark circles under her eyes and she rubbed beneath her glasses in an unconscious gesture of weariness. "So you think you'll be able to figure out who's behind all of this by looking at the tapes?"

"That's what we're hoping," James said as he closed the closet door and wiped his dirty hands on his jeans. Jennifer was taping cable to the floor, her face smudged with dirt and her lovely hair tied back with a kerchief.

"How is Eugene?" Martha Whipple took off her glasses and cleaned them on her blouse.

"Not so good." James didn't know Martha Whipple well, but she was a friend of Eugene's, and he felt he owed her the truth. "He's worried about those kids. This retirement is something he insists on. He says he can't write he's so worried, so he might as well quit."

"I never thought Eugene Legander would stop writing." Her eyes dropped to the floor to hide her emotions. "You know he's been doing it since he was virtually an infant." She pinched the bridge of her nose.

James laughed at the mental picture of an infant Eugene pecking away at his typewriter, but his laughter contained an element of sadness. He was worried about the writer. More worried than he'd ever let on to Jennifer.

"We're hoping to talk Eugene into returning to work as soon as the children are home and this settles down some."

"Yes, that would be the smartest course." Martha Whipple looked at the black cat who sat on her counter. "I've enjoyed the company of the two of you, but I'll be glad to see that cat go. Cats and books don't mix."

"Familiar is very intelligent," Jennifer quickly declared. "He hasn't bothered a thing. He's very careful, and far too clever for a cat."

"And he belongs outside." Martha pointed her red pen at him. "He looks like he's thinking up something terrible."

Jennifer had been biding her time, waiting for the best moment to broach a ticklish subject. "Ms. Whipple, how was it that you didn't tell us that Bobby Fornaro was a redhead?"

Martha Whipple steepled her hands together as if she intended to pray. "I've asked myself that question a million times. I know Bobby. Good Lord, he's one of the biggest torments on the face of the earth. But he's a dear child, and I can't believe I overlooked him." A tear slipped from beneath her glasses and traced down her cheek. "He hasn't been to story hour in the last few months. There was an illness in his family or something. They've been out of town." She looked up and slowly brushed her tears away. "I hold myself completely responsible for his disappearance. I have been heartsick since he was taken, and I know you could have saved him if I'd only been a little more intelligent, a little more thorough."

"Martha." Jennifer went to her and put an arm around her shoulders. "It isn't your fault."

"I should have gone back over several lists. I don't know what I was thinking." She sniffed and held back the tears. "I love those children, and now one is missing because I didn't think!"

"What we have to concentrate on is finding them," James said gently. "And that's exactly what we're doing."

"Those poor little babies. I feel like the shepherd who lost a lamb. You know the song. There were ninety and nine." Her voice broke. "Now, because of me, Bobby is missing."

Before the words were completely out of her mouth, Familiar jumped across the counter and slapped several times at the keyboard of Martha's library computer.

"What is that black devil doing?" Martha started forward, her face still blotched and upset, only to run into James's outstretched hand.

"Wait," James said quickly. When Martha started forward again, James caught her arm and held her. "Give him a minute, Ms. Whipple. If Familiar could talk, or write, he'd be in high cotton."

"If cats could talk, there'd be even more jawboning and complaining going on." Martha Whipple gave the cat an evil look as she pushed her glasses up on her nose.

"I think I know the reason Martha Whipple and Eugene never got to be better friends," Jennifer whispered to James. "If she doesn't like cats, then Eugene has no use for her."

James nodded, but his attention was on the black feline. "What's he doing?"

"I don't know."

"It's the checkout file," Martha said. A tiny smile touched her lips. "I believe he's calling up... Crush Bonbon! Why didn't I think of that!"

All three humans hovered over the screen, and Martha Whipple's quick fingers assisted Familiar as they pulled up the list of books Crush had checked out for the past several months.

"Look at that." Jennifer pointed to the screen. "A book on writing children's stories!"

"You don't think Crush wants to be a writer, do you?" Martha was amazed. "Is that why he's always dogging Eugene's books. Just plain, old-fashioned jealousy. Well, I'll be."

"And there's a book on building a bomb shelter," James said. "Checked out only four months ago. It's been years since anyone seriously built a bomb shelter."

Jennifer touched his arm, her eyes wide. "Except for what Mimi said on the phone. She said she was afraid because it was so dark *in here.* You don't suppose..." She left the sentence unfinished as she saw Martha Whipple's expectant look.

"Did you hear from Mimi?" Martha asked. "Tell me!"

"It was probably a prank," Jennifer backtracked as fast as she could. She'd have to learn to keep her mouth shut or get herself, James, and Eugene in even more trouble than they were in already.

"Well, it seems you've got the culprit. The question is where has Crush put those children? And what does he intend to do with them? Are you going to have him arrested?"

James held up a hand. "Whoa, Ms. Whipple. Everything we have is circumstantial. We don't really have any solid proof. I know Crush looks guilty. In more ways than one. But we can't prove a thing. The worst possible set of events would be to accuse Crush before we know where the children are being held. What would happen if he was arrested and then refused to tell us where they are? The children could starve."

"Or worse," Jennifer added direly. She held a purring Familiar in her arms. She kissed the top of his head as she held him.

"Well, what are you going to do?" Martha asked matter-of-factly.

Jennifer looked at James. They were going back to Crush's—this time to explore the grounds for a bomb shelter. But they couldn't tell Martha Whipple that. They couldn't tell anyone.

"What are you going to do about this retirement announcement if Eugene is still in jail?" Martha asked, readjusting her glasses.

"He'll be out. Grand Street Press sent a lawyer down from New York," Jennifer said. "Eugene will be out in plenty of time to make the announcement. That was a guarantee from the publisher himself."

Martha nodded. "This is a pity, all of this ruckus. Do you think it'll have a serious impact on Eugene's writing?"

Jennifer considered the question seriously for the first time. "I don't know. I really don't know. He says he can't write now because he's so worried about the children. And the kidnapping of Bobby will only make matters worse. But permanent effects—I certainly hope not."

James put his arm around Jennifer. "Most writers recover from this type of trauma. Crush has gone a long way toward making Eugene feel responsible, even though he knows logically that he isn't. That's the devastating part. Someone like Eugene is so concerned for others that he assumes the burden of their welfare, even when it's completely out of his control. He may never recover from this."

"Well, I have to do some record-keeping before I get out of here today." Martha waved a hand around the library. "Make yourselves at home. I'll be in the back office if you need me."

"We have to be going," James said as he looked over the equipment again. "We're set here, so there shouldn't be a problem. We'll see you tomorrow, at three."

"You're a lucky woman, Jennifer, to have a man like James to help you." Martha beamed up at James.

"James and Familiar," Jennifer said, cradling the black cat in her arms. "I don't know which one is smarter, or more attractive."

"Posh!" Martha threw her hands up in the air and walked off to the sound of James's laughter.

"Now she knows you're a very weird woman." He took Jennifer's elbow. "Let's get out of here."

"I need to go down to the police station. When Eugene is released I want to minimize the publicity."

James gave her a sidelong look. "We both need to go downtown." His grin was suddenly wide. "Think permits.

As in, building permits. It's a long shot, but there has to be a record of any construction in Crush's neighborhood. It's part of the historic district, and they have to approve even the tiniest change. I'd also like to check the police docket for the past few months. That's something we haven't done, and it would be interesting to see what type of activity has been reported in Crush's neighborhood. I can't help but think those children are somewhere close by. He has to feed them. And check on them."

"Let's hope they're being fed," Jennifer said darkly. "I wish we could connect Anna Green, or Chief Bixley or Crush Bonbon with some property on Highway 98. That would tie things together."

James nodded his head. "I don't know, but we're getting closer and closer to some answers."

James steered her down the steps, his hand moving seductively at the base of her spine. Jennifer's body awakened to his touch, remembering the details of the night they'd spent together. She cast a look at him from the corner of her eye and saw that he, too, had been affected by the casual encounter. She smiled, a secret, sexy smile that made him stop to look at her a long moment before he spoke.

"I miss your dire threats. Please tell me that you're planning on taking me home tonight and making me beg for mercy?"

At the accuracy of his line of thought Jennifer felt the heat climb her face. "I was thinking no such thing." She met his gaze and knew he read the truth. Her blue eyes sparkled. "But I believe a little begging would be good for you. You're far too sure of yourself. And I'm just the woman who could make you beg."

"That's one challenge I'll accept," James said, his voice a soft, heated promise. "Later this evening. Your place or mine?"

Jennifer got in the car door he'd opened for her. "Mine. As soon as we finish exploring Crush Bonbon's bomb shelter."

James shut the door and walked around the car. "Ah, another evening of adventure with a girl and her cat."

TELEVISION CAMERAS lined the sidewalk by the police station, and Anna Green, with Chief Craig Bixley by her side, was getting ready to have an impromptu press conference as Jennifer pulled up. She parked down the street where she could watch the circus without drawing attention to herself.

"Look at that blister on the butt of humanity," Jennifer said to Familiar as she glared at Anna. "She's worse than dangerous. She could be doing good instead of this stupidity."

"Meow." Familiar gave her a knowing look.

The black feline had taken up with her and showed no signs that he wanted to be anywhere else. In fact, he'd resisted all of Jennifer's efforts to leave him at Eugene's house, or at her own home. He was definitely a cat with a mind of his own. As she watched him, his eyes narrowed at Anna Green. And a cat with his own opinions, which just happened to coincide with hers. Familiar didn't like Anna, and Jennifer understood why.

"She's a witch, isn't she?"

"Meow."

"Well, let's see if we can't set her broomstick on fire." Jennifer opened the door for Familiar, trusting that he would stay beside her. She'd grown to depend on him in many ways. Eleanor Curry was going to have a really hard time getting him back—and Jennifer had never considered herself a pet owner. She'd always liked animals, but had avoided owning one since childhood when her best friend, Sam, a mixed-breed pooch, had died and broken her heart. Now, Familiar had filled a vacancy she'd refused to admit she had. How strange that both the cat and James had come into her life on the same day.

From the podium, Anna did a sound check while Bixley straightened his posture and his chief's hat. There was enough gold brocade on his hat and uniform to blind someone, Jennifer thought as she watched the speakers prepare.

Along with the members of the news media were protesters, no doubt carefully orchestrated by Anna, Bixley and Bonbon. There were several signs that called for Eugene's books to be burned, as well as other books and tapes and videos. She couldn't make out the complete list, but it looked like a long one. Most of the spectators looked bored, but one or two had a fanatical gleam in his or her eye. Those were the ones who scared her. Those were the ones who'd take children to *make* Eugene or some other writer look guilty, believing they were acting for the good of humanity.

A loud call from the audience drew Jennifer's attention to a tall, slender woman dressed in red holding a microphone in her hand. It was one of the television reporters.

"Ms. Green! Have any charges been filed against—"

"I have a speech prepared," Anna said, cutting across the reporter's question. She cleared her throat. "Although no formal charges have been filed against Eugene Legander, I want to assure the public that the police chief and his staff are doing everything possible to protect the children of this community...."

She continued, but Jennifer tuned her out. Anna was eating crow and doing her best to make it look like caviar. Bixley, too, looked more chagrined than proud. They'd arrested Eugene, and it hadn't stuck. She was tempted to hang around and ask a few pointed questions herself, but she had other irons in the fire.

Jennifer's dilemma was how best to get Eugene out of the station and avoid the endless questions. No matter what he said, it would only make matters worse, for the time being.

There had to be a back way out of the station house, and she knew just the cat who could find it.

"Come on, Familiar." She motioned for the cat to follow her. Luckily, neither Anna nor Bixley had spied her. They wouldn't expect her to sneak Eugene out the back while they were warming up the crowd. What they were hoping for was a spectacle of angry parents charging at Eugene. She grinned as she embroidered her "escape" plan more fully.

The building was irregular in shape and design, and Jennifer and the cat made several wrong choices before they found a door that was obviously the patrolman's entrance. "Purr-fect," Jennifer said, bending to pet the cat.

A large shadow fell over her and she looked up into the slitted eyes of Crush Bonbon.

"I thought I might find you here, looking for a back way to sneak out." He stepped back slightly as Familiar growled.

"Why aren't you up on the speaker's box with your friends?" Jennifer slowly straightened. Anger made her square her shoulders and lift her chin.

"I've got something to say to you. Stay off my property. I know you were in my house the other night." He grinned at the startled expression on her face. "Stay out of there. I'm warning you, Miss Barkley. Tamper in my personal life again, and you could get hurt very seriously."

"On the contrary, Crush. I think you're the one who has the most to lose, should I ever admit that I was in your house. Care to explain about that special room, the one for a child?"

She saw his hand ball into a fist and, for a split second, she thought he was going to hit her. Familiar, too, tensed, the hair on his back fuzzing to demonstrate his deadly intent.

"That's none of your business." Red suffused his cheeks. "That's a personal thing. Very private. You'd better not go running your mouth off about that."

"It looks pretty sick to me, Crush. A grown man with a room decorated for a child. A grown single man with no children and no prospects of having any." Jennifer couldn't stop herself. All of the pain that Eugene had suffered was partially due to the man who stood in front of her.

"Watch yourself, Miss Barkley, or you could find yourself in some unpleasant circumstances."

"As Jack Nicholson so succinctly put it, 'I'd like to rip your eyeballs out and shove them up your dead skull.'"

Crush took another step back. "You're as demented as Eugene. The two of you should be in an institution. If I ever had any doubts about Anna and what she's doing, I don't anymore. This violence has to stop, and you're part of it."

He spun around quickly for a heavy man and walked back the way he'd come.

"Let's get Eugene." With the adrenaline dissipating, Jennifer felt a strange uneasiness. Crush hadn't reacted as she'd thought he would. There was something...vulnerable in the way he'd acted about the child's room. She felt a twinge of guilt. No matter how much he'd hurt Eugene, it made her feel bad to strike back.

She shook her head and opened the back door that led into the interior of the police department. "Why am I standing out here wasting time feeling sorry for Crush when Eugene is in a cell?"

Familiar twitched his tail twice.

From the front of the building a loud roar rolled toward Jennifer. "What the hell is that?" She knew even as she asked. It was the crowd. Anna Green had finally roused them to the point where passion overrode good sense.

"Meow!" Familiar darted into the building with Jennifer on his heels. Their only concern now was Eugene.

Chapter Fifteen

Jennifer's dash through the station house was punctuated by a volley of angry shouts directed at her and Familiar. She paid them no mind. Letting Familiar take the lead, she followed him as he made his way unerringly to the small, drab room where Eugene waited.

Jennifer barreled into the room to find Adam Bailey—one of the most respected defense lawyers in the nation—and Eugene hunched over a deck of cards playing gin. She stopped so suddenly that she almost fell over.

"Let's get out of here," she finally managed. "There's a crowd outside waiting to tear you apart."

Eugene waved a hand at her. "Hush, darling. I'm about to show Mr. Bailey exactly how gin is played. Of course, a small glass of port would make this more of a gentleman's game."

"Eugene!"

He finally realized she was genuinely upset and hurried to her side. "What's all of this about teeming masses outside?"

"Anna has whipped up a mob. They're calling to burn your books—and you, if they can manage to get inside here and get you out."

Although Eugene didn't laugh, he was amused. "Ah, it's only April and the fools here are beginning to suffer from the heat. It's a genetic thing, you know, this inability to think clearly on warm days. They should all go home and take a nap."

Bailey stood also, his concern more apparent than Eugene's. "Is there a back door?"

"Meow." Familiar started toward the exit.

"I see. Even the cat is upset." Eugene's amusement was somewhat diminished. "I take it very seriously when Familiar is upset. Maybe we should depart."

"Legally, you can go. The charges have been dropped, as is only proper," Bailey said. "Eugene will receive an official apology no later than noon tomorrow, signed by the mayor as well as Chief Bixley." He nodded. "I don't think they'll be harassing either of you unless they discover some very weighty evidence."

"Eugene?" Jennifer looked down the corridor to where cops were buckling on riot gear as they headed toward the front.

"Maybe it would be best if Eugene and I departed out the back, in my car," Bailey said. "Perhaps you could create a diversion?"

Jennifer nodded. "Good plan."

"But what about Jennifer's safety?" Eugene was planting his feet. "She comes from tough stock, a descendant no doubt of Hippolyta, but we can't abandon her if we're going to flee the mob."

"It isn't *Jennifer's* hide they want," the lawyer observed pointedly. "Besides, I'm paid to protect you. She's a paid employee of the publisher."

"That's the most ridiculous—"

Jennifer gave him a hug and a push. "Go. Familiar and I have some business with the desk sergeant, anyway, and James is meeting me here."

"The intrepid Mr. Tenet." Eugene's face brightened. "Then I'm leaving you in capable hands."

With Familiar leading the way, Eugene and Bailey started down the long corridor to the back.

"Get that blasted cat out of here!" one of the patrolmen yelled.

The angry command was followed by the sound of barking as Eugene went into a series of animal noises, including the trumpeting of an elephant.

Jennifer was smiling as she squared her shoulders and started toward the main entrance. There was a crowd of people there who needed to learn a few things about public conduct, and she was just the woman to teach them.

Even through the tinted plate glass doors, Jennifer could see the angry throng outside. Didn't these people have jobs? How was it possible they were free to participate in Anna Green's obnoxious scheme?

Hitting the door with outstretched arms, Jennifer burst through it and climbed up on the makeshift podium—the tailgate of someone's pickup truck. With a glare that silenced Chief Bixley in midsentence, Jennifer took the microphone from his hand.

She looked into the heart of the mob, waiting until her very silence forced the spectators to take note of her.

"You should be ashamed," she said softly. "Look at yourselves. People opposed to violence and what are you doing? Working yourselves up into a mob." She pointed to the television cameras. "Will your children be proud of you tonight? You've come here because you want to protect your children from the evils of violence on television and in books and records. Well, what will they see when they watch the six o'clock news?"

Jennifer saw guilt flicker across a few faces. Two signs were lowered. "You people are hypocrites. And not very bright ones at that. This woman—" she pointed to Anna Green "—is running for office. She is using you. How much easier it is for her to play on your fears and emotions, on the safety of your children, than to address the many problems that face this state? I ask you, when you're home tonight watching the spectacle of yourselves on television, if you ban all the books at school or in the library, does that solve the problems of our school system? Does it stop the drugs on the street? Does it provide medical care for those who cannot afford it? Does it do one little thing to make your life better? Or does it simply give Anna Green a platform from which to catapult herself to elected office?"

She looked over the crowd again. Then she put the microphone on the stand and jumped from the back of the truck. Eugene had had plenty of time to make his escape, and she was suddenly very tired. So weary she only wanted to sit down someplace quiet and put her head in her hands.

"Well done."

The familiar voice made her look up, directly into the laughing eyes of James Tenet. He held a pad with a pen poised over it. "Shall we step inside...where I can ask a few questions?"

Her heart rate doubled at the sight of him. "We can step inside, but if you try to poke me with questions, I'm going to chop off your head and roll it down the steps."

James's laughter drew the looks of several other reporters as he took her arm and hurried her away. "So much for the reformed Miss Barkley. I didn't hear a single threat from your pickup podium. I was impressed, but a little concerned that you were sick. I at least expected a version of the 'let them eat cake' speech." He nodded at Familiar. "He must be writing your speeches, thank goodness."

"Right." She leaned against a wall as she waited for him to put his pen in his pocket. "Eugene caught a ride with the lawyer. So what's next?"

"Crush hasn't applied for any building permits. Of course, he could be doing it without a permit, or he could be building a shelter in another county."

"That figures." Jennifer was disappointed, but she hadn't really expected anything to go easily.

"Let's take a look at the police reports while we're here. It's a long shot, but you never know."

Jennifer nodded and fell into step beside James. Familiar walked between them as they made their way to the desk.

"The three musketeers," James said, pointing at Familiar. "The forces of evil had better beware now, for sure."

"Meow!" Familiar darted ahead and leapt up on the counter, drawing a smile from the policeman manning the desk. "What a cat," he said, reaching a hand for Familiar to sniff. "What can I do for you people?"

"Put them in jail and throw away the key." The deadly voice came from the back of the room and everyone looked to see Chief Craig Bixley glaring a them. "Get that cat out of here before I have it exterminated."

"You made a fool of yourself once today, Bixley, don't go for two in a row." Jennifer was completely unruffled. "This is a public building, and I want to look at some public records."

"When hell freezes over." Bixley walked toward them. "Take your mangy cat and your biased friend and get out of here."

"Chief—" The young patrolman tried to intervene, but Bixley silenced him with a downward slash of his hand. "You've got two minutes to clear out."

"I'd like to see the log report of calls." James ignored Bixley and spoke to the young officer.

"Out!" Bixley was furious.

Torn between the desire to obey and the law, the young patrolman finally got the logbook and pushed it across to James.

"I said, get out!" Bixley spoke between teeth gritted to a close. He came toward James just as a small black shape jumped from the counter to a desk.

Jennifer watched in horror as the cat batted a large revolver along the desk toward the edge.

"Familiar!" Her cry was lost in the tussle that had developed between Bixley and James. The young officer was doing his best to get between the angry chief and the reporter.

"Familiar!" Jennifer tried again to divert the cat, but with one strong push, Familiar sent the weapon crashing to the floor. The impact of a bullet firing brought all action in the station to a screeching halt.

Silence echoed on top of the loud report. In the back there were loud exclamations and the sound of feet rushing toward the front. Ten officers appeared in the doorway, guns drawn. Crouching, they surveyed the room with the bores of their weapons.

"Take it easy, guys," Bixley said. He'd managed to gain control of his temper, and the situation. No one was injured, but the shot had been a cold dose of reality.

"Familiar." As she saw the police chief eyeing the cat, Jennifer raced around the counter to clutch him against her chest. "They're going to kill you." She held him tight as she made her way toward the exit.

"Wait just a minute." Bixley's hand reached for her shoulder, but James stepped in between. "I want that cat. He's a menace. He could have killed one of us."

"Chief Bixley," the young officer's earnest voice finally caught everyone's attention. "It was a starter pistol. Officer Welford is starting the marathon tomorrow. The shot was a blank." He held up the weapon.

James's laughter was like a slap to Bixley. The red raced up his face. Without another word, he turned and stalked out of the room.

"This should make a great story in tomorrow's paper," James called after him. "Police Chief Threatened By Cat With Blank Pistol."

"I wouldn't push him any harder today," the officer said softly, though he was smiling. "The chief has had a rough day, all in all. Anna Green rides his tail like a tick on a fat hound."

Jennifer's tension eased and she slowly loosened her hold on the cat. "Do you think Familiar knew it was a blank pistol?" She looked at James.

The reporter stared into the gold green eyes of the feline. "I have no doubt he knew." He gave Familiar a scratch under the chin. "Better check the log before Chief Bixley comes back." The officer pushed the ledger toward James. "I'm not telling you what to do, but I'd get that cat out of here, fast."

"If he tries to harm one hair on Familiar's head I'll cut off his—"

James clamped a hand over Jennifer's mouth. "This isn't the time for dire threats." When he felt her nod, he removed his hand and bent over the log. "Let's see here... Why don't we go back to January and skim through this."

They poured over the logbook, noting the multitude of calls that made up the average policeman's workday. There were breaking and enterings, burglaries, hundreds of domestic arguments, UFO sightings, stolen bicycles, dog bites, and family members trying to run over each other with cars.

"Is this the dark side of human nature or what?" Jennifer flipped the page. "Look, there's Anna Green's name. Someone was trying to break into her house."

"Let's take that down." James jotted the information on his notebook. "There's her name again." He pointed with the tip of his pen.

"And again!" Jennifer underlined it with her thumbnail. "All the same complaint. Someone is peeking into her house, trying to enter."

"A Peeping Tom for Anna Green. That might be a good story."

The officer gave them a sick smile. "That might not be a good idea. We've gone over there again and again, but the chief hasn't been able to find a single clue. He's afraid any publicity might push the assailant into more violent action. You know Ms. Green lives in a secluded area, alone. It's not a good situation from a law officer's perspective."

James studied the young man's sincere face, and then the logbook again.

"There are twelve calls in three weeks. That's an average of four times a week. Maybe you should stake out her place?"

"Ah, the chief has done that. It seems the guy knows whenever we set a trap. If we're there, he doesn't bother Ms. Green."

James felt the heel of Jennifer's shoe press lightly into the top of his foot. He knew exactly what she was thinking.

"Does the chief answer these calls himself, seeing as how Ms. Green is a public official and all?"

"Yes, sir. He takes it seriously because she's an elected official. He handles it all himself. If there was anything to be found, he'd have found it."

"I'm sure that's true."

At Jennifer's caustic tone of voice, the officer gave her a curious look. "The chief can be a little difficult at times, but he's a great investigator. Really sharp. He's solved a lot of cases."

"And he's tried to arrest some innocent people." Jennifer knew her temper was rising again.

"He makes mistakes." The officer nodded. "He's only human."

"Me-ow!" Familiar swished his tail.

"I think we have everything we need." James nodded to the young man. "Thanks for your help."

"Please don't put that business in the newspaper about Ms. Green. The chief's going to be upset. That will only make matters worse, and he'll more than likely blame me, even though we both know it's public record."

"I can't make any promises," James said. He took Jennifer's elbow and guided her out the front door into the magical dusk of an Alabama spring.

The sky overhead was a soft pink that intensified to a vibrant fuchsia and purple near the horizon. Mobile's skyline, in contrast, was a series of dark shapes that echoed modern and Gothic.

"Bixley is having an affair with Ms. Green, on the city's time!" Jennifer fairly exploded as soon as they were in the car.

"I think you're right. No wonder he was so upset about us seeing the logbook. One of the reporters for the paper checks it every day, but it's going back over it, seeing all of those calls in accumulation, sometimes as many as five a week."

"And what is Bixley doing working night and day? I'd like to see his overtime pay."

"Another good point."

"If he wasn't so busy looking under Anna Green's sheets he might have better luck at finding those missing children."

James didn't say anything, just started the car. Familiar had taken a seat between them and was watching out the front window intently.

"We certainly didn't find the information we came to get." Jennifer felt a keen disappointment. "All we did was uncover some hanky-panky."

"That's true. But consider the consequences of what we discovered. Hasn't it struck you as odd that Anna Green became a morals crusader overnight? She wasn't harping on those issues six months ago when she was on the school board and had every opportunity to influence the library books in all area public schools. She could have banned Eugene's books and no one would have been the wiser. But it was never mentioned. Not one single time. In fact, as I recall, she pooh-poohed some folks who wanted to ban one of Mark Twain's books." His voice grew more intrigued with every sentence. "I'd forgotten about that until just now."

"That's true enough. I'm not exactly the most political person you've ever met, but I remember that issue. Anna laughed them out of the school board meeting, and that was the end of that. Most of the board meetings were about lack of public funding and disciplinary problems."

"Now, I know Anna is running for a higher office, but this change is interesting. Especially in light of her own nocturnal behavior with Chief Bixley. Or what we suspect to be their behavior. She's left herself wide open for a counterattack from one of her opponents."

"Go on." Jennifer leaned forward and watched the shifting expressions on James's handsome face. He was enjoying this little exploration of possibilities.

"Who's been at every rally, listening to every speech, possibly choreographing everything from the background?"

"Crush Bonbon!"

"Right. It's possible he may be blackmailing Green and Bixley, if he knows about their little tête-à-têtes."

"James, you may have hit on something there." Jennifer settled back in the seat. "That would explain a lot of different things. Such as the lack of evidence in the kidnappings."

James nodded. "The only good thing here is that if this is the case, then Bixley and Green both must be fairly certain those children are doing okay. Now all we have to do is figure out what Crush wants by ruining Eugene, and where the children are being held."

"We already know what Crush wants. I mean, he's checking out books on writing. He wants Eugene's career!"

"Then the retirement announcement is the best thing you could do. It may catapult Crush into releasing those children."

"James?" Jennifer looked at him, suddenly going pale.

"What is it?" He almost pulled over.

"What if those children believe Eugene is holding them? What if they've been convinced that he took them and locked them up somewhere? When they get out, they're going to say that."

James nodded. "I'd thought of that, but I didn't want to mention it."

"What will we do?"

"We'll cross that bridge when we get to it."

ASIDE FROM THE FACT that Chief Bixley is cat-aphobic, there's something not right about the man. He has high blood pressure and sweaty hands. The idea of spending time with Anna Green in an intimate situation is enough to give me both of those, but he seems to have some regard for her.

Crush as a blackmailer fits in nicely, and I think that's the problem I'm having. He fits a little too nicely. Crush as abductor. Crush as blackmailer. Crush as book burner. Crush as jealous would-be author. I mean, how many evil sides can this guy have?

It's true that some humanoids have the capacity to be completely corrupt. There's not a lot about Crush to like, but could he be rotten to the core? Completely rotten?

My mind keeps going back to his house. The person who locked me in the basement with Miss Spitfire was not an overweight man. It could have been Anna Green, and that would fit the scenario that Clark Kent is building.

I don't know. Maybe I'm just being paranoid. There's something not right about all of this. Something that I can't put my paw on right at this time. I think I need some brain food. And maybe a little nap.

Great! We're going to Eugene's house. Miss Spitfire is an extraordinary creature to look upon, but her larder is somewhat lacking. The sardines were an interesting treat, but I could feel my cholesterol level shooting through the roof. Not that I worry about such foolish things when Eugene puts a gourmet kitty spread before me.

And little Judy Luno is here. Judging from the look on her face, though, it isn't going to be a pleasant encounter.

Chapter Sixteen

"I think you're chicken for not doing something to that fat Bonbon." Judy Luno's brow was furrowed and her lips were turned downward in an angry frown. "He's trying to get Eugene in serious trouble. And no one is trying to stop him."

"We are, Judith," Jennifer said softly. "It's just that we have to find some evidence, some proof. Just to accuse him isn't enough. And we have to worry about your friends. They could be in serious danger."

"I know." Judy huffed as she sat back on the sofa. One of her red sneakers had a hole in the toe and there was a scab on her knee from a bicycle wreck.

"I appreciate your concern." Eugene sat beside her and patted her hand. "You're a delightful child, and a very caring one. We'll get Crush yet. That, I promise."

"Eugene, what's your best guess on this? What manuscript will the kidnapper use next?" James had stood slightly removed from the furor with Judy Luno. Now he stepped forward.

"You mean, if I was the kidnapper, what story of mine would fit into the theme of abducting innocent young children?" Eugene's brows were arched as he pondered the question.

"Exactly." James whipped out his pad and pen.

"Well," Eugene automatically lifted AnnaLoulou onto his lap and began to stroke her as he thought. "One of my very first stories was about a little girl who was so curious that she turned herself into a pillar of salt. That story is out of print, though. If I'm not mistaken, there's a copy at the library, but none in any of the stores. It's been thirty years since it was printed, and I doubt anyone remembers it. Grand Street was going to bring it out as a reissue this August, but the publication was supposed to be a surprise."

"Does anyone know about the reissue plans?" James tapped the pen on the pad and refused to look at Jennifer, who was surprised into silence by the question.

"The staff at the publishing house. Jennifer. Her boss."

Jennifer leaned forward. "We did a small press release last month with a listing of all of Eugene's books. He has two other novellas that are out of print, and we plan to reissue one in September and another in October. Grand Street is going to donate a copy of each to every school library in the state."

"So anyone could know about this story?"

"Anyone who reads the newspaper," Jennifer agreed. She sat up straight. "Except we didn't name the novellas in the news story. We simply said three Eugene Legander books would be reissued, one a month, beginning in August."

"Tell me a little about the plot." James took a seat on the arm of the sofa and began to write as Eugene talked.

"The little girl, Audrey Lancer, is a very bright, curious child. A little too curious for her own good. When she tracks down an elf to his home in a sycamore tree in the woods behind her house, he tells her that if she doesn't quit snooping around, he's going to cast a spell on her. Audrey tries hard to leave the elf alone, but he's irresistible. She's a snoop."

"Like me," Judy interjected, proud of the term. "I like to know everything. I'm going to grow up to be an international spy. Or maybe a news reporter."

"God save the fourth estate," James murmured under his breath just loud enough for Jennifer to hear.

Ignoring James, Eugene continued. "There's a good side to Audrey's curiosity. She discovers that one of her schoolmates is being abused and reports it and saves her friend's life. But she goes back to the sycamore tree and even though she's been warned, she tries to spy on the elf. She is turned into a pillar of salt, and she can't be changed back until someone comes to spy on her."

"So what happens?" James asked. He couldn't help the fact that he always managed to get caught up in Eugene's stories.

"Her mother comes looking for her and changes her back. When she sees Audrey, she begins to cry, and the salt of her tears breaks the elf's spell."

"Do you have a copy of this?" James asked. "In fact, I think we should read every one of your books and prepare a list of possible kidnapping suspects."

"Well, Judith would be high on the list to play the role of Audrey. She does have a lively curiosity, and she exercises it regularly." Eugene's brows drew together as he looked at the young girl. "No matter the consequences."

Unperturbed by Eugene's comment, Judy smiled. "I'd rather be curious than brain-dead, like some people I know."

"No chance of that," Jennifer said. "Okay, so let's find that story, and we can each take three of his other books and begin our list of suspects."

"I'll get the manuscript and some books," Eugene said as he crossed the room. "I'll be back in a moment."

"I get to read, too?" Judy was impressed at her inclusion.

"You know the children better than anyone else. I think you'd make an excellent detective in this area," Jennifer said. She didn't add that it was also a way to keep the young girl out of trouble.

"I can't help but feel that there's something we're missing. Something very obvious," James said. "It's nagging at my subconscious, but it won't come through."

Jennifer looked up as Eugene returned to the room. He wore a strange expression. "The manuscript copy of *A Pinch of Curiosity* is gone. It's been sitting on that bottom shelf under those dreadful yellowed clippings for ten years. Now it's gone."

"Are you sure?" Jennifer felt sick to her stomach. She'd seen glimpses of someone lurking around Eugene's house, but she hadn't believed that anyone had actually broken in. The writer was completely vulnerable. He wouldn't own a gun. His only defense was a water pistol, which could get him into more trouble than anything else.

"I'm positive."

"Perhaps the maid might have moved it," James suggested.

"Maid? Are you mad? I don't have a maid!" Eugene shook his head. "It was there not five months ago because I pulled it out to check the spelling of a name. I was reading the galleys for the reprint."

"Maybe you put it down somewhere." Jennifer surveyed the sitting room, the walls covered in original artwork and the shelves stacked two layers thick with rare books. The manuscript could honestly be anywhere in the house.

"I may not be a spring chicken, but I haven't lost my memory. I put it right back on the bottom shelf beneath those yellowed clippings of my book tour in New York." Eugene was adamant. "If I didn't know where I put things, I'd never get a book finished."

"Then someone took the manuscript." Judy Luno steepled her hands. "Now we have to find out who it was, and what they wanted with it." She tapped her fingertips together. "We have to try to think like the thief."

"I'm afraid I already know where this is leading," Jennifer said. "A child will be taken and a manuscript page will be left at the scene of the abduction. It's the perfect way to pin this on Eugene once and for all—the rare manuscript of an out-of-print book! A manuscript that only he has a copy of."

"Except for the New York publisher," Eugene acknowledged.

James cleared his throat and held Jennifer with his gaze. "Is there anyone at Grand Street who might want to harm Eugene?"

Even though she'd been mulling over that same question in the back of her mind, to hear it spoken aloud was a shock to Jennifer. She'd begun work at Grand Street more than five years ago, and Eugene was the figurehead of the house. The company had other fine writers, but none like Eugene. She ran down the editors, assistants, art department, publicists. There was no one who didn't love the writer—and his work.

"If it's someone at Grand Street who means harm to Eugene, they've been able to hide it very well," she finally answered. "Everyone there loves Eugene. Without him, Grand Street would be overwhelmed by the bigger houses. He is our claim to fame."

"No jealousies? No past editors who have left and might carry a grudge?"

Jennifer looked at Eugene. He shrugged. "I've had a few spats with editors. They want to get heavy-handed on the cut and slice, but I don't allow it. Sometimes I had to take a firm stand, but there's nothing there that could result in such animosity."

James studied the writer for a moment. "Are you sure, Eugene? It seems that Crush has a personal vendetta against you. And possibly Anna Green. Is there something from your past that you're not telling us?"

"Exactly what are you implying?" Eugene was suddenly still, his eyes alert.

"He's implying that some people hold a grudge and wait years to get even for some imagined offense." Jennifer went to Eugene and put her arm around him. "You aren't the kind of man who broods about things. Everyone isn't like you. If there's anyone who might have reason to want to see you harmed, we need to have that name. We can check the person out, make sure they aren't around. Just to be on the safe side."

"There were some people who got angry with me, but it didn't amount to a hill of beans. They've gone on to different publishing houses. The past is the past, Jennifer. You have to let go." He frowned and stared down at his hands holding the stack of books. "Remember the good and forget the bad."

"Is there anyone in particular we should be concerned about?" Jennifer asked the question softly, but she wasn't going to let Eugene off the hook.

"There was Josh Wainwright. He left the house because of me. He said he wouldn't work without complete editorial control, and the publisher didn't think that was reasonable."

James wrote his name down. "Where is he now?"

"He left the publishing business," Jennifer said. She felt a tingle of fear. "He left New York. I remember it vaguely. I was still with Alfonso House, but the rumors got out that he really burned his bridges."

"Sounds like a man with a grudge," James said. "A good possible suspect to add to Crush Bonbon."

"Something about Crush has been troubling me," Jennifer confessed. "He's so absolutely guilty, or so it would seem. Is it possible that he's so corrupt?" At the look on James's face, she faltered. "I mean, I know it sounds naive, but it's so...convenient that he's the perfect suspect for everything that's gone wrong."

"Meow!" Familiar sat up from his nap beside Judy and stretched.

"Even Familiar agrees," Eugene said.

"What we need is a test." Judy swung her legs against the sofa. "A test that would show once and for all if he's behind this."

"The evidence, in my opinion, is stacked pretty darn high against him." Jennifer held up a finger. "The room in his house." She held up another. "The telephone in his washing machine." Another. "The fact he didn't report the break-in." The fourth finger went in the air. "The fact that he's always egging Anna Green on with his book-banning tirade." Her thumb went up. "And he's checking out books on how to write children's stories. I think he clearly envies Eugene and wants to ruin him."

"The old dog-in-the-manger theory," James said.

"Me-ow!" Familiar nodded once.

"He can't write, so he doesn't want Eugene to have a successful career." Jennifer pondered that equation. "It fits. It fits perfectly."

"I think we need to explore Crush's house to see if we can find that manuscript," James said.

Jennifer groaned. "We almost got caught the last time. If he does catch us, he's going to throw the book at us."

"I know, but we don't really have a choice."

Judy stood. "Yes, you do. I'll go."

"Absolutely not!" All three adults spoke together, and even Familiar put his paw on Judy's leg and held with his claws.

"I'm the perfect candidate to be kidnapped, you said so yourself. If I could figure out a secret code, some way to communicate with you guys, then you could follow me and find the other children." Judy's eyes grew large and bright. "I'd be a hero."

"Forget it." James's voice cut through her euphoric vision like an ax biting into a tree. "You can't risk yourself. What if he is the kidnapper? What if those other children are in serious trouble? We can't guarantee that we could rescue you, Judy. It's too dangerous."

Judy's full mouth clamped into a thin line. "I can do this. You don't think I can, but I can."

"We can't risk you," Eugene said gently. "What would your parents do if you didn't show up for bed tonight?"

"They'd call the cops and really worry." Judy met Eugene's gaze. "That's their job. They're parents."

"If I had a kid like you I'd chain you to the wall in the bedroom," Jennifer said. "I'd have a digital beeper implanted into your head with a homing device. I'd—"

"Man, you make my parents look cool." Judy gave her a baleful look. "You've got a control problem, Jennifer. You need to chill out."

James quickly covered his mouth to hide the grin. "Jennifer may have a control problem, but she's right. It's out of the question for you to put yourself in danger, so let's move on."

For another twenty minutes they listed children who were potential kidnap victims. "I'll call the parents," Jennifer said. "We don't have time to visit each one individually. And even when we went to the McNairs and Ralstons, we didn't save little Bobby Fornaro."

"You did your best," Eugene responded.

In the silence that followed his remark, Judy stood again. "I'd better go home. My folks will be looking for me for dinner." She gave Jennifer a look and then rolled her eyes. "I don't want to make them worry, you know."

"I'll walk you home," James offered.

"Don't trust me, do ya?" Judy grinned. "It's okay, I rode my bicycle over. And I have to show up for dinner or my folks will have a fit. Sometimes I can sneak out, but if I'm not around for dinner, they worry."

James glanced at Jennifer. "Can we trust her?"

"We have to," Jennifer said. She gave Judy a grin. "We need your help, and if you go and get yourself into trouble, what will we do?"

"Don't worry. I won't get into any trouble." Judy picked up the three books. "I'll talk with you tomorrow. I have my own phone line." She wrote the number down. "Call me in my room. My parents get irritated if my friends wake them up or tie up their phone."

"Great." Jennifer took the scrap of paper. "See you tomorrow."

"And I think I'd like to spend some time reading through these books myself," Eugene said.

"We'd better get busy." Jennifer cast a shy look at James. As the evening had dwindled away, it wasn't reading that was on her mind. They were tired, exhausted and worried about three missing children. But the intimate bond they'd forged could not be ignored. Jennifer felt her pulse quicken as she looked in James's dark brown eyes.

"You two get some rest," Eugene said, his face as innocent as a child's—except for the twinkle in his eyes. "I'd hate to think that you exhausted yourselves on my behalf."

James laughed out loud. "You have my word of honor, Eugene, if we're exhausted, it won't be on your behalf."

Even though she was used to verbal bantering, Jennifer felt the warm color touch her cheeks. Her feelings for James were too intense to bear scrutiny, even by her best friend, Eugene.

"Ah, the maiden does have a modest streak," James whispered in her ear.

"The maiden has an ice pick in her purse, and she's going to plunge it into your massively oversize ego," she answered in an equally soft whisper.

"Good night," Eugene said, ushering them to the door. "Please vacate the premises before there's a bloodletting. As I said earlier, I don't have a maid and I do so hate to clean up bloodstains."

James and Jennifer stepped into the warm night. The smell of wisteria was as strong and sweet as a hidden memory. It seemed to wrap around them, drawing them closer in the thin light of a half moon that peeked through the border of willow trees on the front of Eugene's small lawn.

"Are you too tired for some company?" James asked.

Jennifer tried to think of a teasing retort, something to hide the pounding of her heart. But there was nothing to say except the truth. "I've been waiting for some time when we could be alone."

"Me, too." He slipped his arms around her and brought her so close that his breath was warm on her forehead. "I watch you across the room, and I think that I've been dreaming. Is it possible you really care for me?"

"It's more than possible." Jennifer turned her face up to his, a slight smile curving her mouth in invitation.

As his lips claimed hers, she gave up any attempt to think, to rationalize. The warm sweep of desire pulled her into a state of sensation and the need to give as much pleasure to James as he gave to her was uppermost.

"I think we should go home," she said after a long, breathless kiss.

"Before we're arrested," James added, his own voice slightly rough.

"Alone," she said, brushing her lips once again across his jaw. "Just the two of us."

"Meow!"

James and Jennifer turned to look at the sidewalk where Familiar sat, obviously taking in every nuance of their kiss.

"Maybe not alone," Jennifer added darkly. "I never in a million years thought a cat would be spying on us."

Familiar went to her leg and swatted it with great force but no claws.

"You were spying!" Jennifer insisted.

Once again the paw batted her leg.

"I don't think he's denying the charge." James pondered the cat. He knelt beside Familiar. "Spying."

"Meow!" Familiar started down the sidewalk.

"I have a terrible feeling," James said as the cat disappeared into the shadow of a tallow tree.

"Me, too."

"He's headed toward Judy Luno's house, isn't he?"

"Yes." Jennifer sighed as she found her keys in her pocket. "And I'll bet you the little minx isn't at home as she promised. She's gone spying on Crush Bonbon. And we're going to have to figure out a plan to get her out of there."

"Before it's too late," James added.

Chapter Seventeen

While James was keeping an eye on Jennifer, I should have been the jailer for that little hellcat Judy. As I sat on the sofa and watched the expressions on her face, I could see that she wasn't satisfied with simply reading a few books. That girl wants action, and this time she's going to provoke it.

I have to get to the Luno home before Miss Spitfire and Clark Kent. I can get in her bedroom and check things out. If she's there, there's no point in getting the entire household in a panic. If she's not there, we certainly don't want to scare the grits out of her parents. Maybe we can retrieve her before it all goes to hell in a hand basket. You know, even in times like this I love the phrases these Southerners use. Hell in a hand basket. Now that would be a toasty little means of conveyance.

Ah, the Luno house looms. I have to get Jennifer's attention and let her know that I'm going in alone on this. Humans are too big, too noisy, and too blind in the dark. This is a job for a cat.

"LET HIM GO," James grasped Jennifer's hand and held it tightly as he moved her into the dense shadows of an old oak tree. "Familiar can check on her without waking the entire house. If she's there—"

"I should have hog-tied that little imp and toted her home myself. I'll bet her parents are addicted to Valium. How do they keep from going crazy?"

"My best guess is that they don't know the half of what their daughter gets into. Judy is not only smart, she has developed quite a few covert skills. Pity the government if she does decide to become a journalist."

Jennifer couldn't deny the chuckle that came with his observation. "God, I hope she's okay," she whispered, her fingers catching his and holding tightly. Without James the waiting would be unendurable. Just the fact that he was there, beside her, giving support, made her want to touch him. She shifted closer to him so that she could feel the solidness of his body against hers. How had she grown to love this man so quickly? It was a question without an answer. Truth was, she didn't want to question her feelings. They were right, and she accepted them.

In the darkness James caressed her waist with one strong hand. "Maybe she's home, safe and sound." But James knew better. Though he was determined to put up a cool front for Jennifer's sake, he was silently kicking himself for not walking the young girl home and turning her in to her parents with a strong warning. But would it have done any good?

"He's back." Jennifer nodded to the cat.

"She's not home." James bent down to stroke Familiar. "She would be with him if she was in her room."

"Now what?" Jennifer knew already. They had to go back to Crush Bonbon's house. That's where they would find Judy Luno—if she wasn't already kidnapped.

HOT AND JITTERY with worry, James, Jennifer and Familiar had spent the next half hour covertly working their way to the open window of Crush Bonbon's sitting room. Peering over the sill, James and Jennifer suppressed a gasp of surprise as Familiar crouched, ready to rush to the young girl's aid. Judy Luno sat comfortably on a hassock, a tall glass in one hand.

"No, thank you, Mr. Bonbon." Judy covered the top of her glass with her hand as he held up a pitcher. "One chocolate milk was plenty. I just had dinner not long before I came here."

"Do your parents often allow you to go gallivanting around the streets at night?" Crush sat back in his chair and sipped his own glass of chocolate milk. As he spoke, he helped himself to a chocolate pinwheel off a plate on the coffee table. "This nocturnal behavior must be some influence from that Eugene Legander." He pointed to a glass jar of silver-wrapped chocolate candy. "Help yourself."

Judy shook her head. "My parents understand that I'm in training for the future." She gave him a bold grin. "I'm going to be an ace reporter."

"And you're here to get the scoop on me?" For a moment, displeasure creased the talk show host's features. "Don't you think that's a little presumptuous, especially since I caught you red-handed trying to sneak in my dining room window? I could call the juvenile authorities, and you'd spend an adventurous evening at juvy hall."

"Why don't you show me around your house?" Judy got up and went to an end table beside the sofa. "In particular, where did you get this copy of Eugene's manuscript for *A Pinch of Curiosity*? It's a very valuable manuscript, you know. And it was stolen from his house."

"You're a bold little thing, aren't you?" Crush rose. "There is one room I want to show you. One in particular."

Outside the house, Jennifer grabbed James's arm and squeezed. "He drugged her milk, and now he's going to take her into that horrible children's bedroom. Oh, God, James, we have to stop this."

James was coiled as tightly as a steel spring. Crush was standing right beside Judy. If they tried to get in the window, he'd have too much time to grab her and possibly hurt her.

"Wait until he leaves the room with her. We'll sneak in and then I'll clobber him from behind. Not very gallant, but we can't risk Judy."

Jennifer transferred her death grip to the windowsill, ready at the first moment to boost herself into the room with a little help from James. It was torture to watch the small, dark-haired girl leave the room chatting so determinedly with the big man. "I'm sure you have some interesting rooms," Judy said as she turned the corner. Crush loomed behind her, his shadow a sinister black shape shifting uneasily down the hallway.

Jennifer was right on Familiar's heels as soon as the room was empty. James boosted her from behind, then leapt up after her.

Moving as swiftly as they could without making noise, they hurried to the bedroom that contained the bizarre collection of toys.

Jennifer's mouth was dry and her ears roaring with blood. She should have reported Crush. She should have done a million things differently. Now another child was at risk, and they would have to confront Crush. Once forced into a corner, he might or might not tell them where the other children were being held.

"Step right inside here." Crush pushed open the bedroom door, a tiny smile on his face as he gave Judy a courtly bow.

"Hold it, Bonbon!" James stepped out of the darkness and smashed into the talk show host's face with a strong right followed by an upper punch to the jaw with his left. For a big man, Crush sank to the floor like a balloon slowly deflated of air.

Once seated, he looked up at James with surprise and then anger. "You, sir, have just initiated a lawsuit that is going to leave you without a job, without money, and without any hopes for a future!"

"You're going to prison, Bonbon. We know you were trying to abduct this girl." Jennifer pulled Judy into her arms. "I'm going to strangle you when I get you outside," she whispered to the girl. "You'll wish Crush had you prisoner." Judy didn't bother to reply; she just rolled her eyes in complete disgust.

It had taken a few seconds for James's accusations to sink in, but Crush had finally caught the gist. "*I* was going to abduct her? You're in the wrong house. It's Eugene you have to worry about."

"Give it up, Crush." James hit the light switch on the wall. "Look at this room. You're some kind of sicko child abductor, and we've got the evidence to prove it."

Crush looked around the room as if seeing it for the first time. "There's nothing here but toys."

"And you stole this manuscript!" Judy pulled a page from inside her blouse. "I lifted this from the stack beside his chair, and he never even knew I took it!" She proudly gave it to Jennifer.

As her fingers closed over the page, Jennifer knew it was wrong. It was a page from Eugene's missing manuscript, but it wasn't right. She held it a moment, then her fingers slid over the page. There were none of the indentations caused by the keys of his typewriter. "It's a photocopy."

James, Crush and Judy looked at her as if she had lost her mind. "So?" Crush was the first to speak. "I got that in the mail from an admirer. Someone sent it to me with a warning that another child would be abducted. I had intended to spend the evening trying to figure out the clue, but I was interrupted by a young burglar."

"But it's a photocopy," Jennifer repeated. "Not the original manuscript that was stolen. Whoever took the manuscript from Eugene's has the original." She looked around the room again. The stuffed animals filled the bed and lined the walls. The bookshelf was there, filled with the finest stories of childhood. Everything was just as she remembered it, but now it didn't seem so wrong.

"What is all of this, Crush?" She swept her hand around the room.

"I had this room built for my fiancée's daughter." Crush slowly got to his feet. "This is none of your business, but I'm going to tell you." He glared at James. "It's going to give me great pleasure telling you, because you've created some warped fantasy in your mind about me and this room. Once I tell you the truth, you're going to be really sorry about coming here tonight. All of you."

He took a breath. "When Arlene Mason agreed to marry me, I wanted her child to feel loved and welcomed when she moved here." He looked away as he shrugged. "Things didn't work out and the marriage was called off. By then, the room was decorated and filled with toys."

Jennifer wanted to ask why the marriage was called off, but she couldn't. Her gaze wandered around the room, taking in each toy that had been bought with the idea of pleasing a little girl, of making her feel welcome in a strange home. Damn Crush Bonbon to Hades. He was making her feel sorry for him, and he wasn't even trying.

"Meow!"

Familiar saved her from embarrassing herself with a few tears when he swatted her leg and demanded her attention. As soon as she looked, he hurried back to the den.

"How did that cat get in here?" Crush asked, following James, who followed Jennifer, who was right on the heels of the cat.

"Look." Jennifer pointed to the small end table where Familiar swatted the stack of manuscript pages to the floor.

"Stop that beast." Crush started forward, but Judy grabbed his hand.

"Hold on. He's showing us something."

"Right. And next he'll sing 'The Star Spangled Banner.' "

Judy went to the manuscript and began to pick it up.

Remembering Familiar's last stunt with the manuscript pages, Jennifer bent down. "I'll bet a page is missing."

"Yeah, the one little Miss Sticky Fingers had tucked in her blouse." Crush was standing in the doorway with a glare focused on the entire lot of them.

"No, the kidnapper always leaves a page of one of Eugene's books." Jennifer spoke without thinking. She felt James's gaze on her and looked up to see the warning in his eyes. But it was too late. Crush had heard the tidbit of fact and was ready to run with it.

"Has that been reported to the police? I know they found something when Mimi was kidnapped. But the other children, as well? It wasn't in any of the evidence reports, and Bixley never mentioned it to me." He stepped into the room. "Ah-a. You've been hiding evidence, haven't you? Things that would incriminate Eugene!"

It was too late to distract Crush now. He had a competitive gleam in his eyes as he silently dared Jennifer to lie.

She met his gaze with her own glance of sheer blue willpower. "Let's check the pages and see." She sat on the floor beside Judy, and James sat down beside them and took a third of the pages.

Crush eased himself down into an overstuffed chair and gently began to rub his jaw, which had begun to swell. "After a visit to my dentist, I'm going to see a lawyer." But he made no effort to put them out of his house.

"Look!" Jennifer held up a bundle of pages. "It's page ninety-eight, the exact page that's been written—" She stopped.

James watched Crush during the entire exchange. "You really don't know where the children are, do you?" He took a manuscript page from Jennifer's hand and held it a moment, as if deciding whether to give it to Crush or not.

"Of course, I don't know. You think *I* actually kidnapped those children? For what purpose?" He looked at James, then at Jennifer, and finally at Judy.

"Because you hate Eugene," Judy said simply. "You're jealous of him."

"Of Eugene?" Crush was incensed. "Jealous of what?"

"His success," Jennifer said quietly. "Of the fact that the children love him."

"And we don't like you." Judy was matter-of-fact. "You're always saying mean things about everyone. You try to start trouble. You don't think anyone else has a right to have a say about anything. And when they try, you make them look stupid. Eugene makes everyone feel good. Especially kids."

When Judy stopped speaking, there was a long silence. Jennifer peeked at Crush and saw the redness of his face. James was staring at the manuscript page. Familiar was licking his back leg, oblivious to the entire scene.

"Is that how the children really see me?" Crush addressed his question to Judy.

"You make my parents argue with each other. Especially when you talk about women. My mother wants to get a job. She's tired of staying home. But my dad says her job is to stay home and cook. That's not fair. And he uses what you say as if it came from the Bible. It makes my mother cry." Judy's temper was on the rise. "What you do is wrong. It hurts people."

"I see."

"I think you've made your point, Judy," Jennifer said as she shifted to her knees. "I think I owe Crush an apology. Not so much for what I've said, but for what I've thought." She handed him the page. "This is ninety-nine. The one after the missing one. It's about a little girl who gets turned to a pillar of salt for being nosy." She smiled, a sad, weary smile. "I honestly thought you'd taken the children. I even broke into your house and—the telephone!" Her eyes widened and her voice rose. "Who put the portable phone in your house?" She didn't give him a chance to answer. "Eugene has been neatly framed in this whole mess, but so has Crush. Someone went to a lot of trouble to set him up, hoping that we would put the pieces of the puzzle together. Look—the phone, the attacks, now this manuscript!" She turned to James.

His dark eyes were blazing. "You're right. Someone has just as neatly drawn the noose around Crush's neck. And we've played right into their hands. We've spent all of our time trying to convict Crush, when we've been sniffing a false trail."

"What are you talking about? What telephone? And someone owes me for a very unpleasant cleaning task. How did you manage to get that blood all over the bedroom floor upstairs?"

"Someone knocked me out," James said, and then explained the portable telephone that belonged to Mimi Frost's father. And the fact that they'd found it in his washing machine.

"Is Frost involved?" Crush asked.

James and Jennifer both shook their heads. "I don't believe so. At first I thought it was surely him. You know, one of those custody battle things. But I don't believe he'd do such a thing. And he's as worried about Mimi as we are."

Judy gave them a disgusted look. "Mr. Frost would never do anything to frighten Mimi or Mrs. Frost. He's not a dork."

"Thank you, Judy, for that astute observation." James got to his feet and gave the manuscript page to Crush. "You might as well hear it all. But I'm going to ask you, on your word of honor, not to broadcast any of this information until we've found the children."

"James!" Jennifer shot to her feet. She might have misjudged Crush's involvement in the kidnapping, but he wasn't to be trusted. He was still a loudmouthed blowhard who made his show spicy by devastating other people's reputations and opinions.

Crush had started to take the page that James held out, but Jennifer's objection made him stop. "You don't think I have any honor, do you?"

"Not where Eugene is involved. I think you'd do whatever you could to destroy him."

Crush took the page. "I'm going to prove you wrong." He looked at Judy. "And you, too. Now, what is all of this about?"

James ignored the hand that Jennifer put on his arm. He told Crush the clues they had pieced together. Crush nodded as James talked.

"I can see why you suspected me. So, pages of manuscript, page ninety-eight." Crush sat forward and automatically picked up his milk. He held the plate of cookies and offered them to James and Jennifer, then Judy.

"What about Familiar?" Judy's look was meant to intimidate, and it worked beautifully.

"Oh, okay." He held the plate to the cat who swatted a single cookie onto the floor and began delicately eating the chocolate shell around the cake filling. "I haven't really thought this thing through, but it would appear that whoever is out to get Eugene is also out to get me. The question we have to answer is, who is our mutual enemy?"

"Any possibilities?" James asked.

Crush smiled, one of genuine amusement. "Not the first. Eugene and I are, philosophically, intellectually, and socially, in opposite camps. It would seem that his enemies would be my friends. This doesn't make an ounce of sense."

"No, it doesn't." Jennifer picked up another cookie and began munching it. "I haven't a single—"

The shrill of the telephone interrupted them.

Crush automatically checked his watch. "It's only ten o'clock, but...still." He got to his feet, a worried frown on his face. "Who could this be?"

Jennifer watched closely as Crush picked up the telephone on the far end table. His face showed first annoyance, then disbelief, and finally concern. "I see," he said, but he made no mention of his uninvited guests. "Was it an original or a copy?"

After a pause, he spoke again. "I'll go to the station immediately. We can coordinate television and radio, and I'm sure the newspaper will agree to help." He gave James a look. "Yes, I'm leaving momentarily. Tell Anna to meet me at the station." He replaced the receiver.

"What's going on?" Judy asked. She hadn't missed a moment.

Crush hesitated. "That was Chief Bixley. Anna Green's young daughter has been kidnapped. They found a page of Eugene's manuscript in her bed. She was abducted from her own home while the baby-sitter was watching television. Anna was making a speech in Chickasaw."

"What page of what manuscript?"

"Page ninety-eight of *Pinch of Curiosity.*" Crush stared at the manuscript page he held. "Exactly the one that is missing from this manuscript. And Chief Bixley said it was indeed a photocopied page." Crush pointed to the manuscript. "Both Eugene and I have been perfectly framed."

Chapter Eighteen

Anna Green arrived at the radio station in a swirl of red and blue lights. Craig Bixley, all arrogance replaced by dread and helplessness, stood beside her. Bixley didn't even cast a curious glance at James and Jennifer sitting on a couch beside the young girl and a black cat.

"I can't believe they've taken Amber." Anna covered her face. "It's those crazy, liberal, book people. They've taken my child in retaliation for the strong stand I've taken against violence. They're punishing me because I dared to confront them."

"I don't think so, Anna." Crush walked up to her. "Maybe you should stop this foolishness. The person who took Amber isn't some vengeful bookworm. There's someone out there kidnapping children, and it isn't about books."

"What are you saying? Who else could have taken her?" Anna looked around the room, her anger finally settling on Jennifer. "Are you here to gloat?"

"Hardly." Jennifer rose slowly. "I'm here to help you find your daughter, and the other missing children. But we're going to have to put our differences aside to try to put this puzzle together."

"She's right. We've been wrong about Eugene. I don't think he has anything to do with these children. And I don't think it has a thing to do with his books. There's something else at work here. Some type of revenge. Against Eugene, and me, and possibly you. Maybe against several different people. That's what we have to figure out."

"But—"

"No buts, Anna. This has gone far beyond a platform to launch your political campaign."

"You're scaring me, Crush."

Bixley stepped up to Anna's side. "Do you know something, Bonbon?" His tone grew threatening. "If you know something about Amber—"

"Can the threats, Bixley." Crush's voice was suddenly tired. "Let's get Anna on the air to make a plea to the kidnappers and then we'll talk about what we need to do. In the meantime, I suggest you listen to James and Jennifer, and the half-pint. They have a few clues and some evidence that may help us find those children. Whoever the abductor is, they aren't afraid of political or police power. And that's frightening in and of itself." He saw the technician in the control room give him the wave. "Come along, Anna. Let's get started."

Craig Bixley gave Anna's hand a supportive squeeze, then he motioned to James and Jennifer to follow him into a private office. "Hey!" Judy stood. "What about me and Familiar?"

Bixley gave them a long look and realized it was easier to acquiesce. "Come along, then," he said, opening the door. "I can't believe that blasted cat goes everywhere you do."

Familiar ignored him as they filed into the room and took seats around a small conference table.

"Now what is that idiot Crush trying to say?" Bixley sat down and placed his hands on the table.

James and Jennifer, with a few interruptions from Judy, had just finished laying out the clues for Bixley when there was a soft tap on the door. A police officer stuck his head around the door and nodded. "Mr. Bonbon asked me to turn on the radio in here. He said there was something coming on the air that might interest all of you."

"Okay."

The uniformed officer entered and went to a wall panel to flip a few switches. Crush's voluminous voice filled the room.

"And here's a caller with some information."

"It has something to do with salt." Eugene's voice was distinct and completely undisguised. "I've been mulling it over and over, and the title of each story figures in prominently with the method of kidnapping. There's a theme. All of the children display curiosity, which is what children are mostly composed of. The good ones, at least. But there is also a common theme in the abductions. This final clue is salt. We have to put everything we know together... because I believe the kidnapper wants us to find the children."

"You think this guy wants to get caught?" Crush asked.

"Indeed. The clues are becoming more and more obvious. Think of it, Crush. This kidnapper now has four children to feed, bathe, clothe and keep from whining. I'd say he or she is ready for them to be found. Now I'm not implying the kidnapper wants to be caught, but I think he's ready to give back the children."

"What could Amber's abduction have to do with salt?" Crush asked.

"I haven't gotten that far along, but I feel very strongly. Salt is one of the key issues. I'll keep working on it."

"Thanks, Mr. Legander." Crush actually sounded sincere. "Anyone else out there got some thoughts about finding these children?"

He fielded several calls before Jennifer got up and turned the sound down low. "I wonder what Eugene has up his sleeve?" she said. "Salt. As in 'pinch of salt.' Curiosity."

"Who could have taken that manuscript from Eugene's house?" Bixley asked, looking at them. "I have to tell you,

Eugene is still a suspect. This is all too convenient. Not to mention the fact that I could hit all of you with aiding and abetting charges. You protected Eugene and withheld evidence.'' He rubbed his jaw. ''The trouble is, even Crush is beginning to look suspicious to me. Why didn't he report the incident when you broke into his house?''

Judy sighed and rolled her eyes. ''That kid's room is really incriminating. Besides, he got dumped by his girl. That's embarrassing. Two good reasons to keep his mouth shut.''

''Good points.'' Bixley got up from his seat and swiftly exited the room.

''While he's preoccupied, let's get out of here.'' Jennifer looked at James.

''My thoughts exactly,'' James said. ''Let's make tracks.''

''I don't want to go home,'' Judy said. ''This is building up to a climatic end and I'm not going to go home and miss it.''

''Trust me, I wouldn't dream of letting you out of my sight,'' Jennifer said to the girl. ''If I have to tie you up and leave you in the trunk of the car, I will. But I'll know where you are every second, until this kidnapper is caught.''

''Do you always go around threatening people?'' Judy asked. ''Eugene said you had a forked tongue, but he didn't warn me that you get off on intimidating innocent children.''

''Innocent?'' Jennifer turned to the girl, her blue eyes disbelieving. ''You call yourself innocent?''

''By the way, I've got something to get off my chest.'' Judy looked down at her shoes. ''I was the person you saw sneaking around Eugene's house. I was casing the area. To protect Eugene.''

''You!'' Jennifer felt her temper skyrocket. ''I've been worried to death. I'm going to chew you up and spit you out like bad baloney!''

"Wait!" Judy held up both hands. "I saw someone there! A small person. Like a woman. I was investigating."

"Why didn't you say so before?" Jennifer demanded.

"Then you would have known how often I was sneaking out of my house. You would have told my parents."

"Let's go, ladies—and I use that term loosely." James put an end to the conversation as he nodded to Craig Bixley, who had begun to take notice of their conversation. "If we don't go now, Bixley may detain us."

Sprinting ahead, Familiar led the way out into the night.

"COME IN, DARLINGS." Eugene met them at the door with a silver tray of crystal glasses filled with port. "I knew you'd need a little fortifying liquid as soon as I heard the car stop." He gave James and Jennifer each a glass and waved them into a seat. He handed Judy a glass of chocolate milk and steered her toward the couch. Familiar gave one long look at the kitchen but sat down.

"I've been listening to the radio, and no one has any more ideas about where the children might be."

"If we could only put together what the numeral ninety-eight, kidnapped children, books, and salt have in common." Jennifer held her glass in one hand and rested her chin on the other. She gave Judy a glare. "And don't forget the small person who's been snooping around Eugene's house."

"I think it was a woman." Judy had recovered her poise. "About Anna Green's size."

James sat forward. "Anna could have kidnapped her own daughter, or had her taken. It wouldn't be the first time someone did such a thing."

"To what purpose? There's no motive that I can see. Sympathy? For a vote? Is she going to keep her daughter hostage until the elections?" Eugene was puzzled.

Jennifer's brow was furrowed. "I don't know. But whoever was in Crush Bonbon's house the night we were there was small. A young person or a woman." She shook her head. "It's just that we've wrongly accused Crush, and now we're turning to Anna. I'm not certain she's the criminal behind all of this."

"Perhaps we aren't considering all of the clues," James said. His eyes narrowed. "Ninety-eight is the consistent clue, the one that recurs again and again, even when the kidnapper had to change the page number."

"That's right," Jennifer said. She almost spilled her port when Familiar leapt from the sofa and dashed to the dining room table. With one large black paw he smashed the saltshaker into the wall. The little china chicken splintered into a thousand pieces.

"Familiar!" Jennifer stood and simply stared. She'd never seen the cat misbehave in such a fashion.

James rose, as did Eugene and Judy.

"Oh, my God." Jennifer looked at Familiar. "The saltshaker."

"It wasn't expensive," Eugene said, trying to soothe her.

"No! Salt! Ninety-eight. James was right about the highway." Jennifer was talking at such a speed that she had to force herself to slow down. "Remember the old salt domes on Highway 98? They've been abandoned for years, but it would be the perfect place to hide children."

James pulled the car keys from his pocket. "Let's go."

"Shouldn't we notify the authorities?" Judy asked. She took one look at their faces. "Forget I said that. Bixley would bungle the entire operation. You're right, let's go. And I'm going if I have to hitchhike!"

THE HALF-MOON shone through tall pines that ringed the edge of what had once been a working salt mine on the backside of nowhere in the Alabama piney woods. It was just shy of midnight, and James and Jennifer had begun to circle around the back of the entrance to the dark mine shaft. Eugene and a very unhappy Judy had agreed to stand watch and signal if anyone approached.

"Listen." James put his hand on Jennifer's shoulder and pulled her against him. The sinister call of an owl hooted through the night.

"Someone's here."

"Maybe we can catch the kidnapper red-handed and put an end to this once and for all," James said. "I've been worried that the children didn't see their abductor and might still believe Eugene was behind this."

"Shush." Jennifer ducked lower behind a leafy huckleberry bush as someone approached the mouth of the shaft. The person was small, slender, and carried a large stack of McDonald's bags.

"We've hit pay dirt," Jennifer said. "Now, let's nail the cretin."

With James behind her, they started slowly forward just as the figure disappeared into the cave. There was the sound of keys jiggling, rusty hinges complaining, and finally a loud burst of voices.

"They sound okay." James felt a heavy burden lift from his shoulders.

"They sound hungry and glad to see whoever that is." Jennifer was perplexed. The children's greeting wasn't one of hostages to a captor. It was more of children to a benefactor. Something was still screwy about the entire scene.

Moving as swiftly as possible across the opening to the shaft, they stopped at the heavy door. James inched it open and was surprised to hear animated chatter. The smell of hamburgers wafted on the air toward him.

"When are we going home?" Mimi Frost's voice sounded plaintive yet composed.

"Yeah, my mother's going to kill me," Tommy added.

"Soon, children. Very soon now. Eugene said the experiment is almost over." The voice was soft and motherly.

"I'm ready to go home now," Mimi insisted. "It wasn't fair of Eugene to take us without asking. Mama's going to be terribly upset." Mimi's voice filled with emotion. "And Daddy, too."

"Yes, it was wrong of Eugene to trick you like he did." Martha Whipple's voice was unmistakable. "I've left clues for your parents to find you, but you have to promise not to tell anyone I brought you food. Right?"

The children gave a chorus of agreement. "It's Eugene's fault. He started the experiment," Bobby said. "That was a nasty trick."

Jennifer put her hand on James. Her heart was beating a rapid tattoo, but her thoughts were clear. Of all of the people in Mobile, she'd never suspected Martha Whipple. The librarian. Eugene's old friend. Now she knew everything but why.

"On three, we'll rush in and I'll take Martha while you get the children out and safe." James tapped her shoulder. "One, two, three!"

Together they pushed opened the heavy old door that had sealed the shaft from curious children for decades. Jennifer saw the children, all sitting at a plastic table. Martha Whipple stood over them, a revolver tucked discreetly in one hand. It was the sight of the gun more than anything that put speed to her feet as she launched herself across the table. Her body knocked burgers, colas and children to the floor in one grand, dramatic sweep as James tackled the librarian and sent her sprawling.

The gun flew out of her hand and Familiar, waiting at the doorway, fielded it neatly, pushing it out of the reach of Martha Whipple and the children.

Twenty seconds later, Eugene and Judy burst into the room and hurried to help Jennifer comfort the children, who were too stunned to do anything except look at the ruination of their meal and the strange sight of Martha Whipple being held tightly by James.

For a brief moment Martha struggled, then gave up as she glared at Jennifer. "You stupid interfering witch. Ever since you came to town you've ruined my plans."

"Martha?" Eugene stepped toward her, then stopped at the venomous look she gave him.

"I hate you," she snarled. "Everything you write is wonderful. The children love you, and the critics rave over each stupid word. You had everything I ever wanted, but you couldn't even throw me a scrap."

"Martha, what are you talking about?" Eugene picked up several pages of manuscript that had scattered across the floor of the mine. Understanding dawned on his face.

Martha sneered. "That's right. My stories. Remember when I showed them to you?" She struggled, but James held her. "You said I was the perfect librarian, but that I was no writer. You said my stories were *interesting*. That word that means nothing." As she talked, she slowly sank back against James until he was supporting her. "You took away my dreams, my hopes." She started to cry.

"Martha, I said you needed to write more."

"You ruined everything!" Martha lunged toward the writer, foiled only by the strong grip James had on her.

Aware that the children were watching with the beginnings of genuine fear, Jennifer signaled to James to move Martha Whipple away from the children. "We're going home," she said, kneeling to their level.

"Eugene." Bobby Fornaro stepped forward and addressed the writer. "You're going to be in big trouble for kidnapping all of us. Are we going to be in your next book?"

"Without a doubt," Eugene said, gathering them into his arms.

"And I'm going to be the detective," Judy said. She looked at Eugene. "Right?"

"Right. Now, it's time to go home. I think some parents are going to be very happy to see you."

"Is my mother mad?" Amber Green came out from behind a chair. "She has a terrible temper."

"I think even Anna will be sufficiently relieved to see you not to be angry," Eugene said. "Now, we'll have to pack in the car like sardines, but we can manage."

"Miss Whipple has a van," Tommy offered. "She blindfolded us and told us all about the experiment for one of your books."

"But she wouldn't take us back home," Mimi said, her voice becoming choked again. "I was getting scared. And this place is boring, being locked inside all day and night."

"Well, we're going home now," Jennifer said as she ruffled Mimi's bangs. As they started toward the door, Familiar in the lead, Jennifer turned to Martha Whipple. The woman was obviously off her rocker, a woman consumed with petty jealousies and meanness. But there was one thing that didn't make any sense. "I can see why you hated Eugene, but why Crush Bonbon? He was Eugene's rival, his enemy. And you tried to implicate him in the kidnappings. Why?"

Martha Whipple's glasses had slipped down her nose and the blue eyes that gazed back at Jennifer were slightly crazed. "It was for my daughter. He asked Arlene to marry him, but I fixed that. He wanted my only child, and her daughter. But I told her he was running around behind her back. I put a stop to that marriage. But Arlene moved away from me, anyway." Her burst of anger faded and she slumped against James once again.

"Come along, children." Wanting to spare them any more trauma, Eugene led them out into the night. "Now, where is the van? Jennifer will drive us and Familiar, and we'll leave James to help Martha. She's unhappy right now, but things will get better soon. Remember in the story where Kevin is tempted by the Gypsy. . . ?"

Jennifer watched as the children obediently followed him to the van. Whatever trauma they'd suffered was momentarily lost in the joy of one of Eugene's stories. They would be okay.

James's touch was as comforting and expected as the sweet kiss of the night, and Jennifer turned into his arms. Martha Whipple's arms had been bound with a length of jump rope and she was safely tucked into the car, waiting for James to drive her to the police station.

"Are you okay?" James whispered into her ear.

"I'm better than okay." She lifted her face and brushed a kiss across his lips. "Should I say 'my hero' now, or wait until later?"

"Even in moments of glory you are still sarcastic." His tone was slightly chastising.

"I can't afford to let you think you're as terrific as I think you are."

"No, we wouldn't want to say anything kind at all." He laughed as he pulled her hard against him. "But I can make you beg for mercy."

"You can make me beg for a lot of things, most of them a lot more pleasurable than mercy." She kissed him, her body yielding against him, her desire for him instant and hot. "Let's continue this discussion at my place as soon as we deliver Ms. Whipple and the children."

"That's *Mrs.* Whipple, and it will have to wait until I file this story." James sighed. "If I'm going to make you a star in print and save Eugene's reputation, I have to hurry to the paper and get to work."

"Slave over that hot keyboard, and then—" she kissed him again "—we'll lock the doors, bolt the windows and take the telephone off the hook."

"For about five days," he said, returning her kiss.

"Hey!" Jennifer looked down her leg into the golden eyes of Familiar. He popped her shin again with his sheathed claws.

"I think it's time to drive," James said, sighing. "That cat knows how to ruin a romantic moment."

"Until later." Jennifer blew him as kiss as she ran through the pines to catch up with Eugene and the children. Familiar was a streak of black at her side.

EUGENE'S LATEST BOOK has skyrocketed to the New York Times' *bestseller list. Imagine that. Nothing like a little controversy to set things in motion in the book world. And believe me, this entire kidnapping episode has raised the roof around here.*

To the credit of all the voters, Anna Green's behavior has led to a coalition against book burning, which has destroyed her political future. Chief Bixley is under scrutiny for his nocturnal investigations, and James has been promoted to the ace reporter slot.

The best news of all is that Jennifer has been permanently assigned to Mobile to look out for Eugene. They realize it's a full-time job down here, and she's the woman for it.

I think sharing the same geographic space, or at least the same coast, is vital to a new marriage. And along with a job promotion, Jennifer is sporting an engagement ring.

Poor Martha Whipple. She's undergoing extensive psychiatric evaluation. As a Trained Observer, I can diagnose her condition—driven completely mad by jealousy. Imagine, she had checked out all of those books on writing and put them on Crush Bonbon's library card. She wanted to write. She wanted the glory. And when Eugene had looked at some of her manuscripts and said they weren't polished enough to be published, she lost it! The irony is that she never even tried to rewrite them and send them in. She just plotted and schemed how to ruin Eugene.

Ah, humans. They see what they want and then they screw it all up by doing something stupid. But they are interesting. That is their redeeming quality. They're endlessly interesting. And some of them, like Miss Spitfire, are enough to make a cat's heart go pitter-pat.

Now I'm settled in with Eugene. AnnaLoulou and I have developed a friendship that puts no strain on my vows to Clotilde. And Eleanor's on her way to retrieve me—and hold a bridal shower for Jennifer. Then it's home to Washington for a few weeks. There's no telling what can happen in Washington. A cat with a love of adventure knows no bounds.

FLYAWAY VACATION
SWEEPSTAKES

OFFICIAL ENTRY COUPON

This entry must be received by: MAY 30, 1995
This month's winner will be notified by: JUNE 15, 1995
Trip must be taken between: JULY 30, 1995-JULY 30, 1996

YES, I want to win the San Francisco vacation for two. I understand the prize includes round-trip airfare, first-class hotel and $500.00 spending money. Please let me know if I'm the winner!

Name______________________________________

Address ____________________ Apt. ____________

____
City State/Prov. Zip/Postal Code

Account #__________________________________

Return entry with invoice in reply envelope.

 CSF KAL

FLYAWAY VACATION
SWEEPSTAKES

OFFICIAL ENTRY COUPON

This entry must be received by: MAY 30, 1995
This month's winner will be notified by: JUNE 15, 1995
Trip must be taken between: JULY 30, 1995-JULY 30, 1996

YES, I want to win the San Francisco vacation for two. I understand the prize includes round-trip airfare, first-class hotel and $500.00 spending money. Please let me know if I'm the winner!

Name______________________________________

Address ____________________ Apt. ____________

____
City State/Prov. Zip/Postal Code

Account #__________________________________

Return entry with invoice in reply envelope.

© 1995 HARLEQUIN ENTERPRISES LTD. CSF KAL

OFFICIAL RULES

FLYAWAY VACATION SWEEPSTAKES 3449

NO PURCHASE OR OBLIGATION NECESSARY

Three Harlequin Reader Service 1995 shipments will contain respectively, coupons for entry into three different prize drawings, one for a trip for two to San Francisco, another for a trip for two to Las Vegas and the third for a trip for two to Orlando, Florida. To enter any drawing using an Entry Coupon, simply complete and mail according to directions.

There is no obligation to continue using the Reader Service to enter and be eligible for any prize drawing. You may also enter any drawing by hand printing the words "Flyaway Vacation," your name and address on a 3"x5" card and the destination of the prize you wish that entry to be considered for (i.e., San Francisco trip, Las Vegas trip or Orlando trip). Send your 3"x5" entries via first-class mail (limit: one entry per envelope) to: Flyaway Vacation Sweepstakes 3449, c/o Prize Destination you wish that entry to be considered for, P.O. Box 1315, Buffalo, NY 14269-1315, USA or P.O. Box 610, Fort Erie, Ontario L2A 5X3, Canada.

To be eligible for the San Francisco trip, entries must be received by 5/30/95; for the Las Vegas trip, 7/30/95; and for the Orlando trip, 9/30/95.

Winners will be determined in random drawings conducted under the supervision of D.L. Blair, Inc., an independent judging organization whose decisions are final, from among all eligible entries received for that drawing. San Francisco trip prize includes round-trip airfare for two, 4-day/3-night weekend accommodations at a first-class hotel, and $500 in cash (trip must be taken between 7/30/95—7/30/96, approximate prize value—$3,500); Las Vegas trip includes round-trip airfare for two, 4-day/3-night weekend accommodations at a first-class hotel, and $500 in cash (trip must be taken between 9/30/95—9/30/96, approximate prize value—$3,500); Orlando trip includes round-trip airfare for two, 4-day/3-night weekend accommodations at a first-class hotel, and $500 in cash (trip must be taken between 11/30/95—11/30/96, approximate prize value—$3,500). All travelers must sign and return a Release of Liability prior to travel. Hotel accommodations and flights are subject to accommodation and schedule availability. Sweepstakes open to residents of the U.S. (except Puerto Rico) and Canada, 18 years of age or older. Employees and immediate family members of Harlequin Enterprises, Ltd., D.L. Blair, Inc., their affiliates, subsidiaries and all other agencies, entities and persons connected with the use, marketing or conduct of this sweepstakes are not eligible. Odds of winning a prize are dependent upon the number of eligible entries received for that drawing. Prize drawing and winner notification for each drawing will occur no later than 15 days after deadline for entry eligibility for that drawing. Limit: one prize to an individual, family or organization. All applicable laws and regulations apply. Sweepstakes offer void wherever prohibited by law. Any litigation within the province of Quebec respecting the conduct and awarding of the prizes in this sweepstakes must be submitted to the Regies des loteries et Courses du Quebec. In order to win a prize, residents of Canada will be required to correctly answer a time-limited arithmetical skill-testing question. Value of prizes are in U.S. currency.

Winners will be obligated to sign and return an Affidavit of Eligibility within 30 days of notification. In the event of noncompliance within this time period, prize may not be awarded. If any prize or prize notification is returned as undeliverable, that prize will not be awarded. By acceptance of a prize, winner consents to use of his/her name, photograph or other likeness for purposes of advertising, trade and promotion on behalf of Harlequin Enterprises, Ltd., without further compensation, unless prohibited by law.

For the names of prizewinners (available after 12/31/95), send a self-addressed, stamped envelope to: Flyaway Vacation Sweepstakes 3449 Winners, P.O. Box 4200, Blair, NE 68009.

RVC KAL